BAD

LUCK

SIMON KANE BOOK ONE

Brad Younie

First paperback edition: November, 2019

Book design by Brad Younie
Cover Art by Alex McVey

ISBN 978-1-7333715-0-6 (paperback)
ISBN 978-1-7333715-2-0 (hardcover)
ISBN 978-1-7333715-1-3 (ebook)

www.bradyounie.com

Chapter 1

Brookline; a charming Boston suburb. More upscale than most, this was the home of business VPs and other upper-middle-class professionals. The spacious houses with immaculate lawns and two-car garages. The Mercedes, Audis, and Cadillacs in each driveway. Just cruising down a street like this made people feel inadequate.

But not me.

I pulled my Ferrari to the curb behind Detective Ross' unmarked Impala and turned off the engine. The officers in the yard stared at my shiny new 458 Italia, a top-of-the-line sports car. In red, of course. When I do something, I do it right.

The house before me stood out from the others. As big and beautiful as any in the neighborhood, the two police cruisers parked in the street before it drew attention. All the neighbors stared at the place with undisguised contempt. Rich people. Always ready to turn on their neighbor at the slightest indiscretion.

A fine mist of rain greeted me as I walked up the driveway. Despite the weather, I left my jacket unzipped to provide access to my gun, just in case.

"If it isn't our friend, Simon Kane." The asinine words came from Officer Pope. He had been with the Brookline PD for twenty years and was still a street cop. With a wit like that, I was surprised he hadn't made captain.

I continued my stroll up the driveway. It would bring me past Pope, but I wasn't getting my shoes wet on the rain-soaked lawn.

"Hey," Pope's expression promised another insightful witticism. "You think the suspect's a vampire? No, wait! A werewolf! You believe in them, right?"

Yup. Pure genius.

"Failed the detective test again, I see." Grabbing his wrist, I shoved a hundred-dollar bill into his sweaty palm. "Go buy yourself some Cliff Notes." Without a second glance, I continued past him to the door. Guffaws from the other cops followed, and his eyes burned on my back, but I didn't care. He would be a good boy and leave me alone. The cop at the door said nothing as I passed him and entered the house.

The place was clean and comfortable with classy décor. They had some taste for middle-class. The sound of Ross' voice led me through a doorway off to the left, and I found myself in an equally well-decorated living room. A large, flat screen TV dominated one wall, with the couch and other chairs positioned toward it. Photographs and nick-nacks lined the mantelpiece above the fireplace. The room felt warm and homey. A playpen sat by the bay window, and a baby held itself up on tiptoes, gripping the railing for support. A woman stood in front of the sofa near the center of the room. She crossed her arms nervously over her chest, her face a wreck from crying. Detective Joseph Ross hovered between her and the crib. He wore a beleaguered expression as he watched the woman. My entrance got his attention, and he showed relief when he saw me—a rare thing.

My brow wrinkled in consternation as I scanned the room. There were no bodies. No stench of death. And no occult symbols or artifacts anywhere. Only Ross, a few cops, and a distraught housewife.

"Simon," the detective said, taking a professional tone and waving me over.

In three long strides, I stood beside him. "Why am I here? I don't do domestic disputes."

Ross ignored my greeting and turned to the woman. "Mrs. Mann, this is Simon Kane. He's a private investigator but is well suited to help sort this out."

Mrs. Mann stared past me at the baby with undisguised hatred. Odd. Wasn't she the child's mother?

"Simon," he said, undaunted. "I'd like you to give this woman your professional opinion about her son—"

"He's *not* my son!" the woman shrieked, tearing her gaze from the child to scowl at the detective.

"Ross, I'm not an expert on babies, you know that." Domestic disputes were number one on my list of reasons not to be a cop.

"You *are* an expert on the supernatural, aren't you?" He said that loudly, as much for the woman's benefit as for mine.

"Yes, that's why I consult for you. What does that

have to do with the baby?"

"Mrs. Mann believes little Jacob over there is not hers."

"It *isn't* Jacob!" the woman sobbed. That explained the look she gave the child.

"But you think it is?" I said to Ross.

The detective nodded. "A photo comparison matches."

For the first time, I turned to face Mrs. Mann. She gazed at me with teary eyes as I examined her. She was pretty for a woman in her mid-thirties. Though she had that soccer mom look that turns me off. She held a wild, hysterical expression that made her appear desperate, but she wasn't a nut-job who wouldn't recognize her own child. Okay, I was curious.

I affected my best professional tone as I addressed Mrs. Mann. "Why do you think the baby isn't yours?"

She gazed at me for a moment. "You have to be a mother to understand. That—that *thing* is not my son!"

"Hmm." Not really an answer, but there was one thing going for it: sincerity. The woman believed what she said. The time had come to interview the kid.

Crossing over to the crib I knelt and examined the thing that stood inside, holding onto the railing. I say *thing* because it was no kid—I could tell that much. Oh, the creature looked like a baby to everyone else. To me—well, let's just say I have a nose for the supernatural—or an eye, in this case.

It's one of my unique talents. You see, I'm not entirely human. Somehow, my DNA got mixed with something paranormal. I have no idea what I am or how

I got to be this way. Whatever the case, I've found I have certain abilities, one of which is seeing supernatural beings for what they are. This is why I'm a PI. To learn more about these beings, and exactly where I fit in.

Identifying a supernatural being—or *supey*, as I like to call them—is hard to do. This is, in part, because I was raised like a human, and had to figure it all out myself. Some supies look different to me than they do to ordinary people. Those are easier to identify. But some are tricky. This one had the body of an infant, but something was off about Little Baby Jacob. The expression with which the baby's face considered me was too adult to be real.

"What are you?" I whispered. The fake Jacob stuck its tongue out at me. Nice.

"Fuck you," the baby said, so quietly only I heard. But instead of the surprise and revulsion the faux infant expected, I smiled. Yeah, I knew what it was.

As casually as I could manage, I turned and walked a few steps away. The timing was important. I didn't want to tip my hand, or things could get nasty. In one fluid motion, I drew as I turned, flicking off the safety as I aimed. My handgun was always cocked, so the thing only managed to gape at me, its blue eyes bulging in surprise as I squeezed the trigger.

I always forget how loud a gun is. The report filled the enclosed space of the room in a deafening roar, leaving my ears ringing. Cops ran into the room from outside, their guns trained on me within seconds.

"What the hell!" Ross was beside me in an instant and pulled the gun from my hand. I let him take it.

Ignoring Brookline's finest—and their weapons,
I turned to the grieving mother. "You were absolutely
right, Mrs. Mann. That was not your son."

"Sir!" Officer Pope said to the detective. "Look!"

All eyes turned to the crib. Where the bloody body
of a baby should have been, instead lay the bloodless
empty skin of a child. There were no bones, no meat,
no organs. It was a baby suit, like the skin of a snake
after it molted.

Ross whirled on me, his face twisted in disgust and
confusion. "What the hell was that thing?"

I shrugged. "A changeling, of course."

Chapter 2

Ross bobble-headed from the playpen to me, gaping stupidly. He took the revelation better than most people would. At least half of the cops turned away, and one of them vomited. Mrs. Mann screamed. Perhaps she *did* think it was her son, after all.

My gaze switched to the detective. "May I have my gun back?" The request was reasonable. The thing in the playpen wasn't human, so no murder was involved. In fact, I might have even saved their lives. After all, fairies could be extremely dangerous when pissed off.

"The Hell I will!" Ross exclaimed ungratefully. "You shot a baby!"

I rolled my eyes. Sometimes, I just couldn't help it. The detective had always been more sensitive to the supernatural than most people, which he stubbornly refused to accept. "Didn't you hear me?" My tone was calm, matter-of-fact. "The creature was a changeling, not a baby."

"That was a baby in the crib, Kane. We *all* thought so. Even you did when you first came in."

"But when I took a close look the thing in the crib,

I became certain."

"Christ, Kane. *I* looked at the baby, and all I saw was little Jacob Mann."

"I'm not like you, Detective Ross . . ."

"That's for damn sure," he cut in gruffly. I chose to ignore his bad manners.

"You know I can see supernatural entities, even when they're in disguise. When I went to the crib, a changeling looked back at me. I knew exactly what I was doing when I pulled the trigger."

"So, you're saying you expected Baby Jacob to turn into *that*?" His frown betrayed his disbelief.

"Well, I expected the important part. The changeling would be sent home, and its disguise would be lifted."

"Mr. Kane," Mrs. Mann said in a shaky voice. She had gotten over her screaming fit, and now only sniffled. "You said *that*—" she pointed at the crib "—is not my son."

"That's right."

She clenched her jaw, taking control of her emotions for the first time. "Then where is he? Where is my Jacob?"

The two waited expectantly for my answer. "Let's go to the kitchen, and I'll explain changelings to you."

Ross stepped away to tell his men what to do with the mess in the playpen before ushering the woman into the kitchen. We sat at the table, and they both stared at me—her expression full of desperate hope, his grim understanding. He thought the kid was gone for good. He might be right.

"A changeling is a type of fairy that loves to cause

suffering in humans. It disguises itself as a human child or an elderly person and behaves in ways that drive the victim's loved ones crazy. The thing made you hysterical today, but trust me, that was only the beginning."

The two of them stared at me. Both of their expressions changed. Mrs. Mann's became one of confusion and Ross' one of disbelief with maybe a touch of impatience.

"Cut the crap, Kane," he growled.

My eyes rolled again. "Detective Ross, you know I wouldn't lie about something like this."

"But a fairy?"

"Fairies exist. I've seen them. You need to get over your mundane beliefs." He should have trusted me more than that. I was a professional.

"You're serious?"

"Yes."

"Are you saying," said Mrs. Mann timidly, as though she felt crazy just thinking of it, "that my son is a fairy?"

"Of course not. I'm saying your son was exchanged with a changeling."

"By whom?"

"By other fairies."

"Why?"

"Because, Mrs. Mann, you made them mad."

"What?" she said, surprised. "That's absurd! How could that happen? I don't even believe in them."

"Well, somehow they got angry with you or your family, and so they switched your kid with the changeling. They're punishing you."

Mrs. Mann opened her mouth to speak, but Ross

spoke first. "How can you make a fairy mad?"

Now he came around. "How do you make anyone mad? Maybe you stepped on its favorite flower, or you cut down a tree it liked to play in."

"You mean a fairy would do something this extreme for stepping on a flower? Come on, Kane. That doesn't make sense."

"You're assuming fairies think like humans. The truth is they have more respect for flowers, trees, and other parts of nature than they do for us. Did you ever torture bugs when you were a kid, Detective? That's what we are to them. And they can act like kids. They're fickle and easy to anger."

"But you're right," I said. "It probably took something bigger to make the fairies this mad."

"How can you fight them?" Ross asked.

"You don't fight them," I said with a chuckle. "You say you're sorry. You do things to appease them, to make them happy. Then, hopefully, they'll leave you alone."

"I just want my son back," Mrs. Mann said.

"Then find out how you made them mad and make reparations. And not just to get your kid back. They haven't finished messing with you. They'll do something else. And no matter how many times we stop them, they'll keep attacking your family. You need to make them happy. And you need to do it soon."

"But I couldn't have done anything to upset them," she said. She was about to lose it again.

"Maybe your husband did, or someone else in your family. Find out what happened and put an end to it. Then, do things to appease them."

"Like what?" Ross asked.

"In the olden days, people used to set food out on their doorstep. But you'll think of something better once you've found what made them mad."

"I'll talk to Richard. Maybe he can think of something. Can I call you when I find out?" Mrs. Mann looked at me all teary-eyed.

The truth was, I had hardly ever seen a fairy, and I wanted to. I had questions for them. I was curious about this case. Reaching into my jacket pocket, I pulled out a business card and set it on the table.

"I'm a professional, ma'am. I charge for my services."

She took the card.

"You're a private investigator?" she asked.

"And occult expert," I added. "The supernatural is my specialty—it's all I do."

"That can't earn you a living."

A smile tugged at my lips. "I don't do it for a living."

Ross handed her a tissue, and she blew her nose. She did it daintily.

"Thank you, Mr. Kane." She sounded grateful. That was surprisingly accepting, given the circumstances.

"Is that all?" I said to the detective.

He nodded.

"Good. Then I'd like my gun back."

Ross just stared at me. He didn't want to. The muscles in his jaw tightened at the prospect. "Okay. But next time I keep it."

"Whatever you say." He would never be able to keep my gun. My father had connections. He was one of the most influential men in Boston, which gave me certain liberties with the police.

Ross pulled my gun from his belt and handed it to me. "I'll walk you out," he said.

After cocking the weapon and making sure the safety was on, I holstered it. We went to the door.

"Are you serious about this fairy crap?" he said once we were out of earshot of Mrs. Mann.

"Yes, I am serious about this crap."

"Look," he said, his tone still hushed, "I'm okay with ghosts and some of the other paranormal stuff. But fairies—that's going a bit far."

"It took me a while to believe in them, too. My eyes are tuned differently. You and I see a very different world out there. But they're real. You saw one today. How else can you explain what happened?"

He shrugged. "But it didn't look like a fairy."

"How do fairies look? And please don't tell me they're like Tinkerbell. You're too smart for that."

Ross glared at me. "Fine." He did expect Tinkerbell. "So, do you think they'll give the kid back?"

At the door, I turned to face him, looking him squarely in the eyes.

"Honestly, I have no idea. Fairies sometimes give them back. But not always. It's said they occasionally kill the child. Other times, they raise it as their own. I think you should be prepared for the possibility the baby is gone for good."

"Is there a way to rescue him? You know. Do your supernatural thing and bring him back?"

"Who do you think I am? Gandalf the Gray?" The chuckle that followed was more for the absurdity of this conversation than at my joke. "Being rich doesn't help. Fairies don't care about money. And I may have 'special abilities,' but there's a limit to what I can do. To my knowledge, no one can force them to do something they don't want to do."

The expression on Ross' face was grim. He cared. He cared for the kid, and for Mrs. Mann. He was setting himself up for a fall, but I bet he understood that. "The woman's best chance is to try to appease them. If they can make up for what they did—whatever that may be—then they might give the baby back. It's a long shot, but it's all they've got."

Ross frowned. "I'm reporting this as a missing child. After all, I can't go to my superiors and say, 'the child was taken by fairies.' We'll send the skin to the Medical Examiner for analysis and hope they find something useful.

"In the meantime, I'll talk to the husband. He might think of something that could have pissed off the fairies. Although, I might use the term 'ecological extremists.'"

"Fair enough," I said with a laugh. "Call me if you find anything." And with that, I walked out into the chilly spring air.

A changeling.

The drive back to my office was spent thinking about them. Fairy lore was a subject I put extra effort into because I suspected there might be some Fae blood in me. My knowledge of them was pretty impressive. In fact, I would say I knew more about them than just about any human being. When it came to the supernatural, there were two lines of research. One was to study the folklore, mythology, and experiences people had. The other was to investigate using supernatural means. Normal humans couldn't follow that second line of study. I could.

In history, many of the worst diseases and illnesses were blamed on changelings. But not all of them acted sick. Some were abusive or even violent. Whatever it took to punish the real victims—the loved ones.

Why did the changeling target the Mann family? In this day and age of non-belief, what could someone do to upset fairies that much? People destroyed acres of forestland every day, and they're never targeted. It just didn't seem possible that an average family could accidentally anger them to the point where they would use a changeling. There had to be more to it.

Well, whether or not Ross wanted it, he managed to get my attention. I decided to do a little research on the Manns. Maybe one of them was doing something out of the ordinary, something I could work with.

Chapter 3

I rented a nice little office with a street-side entrance only a short walk from Faneuil Hall. It was comfortable, convenient, and too expensive for my business to afford. Luckily, my father was one of the richest men in the city, and so money was never a problem for me.

A young woman stood at the door to my office, bracing herself against the chilly wind that continually blew down the tunnel-like Boston streets. She was at least seventeen, but I doubted she was twenty-one. The girl looked like she just came from an Addams Family audition with her black, baggy shirt underneath a matching wool coat that blew open in the breeze. A knee-length black skirt covered dark stockings. Top that with black eyeliner and long, straight black hair that partially obscured her face, and I was looking at a Wednesday Addams lookalike. The baby goth leaned casually against the door and stared at the people who walked by on the sidewalk.

The girl raised her eyes as I approached. "You Simon Kane?"

"I'm not taking cases right now," I said, stepping

up to her.

The girl regarded me with cool detachment. "I've been waiting for an hour. The least you can do is talk to me."

"That was your choice. Now, excuse me." Keys jingled as I held them up and gestured toward the door she leaned against.

She stayed put.

"I can move you."

"I can scream."

Ugh. It wasn't worth the hassle. Besides, I could say "no" as easily inside as out.

"Fine. I'll hear you out, but I'm busy right now."

The girl stepped aside to let me open the door.

A brochure taped to my office door flapped in the wind. A title, in bright yellow letters, said, *The People of the Wing: Followers of the Fae Path.* They were fairy worshipers, which would have been quite a coincidence if I didn't know them. A note was stapled to the front page, which read:

Mister Kane, we would like you to come and speak to our group about the supernatural. Call us to schedule. We will pay.

Some people really had the gift to commune with supeys. Not them. I met some of that group at a few psychic fairs. They cosplayed as fairies and pretended they knew them by name. But they had no real connection to the Fae whatsoever. It was a good thing I didn't need to put up with losers like them.

My office was made up of three rooms, plus a bathroom. We entered the building into a reception area. Sparsely decorated, it held a few pictures on the walls and no plants. A handful of chairs lined the right-hand wall, while a desk was set up opposite them, which had a computer, a phone, and a notepad. The door to my office was beside the empty receptionist's desk. I didn't have a receptionist because I didn't get much business. My entry in the Yellow Pages clearly stated I only handled cases involving the occult, the paranormal, and the bizarre. Occasionally, someone called about a haunted house, but I turned most of those down. Ghosts didn't interest me. But the office came with a reception room, and I figured I ought to make the place look official for the few clients that mattered.

The girl glanced around the room. "You don't get much business, do you?"

A wry grin was all she got in response.

I held the door to my office open and gestured the girl through, then led her inside. My office was almost as sparsely decorated since I did most of my work at home. A bookshelf filled with books on the paranormal was against one wall, and my PI certificate hung framed on another. Someone told me I should, and he seemed to be right. Everyone had to look at it, as though they couldn't believe I was legitimate. The girl, however, took a seat at my desk without looking at the certificate and waited patiently as I went around to take mine.

"How can I help you?"

"I want to hire you," she said in a detached tone.

"I'm sorry. I'm already on a case." Short and sweet,

I thought it was best to let her down quickly so I could go back to the real work.

"I'm not leaving until you hear me out." This time, there was a hint of something in her monotone. Was it determination? Desperation?

"What's the job?"

"I need you to find out what my stepfather is doing."

My eyes rolled a lot that day. She noticed, and her expression hardened almost imperceptibly.

"I'm sorry, but I don't take that kind of case."

"You're a private eye."

"And I only deal with the supernatural."

Not even a twitch of an eyebrow.

"He's doing something supernatural."

Another long breath. That was the second today, and that didn't bode well. Sighs meant I was annoyed, and I didn't like being annoyed. "You're lying."

"You'll never know unless you take the case."

"What if I don't *want* it?"

"I'll pay you."

"I don't need the money."

"Then why do you own a business?"

The wry grin returned, which was an improvement. The gothlet was growing on me. "What's your name?"

"Liz. Liz Borden."

"You're kidding me?"

"No," she said with an annoyed roll of her eyes. She'd been through this before.

"Who names their kid after an axe murderer?"

"My parents. To be fair, they'd never heard of her."

My head shook slowly. Now I felt bad about turning her down. "The truth is, Miss Borden, I'm on a case, and I don't want any distractions. You would have to be pretty convincing to get me to help you."

Liz paused. Desperation. That was what I saw under her emotionless facade. Nobody can keep a completely blank face—at least no *human*. The kid might be odd, but she was human.

"My mother's in danger."

The bored expression on my face shifted to a frown.

"Your stepfather threatened her?"

"No, but he's mixed up in something dangerous, and he has no regard for the welfare of any person. He thinks people are something to own and use."

"You're saying he's a psychopath?"

She nodded.

"What is he mixed up in?"

"That's what I need you to find out. My stepfather's doing something big and bad, but I don't know what. If I did and had proof, I could convince my mother to leave him. He stays out late every night, and there's something strange about him—about his behavior when he finally comes home."

"You want me to follow him, find out where he's going and what he's doing, and then take some pictures? It's going to cost you."

"I've got money. My parents are rich."

Ah, neglected kid of rich people. Something I could relate to.

"All right. Three hundred up front, plus four upon completion. That'll buy you a standard investigation.

If it gets difficult or needs more time, we'll have to negotiate."

Miss Borden said nothing. Reaching into her coat, she pulled out an envelope with a bank logo. She counted through a large wad of cash and then dropped three one-hundred-dollar notes onto my desk. On the stack, she set a business card, which read, "Sebastian Gray, Chief Operating Officer, Dynamo Software."

I picked up the card and examined it. A phone number was written on the back in ink.

"My cell," she said. "Call me when you find something. He always comes home after midnight, saying he's working late. He's lying."

"How do you know your stepfather is lying?"

"Because I've gone to his work and watched his car. He drives off every day at five o'clock sharp."

That earned a raised eyebrow. "He does this every day?"

"Yes."

"Have you ever followed him?"

"I tried, but he lost me."

"Don't try again. That's my job. You just tell me where your stepfather parks, and I'll do the rest."

I wrote down the directions. Sebastian Gray had a private parking space, so finding his car shouldn't be a problem. Liz said it was a white BMW and gave me the plate number. That would be an easy car to watch.

"Okay. I'll follow him tonight and see where he goes. Then pictures. Information. The usual."

"Thanks," she said.

Miss Borden rose and walked to the door. Before

leaving, she turned to me and said, "Don't let him know I hired you. He can be . . . easily angered." And with that she went through the door, closing it behind her.

Stuffing the card in my pocket, I locked the cash in my desk drawer. I guess my research would have to wait.

Chapter 4

I drove home. If I was going to tail someone, I needed a less conspicuous car.

My home was a penthouse apartment in a major high-rise with the entire east side providing a great view of Boston Harbor. The strong coastal breezes were a welcome relief during the summer months. Spacious, it was well decorated with the best my father's money could buy.

Shoes echoed in the vast lobby as I strode toward the elevators, pausing briefly as I passed the concierge desk. I winked at Carrie as I leaned against the counter. The attendant grinned from behind the desk.

"Anyone ever tell you how hot you are?"

"You do, every day." Yet she smiled as she said it.

"Any sign of my dad?"

She shook her head, her blond ponytail bobbing behind her. "The coast is clear."

"Thanks," I said and walked away.

"Hey, when are you going to take me out?" she called as I beat my retreat to the elevators.

"You know I respect you too much, Carrie," I said

over my shoulder and pressed the button. If I took her out, we would eventually fall apart. That would be inconvenient. Never date someone who serves you.

"Sometimes, I wish you didn't," she said wistfully as the doors slid shut between us.

Being one of the few apartments on the top floor, the hallway was empty when I left the elevator. After unlocking the door, I pushed it gently open. Nobody was in sight, so I entered and listened, and heard nothing but the fridge whirring. All looked normal. Nothing out of place. Good. I tossed my keys onto the kitchen counter and closed the door. My parents sometimes dropped in unannounced. They had a key, of course, because their money got me the place—a stipulation on the deal. Someday, I kept telling myself, I would be independently wealthy and be able to lock them out.

The apartment had a spacious living room with the east wall made up mostly of picture windows and a sliding glass door giving access to the roof. The rest of the room was predominantly white and included a sofa, love seat, several other chairs, a bar, and a white piano. I didn't play—I just thought it looked good. The roomy kitchen and dining room adjoined the living room. A revolving staircase and catwalk style balcony overlooking the main room gave access to my bedroom and the guest room. All in all, it was a modest apartment—at least compared to my parents' house. They kept telling me I needed a bigger place, but I insisted that my needs were small.

A glance at my watch showed 3:45 pm—not much time. To be unobtrusive, I should be in Dynamo's parking lot for a while before five. Now to dress the part. A pair of blue jeans was a must, with old work boots and a camouflage t-shirt. On my belt went my gun. In a duffel bag, I packed my standard investigating gear. It included a camera, binoculars, spare clothes, my tablet computer, and a few other tools of the trade.

I drew my handgun, an M1911 in .45 ACP. A classic type of weapon, but for a good reason. It had power, handled well, and was reliable. Of course, mine wasn't typical—a Kimber Custom Combat, all tricked out with special features. With a shiny, stainless steel frame, black slider, and rosewood grip, it was a beauty. Unique, stylish, and deadly effective. From a drawer in my desk, I pulled a box of ammo and set it on the tabletop. I ejected the magazine, added one round to replace the one I fired, and then re-inserted it into the grip.

Lastly, I threw on an old Army coat my uncle gave to me. It was the only unfashionable clothing item I owned that I actually liked, so I always wore it when I went undercover. Also, the jacket hung down far enough to cover my gun.

Throwing the duffel over my shoulder, I left my apartment and headed to the parking garage. An entire section of the place was reserved for me. There, I stored all my cars—all seven of them. But only a few were expensive. A handful of them were run-of-the-mill vehicles I used for work. Blending in with the crowd was a must when I was on a case. For this job, I picked out a shiny new Ford Focus. If I had to drive bland cars, they would at least be new.

Dynamo Software dominated a small office park not far from Cambridge. The park pretended to be a quiet oasis amid the chaos and bustle of the city. A maze of roads lined with small decorative trees wound its way through a collection of long and wide two-story buildings that made up the neighborhood. Dynamo Software didn't occupy the largest of the structures, but it was the newest and most well maintained. The company did quite well for itself. Its expansive parking lot was full of cars, but I had no trouble locating Gray's BMW shining in its reserved space near the front entrance. The only available spaces for me, however, were at the far end of the lot. So, I parked there and moved to closer ones as it began to empty at four o'clock.

Sebastian Gray exited the building at precisely 5:05 pm. Dynamo's COO wore business slacks, shiny black shoes, and an expensive-looking dress shirt and tie. A briefcase was in one hand as he unlocked his car with the other. My camera clicked as I snapped a few pictures, while he walked briskly to his car and climbed in. He pulled out with a slight squeal and drove off, showing off the Beemer's powerful engine.

That turned out to be a problem. My Focus, although adequate as a nondescript stakeout car, was decidedly inadequate at tailing a fast-moving BMW. He kept outdistancing me on his way into the city. Luckily, rush-hour traffic worked in my favor as we delved deeper into the city. Soon, speed didn't matter because we were stuck in line after line of slow-moving vehicles. Tailing cars is not something I often did, but I wasn't bad at it.

Navigating traffic is an acquired skill, and I drove like a pro as I stayed behind him, taking an occasional picture when he turned onto another road.

Boston wasn't a massive city in square mileage but was built upward as much as outward. The closer we got to the center, the taller the buildings rose. Soon we drove in a veritable forest of skyscrapers that blocked most of the sunlight. It was always impressive to drive down a narrow street with thirty-some-odd-floor high-rises all around you. But it made navigation by sight tricky. You often couldn't see side roads coming until you were on top of them.

Stuck two cars behind, I temporarily lost him in the traffic. Glancing down a narrow, one-way side street as I drove past, I saw the back of his car shooting away from me. He was already near the other end by the time I saw him, and it was too late to turn. The small engine whined as I raced down the next road. I worked my way around to where his getaway emptied onto the main street. By then, he was gone. A half dozen possible directions confronted me as I scanned the intersection, looking for his Beemer.

Curses pouring in a constant stream from my mouth, I looked frantically around. The skyscrapers that rose so close to the streets prevented me from seeing far down any of the other roads. Gray gave me the slip, *intentionally*. The street he took was only good for changing directions. And the fact that I didn't see him make the turn meant he timed it perfectly.

I prided myself on my skills as an investigator, so this hurt on a professional level.

There was nothing I could do here, so I turned around and headed back to my office. An evening studying Gray's path and doing some research on the guy lay before me. So much for working on the fairy case, for now.

After parking in the garage down the street, I walked to the front door, still in my stakeout clothes with the duffel bag over my shoulder. Keys clinked as I slid one into the lock.

"I'd like a word with you," came a voice from behind me, strong and commanding.

I whirled about, my hand going instinctively to my hip.

A tall man with neatly groomed black hair and expensive slacks, shirt, and tie stood before me. His briefcase was gone, but I recognized Sebastian Gray as he glowered at me, his knuckles white in the clenched fist he likely planned for my face.

"Who hired you?" His anger stabbed out at me with each word.

"Who wants to know?" Playing dumb. Not original, but, well, he took me off guard.

"Cut the crap!" His expression hardened, but he still controlled his rage. "You were hired to follow me. Tell me who did it."

"Why would somebody want you followed?"

That anger rose again, threatening to burst. Gray took a step forward. I took a bigger one backward, my left hand out as a warning as I brushed my coat back to reveal my sidearm. His eyes went from my face to my gun, then back to my face. One slow, measured breath and he regained his composure.

"I can have a restraining order put on you."

"You can try," I replied. "But you're the one who approached me and none too politely. To my security camera, I'll bet it looks like you're the one accosting me."

He glanced up at the device that hung above my door and took a step back. "Stop following me. Stop investigating me. As of this moment, your case is done." With that, he turned on his heels and strode off down the street.

"Don't bet on it!" My shout was muted as it blew away in the wind. Kind of crass, I know, but no one got the last word with Simon Kane. And no one told me what to do. No one.

Chapter 5

I spent the next few hours doing research. First, I went over the path we had taken when I followed Gray. It led, in as direct a line as possible, toward the middle of the city. My consternation grew as I stared at the map. This was one of the most densely populated areas of Boston, riddled with businesses, apartments, hotels, restaurants. Gray's path wound its way to the center of that area before I lost him. Dozens of roads spidered out in all directions from there, each with hundreds of possible destinations. It was a veritable dead end.

With nothing more I could do right then about Liz's case, I spent time researching fairy lore. After an hour's more work, I hadn't found anything I didn't already know about them. A surprising number of people in Ireland still believed in them. They could be quick to anger. And fairies had been known to play "pranks" on humans that often ended in the victim's death. The Fae were not to be trifled with, and it appeared someone in the Mann family had messed with them. Things were likely to turn from bad to worse for them soon.

The westering sun dipped below the buildings,

casting the street in shadows when I left for home to finish my research. Hoisting my bag over my shoulder, I headed out to the garage and my car.

The dark, damp, and cold place smelled like a mixture of gasoline and exhaust. My footsteps echoed in the cavernous place as I walked past rows of filled spaces, even at that hour. A cold, salty breeze blew in from the harbor. An odd chill crept up my spine. My car sat on the second floor in a lonely corner, the spots on either side vacant. I pressed a button on my keychain remote. The Ford's lights flashed, and I heard the locks click.

A sudden groan resounded from somewhere ahead of me, sounding like a submarine that dived too far and got crushed by the pressure. Only a few seconds later, it passed, and I continued more slowly. Something was wrong, I could tell, but I didn't know what. The noise came again, but with greater fury.

A massive steel support beam broke free from the ceiling and crashed down on top of my Ford, bringing with it most of the concrete around it. I ducked and threw my hands in front of my face as debris flew all around me. The vehicle's alarm reverberated throughout the garage, before finally quitting, its dying gasp. Cautiously, I uncovered my face and stared at the heap of metal, glass, and stone that had once been my car.

Retreating to the elevator, I called 911, then waited for help to arrive.

Anyone would say I was lucky to survive such an accident. But I wasn't sure. The whole thing screamed intentional to me—like an attack. Gray tells me to stop tailing him, I refuse, and my car gets crushed. Yet how could Liz's stepfather make that happen, in the space of just a couple hours?

Before long, police cruisers came up the ramp to level two. Two of them blocked access to the corner where my poor car was, while the third pulled into an empty space nearby. Two cops positioned themselves to direct traffic, while the rest approached the rubble and looked it over.

That was my cue. Boots clopped on the concrete as I strolled up to the police tape and smiled at the cop who moved to intercept me.

"Sorry, sir. This section's closed. There's been an accident."

"I know. That's my car." I motioned toward the pile his partners examined.

"You called it in?"

"I did."

He craned his head toward the others. "Hey, I've got the caller here."

A couple of the officers turned to see who had arrived. One of them groaned when he saw me. He came over.

"Of all the rotten luck," he said. "It had to be you."

"It's nice to see you, too."

Officer Finn looked the part of the perfect cop. He stood just over six feet, with broad shoulders and well-muscled biceps. His hard, angular face never smiled—at least, never around me—and the black fuzz of his military haircut was barely noticeable with his hat on. He was all business, and he didn't like me. I'm not sure why, but it might have had to do with all those speeding tickets he gave me that I never had to pay.

"That's your car under all that rock?" He glanced back at the mess. "What happened to the Ferrari? Repossessed?"

"Just slumming," I said.

"Too bad. It would have done you good."

He pulled a notepad and pen from his shirt pocket. "Why don't you tell me your story."

"Well, I was walking to my car and pressed the unlock button on my keychain. There was a big groan, and the ceiling caved in. That's all."

Finn watched me for a moment with that suspicious look he always showed me.

"Right. Then I guess you're all set. We'll take it from here. But you might want to call your insurance company—if people like you even care about that kind of thing." He turned away and went quickly back to his post, as though escaping something unpleasant.

He was right, though—my part was over. So, I left the garage. There were three options for getting home, and I didn't like any of them. It was too far to walk, and I hated taxis. Subways weren't fun, either, but after seeing my crushed car, the trains felt safer than a cab.

Chapter 6

The subway was every bit as disgusting as I remembered. Only a handful of times had I taken the damned things, and only in the line of duty. Walking would almost be preferable.

Now, sure, they were dirty, and smelly, and filled with homeless people. But it was the creepies that made me hate them. That's how I referred to the nameless supies that inhabited the dark places of the world. Nobody could see them but me, and I tried to pretend I couldn't just in case. They weren't friendly monsters. One deep breath steeled myself as I stood in the cavernous entrance and descended the stairs into the underground station.

The "T" station—"T" being the shorthand for MTA, or Massachusetts Transit Authority—was relatively clean but appeared dingy in the flickering glow of fluorescent lighting. Yet so far, no creepies. The turnstile clicked as I inserted the token and it let me through to descend another flight of stairs onto the landing.

A dozen people stood waiting for the train. Against a wall, a street musician played an electric guitar plugged into a portable amplifier. The instrument's case was open with a handful of coins scattered about inside. A combination of green and white tiles adorned the walls, signifying the Green Line. The subway tunnel gaped at both ends of the place like the maw of a giant snake.

And creepies wandered in and out of it.

My stomach churned. These were of the humanoid variety. Creepies came in all shapes and sizes, sometimes looking like grotesque parodies of rats and other vermin, or of skeletal dogs and cats. They all appeared emaciated, with long, bony legs and their skin so thin and stretched, their ribs protruded underneath. The human-like ones were the worst. You see, creepies lacked all facial features except for their eyes, which always glowed red. Some people found featureless mannequins unnerving. But they aren't alive. They didn't turn their heads to regard you with their crimson eyes set on their blank faces.

They skulked around the tracks, staring up at the people above. It made me wonder if the creepies could leave the tunnel and climb up onto the landing, or if they were stuck down there. I hoped for the latter.

One of the creatures showed interest in a young college woman who stood dangerously close to the monsters. She leaned over the edge to gaze up the shaft, as though hoping to be the first to spot the train's lights. Her purse dangled over one of the horrors in the ten-foot pit below her. The creepie reached up with an unrealistically long arm that seemed to grow longer as the monster strove to grab the dangling pocketbook. Its intentions were plain even with its lack of expression. The sick, lidless eyes bulged, and I bet it would have licked its lips if it had any.

With a force of will, I crossed the landing and stepped up next to her.

"Excuse me," I said.

The woman started and took a step back instinctively from the ledge. My eyes strayed to the creepie, which stared at me for a moment, as though trying to tell if I could see it, before slinking away down the tracks.

"Yes?" the woman replied, eying me curiously.

"Oh!" I hadn't had time to make an excuse to talk to her. "I-I thought you were someone else. A model I once met. My apologies."

Her eyes rolled noticeably. "Really? A model? You need to work on your lines."

A chuckle escaped my lips as they spread into a smile. "It's been a rough day."

"I'm sure," she said, turning away and facing the tracks with her arms over her chest. She took me for a loser. That was unacceptable.

I turned my attention from her to the creepie-infested tunnel. "For the record, I wasn't trying to hit on you. I *did* mistake you for someone."

A derisive snort came from her pretty lips. "A model?"

"Okay, that was an unfortunate error. You *are* attractive, so I guess it just slipped out."

"Thanks for the clarification." No eye contact. Bored expression. The woman wanted me to go away. The problem was, I couldn't. Though undeniably awkward, flirtation had begun, and I always won out.

My most disarming smile transformed my face as I

turned back to her. "Let's start over. I'm Simon. Simon Kane. How do you do?"

A tired purse of her lips went along with her bored expression. "Look, I appreciate your interest, and you do have a certain charm. But I don't think I have time for second chances. They don't end well."

Ah, a bad relationship. That would make it challenging.

"Then something simple. Dinner, perhaps—and no expectations. We meet for a bite and conversation, and nothing more."

The woman looked me over for the first time, considering my offer. Her long, brown hair was tied in a ponytail, her matching brown eyes large and expressive—at that moment showing curiosity. Much better!

"Tell me, Simon Kane, why do you talk so smooth, yet dress like a bum?"

A frown creased my face, then I looked down at myself. My Army jacket, jeans, and boots greeted me in their somber way. "Because I'm undercover." From inside my coat, I withdrew a business card and handed it to her.

Her eyes scanned the white rectangle and chuckled. "A private dick? Are you hitting on me for a case, or are you on the level?"

"Oh, this is strictly for pleasure."

The young woman thought for a moment, biting her lower lip. Why did such a simple act turn men on so? She slipped the card into her pocketbook. "I'll call you. My schedule's crazy, it'd be easier this way."

At that moment, there came a rumbling on the tracks. The creepies all scattered down the tunnel and vanished, and the people picked up their bags and got into place for boarding.

"Can I have your name?" I said as people crowded between us.

She smiled, "Summer." Then, she disappeared onto the train.

As I climbed aboard through a different door, I grinned with satisfaction. The little back-and-forth ended with me the victor. Standing like a sardine in the aisle with one hand holding the bar above me, the details of the tunnel whizzed by through the window. Now that I had time to think, it occurred to me that I didn't plan to ask her out.

My lips curled into a wry grin. Perhaps I hadn't won the exchange after all.

Chapter 7

It was good to be home. Once through the door, I tossed the duffel on the couch, dropped my jacket on the floor, and kicked off the godforsaken boots. They were stylish, in a brutish sort of way, and they were comfortable when worn in small doses. After walking all around Boston, my feet were killing me.

I poured myself a glass of wine, drained it, and poured another. By the fourth, I finally slowed to sips.

Now, down to business. After calling in my dinner order, I adjourned to the dining room, where I had my laptop set up.

Though frustrating as the stakeout was, it failed to take my mind off the changeling. When deciding between a mundane case and a supernatural one, the supernatural won out every time. Fairies were not an easy topic to research. All there was online was folklore and fiction. For this mystery, I needed more, which required some real thought. The chances of that girder falling on top of my car—and only my car—was low. That it happened on the same day, I shot a changeling meant they were related. Shooting the little bastard may have made me a target, which was fine since I wanted to talk to one anyway. With that in mind, I typed.

Fairies taking vengeance.

The web browser filled with links to a lot of garbage. I forgot that people used the word *fairy* to mean something else. Several more attempts with stricter search filters and I had a list of healthier hits. I avoided all that looked sketchy, like *A Sorcerer's Guide to Magic, Monsters, and the Mythic World.* That site screamed "pretend real," what I called those sites that presented fictional data while trying to look like they were legitimate.

After some time and much scrolling through search pages, I found some links that looked promising, and I started to read. Fairies could be vicious, which I knew. They'd been known to send monsters at people, drawing people into trouble with will-o'-the-wisps, and of course, the changelings. Apparently, fairies didn't drop things on people or their possessions. At the bookshelves in my bedroom, I pulled down all my books on fairy lore. With five of them stacked on the table, I started poring through them.

It was almost ten o'clock, and half the stack remained untouched when the sound of fumbling at the apartment door got my attention. Gun in hand, I ran into the living room. In my profession, it was best not to trust unexpected visitors.

A key turned in the lock, and the door opened.

"Freeze!" I called as a man stepped into the room.

"Jesus!" The man jumped, then stared in horror at the barrel of my gun.

With a muttered curse, I lowered the weapon.

"How many times have I told you never to barge in?" My dad saw my back as I went back to the table and my dinner.

William Jonathan Kane was about my height, his slick black hair graying on the sides. As always, he dressed like a businessman, in a suit and tie. Though most businessmen couldn't afford to dress like him.

"I came here to talk to you," he said, his voice stern.

"You mean to yell at me," the bitterness was evident in my tone.

"Only if you make it go that way." A hand reached down and took a book off the table, and he examined the cover. A familiar frown creased his face as he held it up.

"*Fairy and Folk Tales of the Irish Peasantry?*" he said, disapproval dripping from each word. He let the tome drop to the table with a solid *thud*. "What's gotten into you, Simon? I mean, I can handle this 'private investigator' thing—sowing your oats, so to speak. But *fairies*? It sounds like you're going off the deep end."

"You wouldn't understand," I said, lifting noodles to my mouth with chopsticks. The old argument started anew, but I was too tired to play along.

"You're right, I don't. No one would understand." He paused, and I watched as he built up to the big one—the reason he had come here. "Now you fired a gun in a woman's home—a *mother's* home. And there are rumors you shot a child. Are you out of your mind?" His voice rose, and his face flushed with anger.

"If that were true, I would be in jail right now."

"But you shot *something*. In front of the police. I didn't raise you to be so reckless—"

"You didn't raise me at all." My voice remained even, held there by sheer force of will. Yet I didn't need to yell. It hit home as cleanly as any bullet could have. Dad stopped in mid-tirade. His jaw stiffened, and his hands balled into fists.

"Ungrateful little brat," he hissed through clenched teeth. "I could take this away. Take it *all* away. You would have nothing. Then, maybe you would appreciate what I've done for you."

My smile wasn't warm with love for my father. Mockery was the theme of the day. This wasn't the first time he made that threat, and it wouldn't be the last. A deep breath pushed my anger down. There was no need for it—the argument was nearly over.

"You and I both know that won't happen."

"You don't think so?" he said, trying to regain his composure.

"The money, the apartment, the cars. They're all to keep me quiet—to not make a scene. You need me to be the good, quiet little boy, so your precious reputation remains untarnished."

"You call what you did today 'keeping quiet?'"

"We both know just how noisy I can be if properly motivated."

William Jonathan Kane, one of Boston's wealthiest and most respected men, turned his back on me, and his shoulders slumped just a little. He walked into the living room and stood at the picture window, staring over Boston Harbor. It had a calming effect on the mind. The man who was my father stared for a while beyond the wall of glass at the twinkling lights of boats and ships, silent. Then I heard him take another long breath, this time louder—intentional.

"What happened to us, Simon?" His tone wasn't angry. It sounded defeated, as unfamiliar in his voice as caring would have been. This wasn't like him, and I frowned as I joined him at the window. A long freighter edged its way into the harbor, a handful of small tugboats working to steer it into port.

"You had your work. There was never time for me."

"I had to make a living. I had my responsibilities. Surely you can see that?"

"You had a responsibility to your family."

"I had so many responsibilities. The key to success is to pick and choose which ones to focus on."

"You chose wrong."

He paused. "But you turned out okay. You're intelligent. Tough. Strong-willed. These are all valuable traits."

"You hardly know me, and you drove Mom away. Are you sure you made the right choice?"

He never answered my question. Instead, he left. Pausing at the door, he turned to me.

"Don't do anything like that again. I don't want to hear about more trouble with the law." He closed the door gently behind him.

The visit had been tame compared to most, and *different*. For the first time, My father acted like he cared. He acted human. This was significant somehow, and it bothered me. Though ugly as hell, I could deal with the angry father routine. This new caring Dad confused the hell out of me.

More research tonight was out of the question. My appetite vanished, too. The boxes went in the fridge, then I turned on some music and sat by the window, a drink in hand—scotch this time. Thoughts of the creepies in the subway and the woman they almost got swirled through my mind. The woman. Summer. Now that cleared my head. She was pretty, with her brown hair in a ponytail and expressive eyes. She wore a bulky jacket so I couldn't see the rest of her. Whatever. The ball was in her court.

Bare feet slapped on the kitchen tile as I went to pour another drink and turn on the news. An eyebrow raised when I saw film footage of my wrecked Focus. The camera zoomed in on the support beam and the ceiling of the garage. I turned the volume up, and the reporter's voice tore through the silence of the apartment.

"It happened around seven o'clock tonight. The girder broke and fell as a man walked to his car, landing on his vehicle. According to experts on the scene, the girder was worn, but should not have fallen."

They cut to a construction worker. "It was a perfect storm," he said in a gruff voice. "Several support bolts were missing. By pure chance, the cars above it had just the right amount of weight to make the beam fall. If one of them weren't a Hummer, none of this would have happened."

"Have you determined why the support bolts fell?" the reporter asked.

The man shook his head. "By accident, we think.

They weren't secured as firmly as they should have been, and years of stress from the vehicles above just loosened them. They were bound to fall off sooner or later. It was just bad luck that a car was underneath when it happened."

Bad luck, I thought. Could fairies cause bad luck and use it for revenge?

Chapter 8

The Mother Load was a curio shop in Cambridge. A veritable hole in the wall, the small basement store was accessed via a narrow staircase that descended parallel to the sidewalk. The sign was small and hard to notice. Most people who went there just browsed, and the place was always nearly empty, yet somehow he stayed in business. Nick Ibori owned the place. Tall, dark, and broad-shouldered, he could have been a football player but chose science instead. An archaeologist, he traveled the world and amassed an amazing collection of artifacts. The store began as a place for selling many of those items, but he had acquired more over time. He charged a lot for the trinkets, but considering their properties, they would still sell to the right buyers.

The Mann case reached a dead-end, so I switched back to Liz. Tailing Gray was problematic, so I needed some help. Nick was just the man to go to.

The bell above the door tinkled as I walked in. The owner glanced up and smiled a toothy smile, his pearly whites in stark contrast to his dark face.

"Simon," he boomed. "It's good to see you. How are you, my friend?"

"Couldn't be better." My gaze scanned the room with its aisles of shelves filled with all manner of strange objects. We were alone. "I see things haven't changed. You know, I've heard selling things is good for business."

Nick's laugh was as deep as anything James Earl Jones could muster. "I'll stay afloat as long as you keep coming here. What can I do for you?"

"I'm looking for an artifact."

"Then you've come to the right place," he said, waving his hand toward the room. "I have a whole store full of them."

"This would be one of your *special* artifacts. One meant to serve a specific purpose."

"Ah, a magical talisman!" he said. "You can say it here, you know. It won't hurt business."

That elicited a chuckle. "Okay, Nick. Whatever you say. A while back, you showed me one that can be used to track someone."

"If I recall, you weren't interested—you said it sounded stupid."

"Now I am. Do you still have it?"

"Of course I do. I'll go fetch it." Nick disappeared through a door in the back of the shop, taking far fewer strides than I would have.

When I first set foot into The Mother Load two years ago, I saw that many of Nick's curios had magical properties. Yes, the magic had a look, but it was hard to describe. The best I could say is the items radiated the stuff, like when things appear wobbly in extreme heat. I'm not sure how Nick knew they were magical, and he never explained. Browsing the aisles while waiting for his return, I noticed some of the items I had seen before had been replaced by artifacts new to me. Maybe I wasn't his only customer after all.

Nick returned after a few minutes, and I met him at the counter. He held up the artifact for me to see.

It was a stone, buffed smooth and shaped like a slim egg. A hole had been drilled through the top to accommodate a rawhide string so you could wear the thing around your neck. Strange writing wrapped its way around the circumference of the object. Etched in a thin script, the characters resembled no language I had seen before. Nick examined the thing with reverence.

"It's beautiful," he said.

"It's a rock."

He rolled his eyes. "Perhaps I shouldn't sell this to you. You have no respect for it."

"I'll respect it a lot if it works."

"I'm sure you will."

He offered the stone to me, which I turned in my hand, looking it over. "How does it work?"

"First, you must activate the talisman, tune it to your will. Then, you can always find it."

Now I remembered calling it stupid. "Are you saying the artifact is used to track itself?"

"First, create a bond with the stone. Then, whenever you want it, you can know where it is."

My brow creased as I thought about that. To use the device to find Gray, I would need to plant the stone on him, or in his car. That could work. No more tailing—I just let him go where he wants and then show up.

"How do I activate it?" I asked.

"Meditate on it. Hold the stone in your hands and concentrate. Bind your will to it—take control. After that, keep the stone against your skin for several hours. Then the artifact should be yours."

"That's all? What if I can't bind to it? Can I return it?"

Nick shook his head. "All sales are final, Simon. You know that."

"How much?"

"Ten thousand."

"Deal." My credit card exchanged hands, and he rung up the sale.

Another smile spread across his face. "It's easy doing business with you. You never haggle."

I shrugged.

He rang up the transaction and gave my card back, and I signed the receipt. Nick put the artifact into a small box, nestled in a bed of tissue. The box then went into a bag that had "The Mother Load" emblazoned on its side.

"As always, it is a pleasure doing business with you."

"I'm certain it is." But I smiled. He meant it, I was sure. Nick liked dealing with me, partly because of the money, and because of my interest in the supernatural. We weren't friends since we never met outside of the shop. Yet we got along, and he knew I would pay well and never rip him off.

"Thank you, Nick," I said. "You come through for me every time."

The big man shook my hand. He had a firm grip with those huge hands, but he shook mine with sincerity.

"Take care of yourself, Simon Kane. And remember: the world can be a dangerous place, for those with their eyes open."

Chapter 9

I've never been good at meditation. Stray thoughts always invaded my mind, and I had a hard time pushing them aside. This was no exception, so I pulled out all the stops, lighting candles and burning incense. Sitting as comfortably as possible in the middle of my living room, I held the artifact in the palm of my hand. My breath went in and out in long, slow draughts to calm myself and prepare me for meditation. The coffee I bought on my way to Nick's didn't help any. But finally, I achieved my restful state and was ready for the job at hand.

My eyes closed, and I reached out with my senses to the object in my hand. The cold surface slid smoothly under my fingers without blemish. My finger ran along the runes etched around its circumference, and its power sent a warm tingle up my arm, making the hairs stand on edge. Its magic swirled around inside the stone, like an animal searching for escape—and I had to bind that force to my will, to tame it, so to speak. My mind shifted its focus, and I found the magical energy within myself and pooled some together. It appeared to me as glowing strands of smoke, flowing throughout my body. At my command, those tendrils snaked their way toward my chest, where they gathered into a glimmering ball. Slowly, I directed the orb of mystical might down my arm and into the artifact. There, my power meshed with that which swirled inside the object. At first, the talisman shied away from me, but I persisted, thinking only calm thoughts, trying to make friends with it. Eventually, the two glowing smokes mixed and became one, and I now controlled the device. Our energies remained like that for some time, getting used to each other. As they mingled, understanding of the talisman came to me, as though I acquired a new limb. At any time, I could call out with my will, and the artifact would respond, letting me The energy released and I broke softly from my trance, my living room returning just as I left it. The rawhide string fit around my neck with room to spare and, once tucked under my shirt, made a constant connection with the skin of my chest. Nick said to let the talisman stay there for several hours, so that let me move on to other things.

Drawing out my cell phone, I called Liz Borden. Four rings later, she picked up.

"Hello?" I recognized her voice right away.

"Miss Borden?"

"Mr. Kane." Anger shot at me through the speaker, the first sign of emotion I'd ever heard from her. "You screwed up. I thought you were a professional."

That took me off guard, and I nearly retorted unprofessionally. A deep breath, like those from a trance, saved the conversation. "What are you talking about?"

"My dad went on a tirade last night about you. He accused my mom of hiring you to spy on him. I thought he might hurt her."

Damn. I hadn't considered how my failure would come back to Liz or her mother. That troubled me.

"I apologize for letting him notice me. I assure you I *am* professional and my attempt to follow your stepfather would have worked had he been anyone else. Did he have any reason to suspect he would be followed?"

"You mean aside from lying and sneaking around? Wouldn't you think that would make him cautious?"

The girl's tone bothered me, but I gave her that luxury, considering I had slipped up. "Not if he was only cheating on his wife. There must be more to it."

"Of course there's more. I told you he's doing something *bad.*"

"Most people would consider adultery bad," I said.

"You know what I mean."

This was going nowhere. Though Liz had every right to be mad, I didn't want to waste my time with her complaints.

"I have a reason for calling," I said.

Silence followed the kind of silence that often preceded a hang-up. Yet she did respond, and her voice took on the even, unemotional tone she used at my office. "What is it?"

"I need to give you something. It needs to be hidden in your stepfather's car. It will help me track him."

"A tracking device? Isn't that kind of high-tech for a

private investigator?"

That won her a chuckle. "Will you do it?"

"Sure. I work at Bullfrog Records in Cambridge. I'm there now, until five. Bring it by any time before then."

Sebastian Gray. Though I only met him once, I already didn't like him. That pushed Liz's case up on my priority list by a notch. It still wasn't as important as the Mann family's Fae problem, but it came close. A cup of freshly brewed coffee in hand, I took a seat at my dining room table. My office, though comfortable, was only for show. My real work happened at home. Now, I suppose I could have gotten a desk and did it right, but I never bothered. The long table served me well.

Finding information on Gray was simpler than I expected. He had been the Chief Operating Officer at Dynamo for less than a year. Before then, he was a manager of a technical team within the company. Drilling down below that took more time and research, but judging from the posts he made on computer programming websites, he was just another programmer at the same place. Gray rose from being a grunt developer to COO in the space of two years. Though I knew nothing about that industry, my gut told me that kind of thing didn't happen.

The man's extracurricular activities, however, proved far more interesting. For years, Gray had been involved with the occult. He frequently posted on a variety of sites focusing on ceremonial magic, Satanism, demonology, and other such topics. Magic was his focus, and he asked plenty of questions regarding magical theory and the mechanics of specific rituals. Then, his posts just stopped. The most recent one I could find was almost two-and-a-half years ago. Either he got trickier with his choice of usernames, or he ceased posting online altogether. I suspected the latter. After meeting him the previous day, I knew him to be pompous and arrogant, considering himself to be an expert in whatever he did. It wouldn't take long for him to become a self-proclaimed master wizard. And if he needed more research, he would do it in a more discreet, less social way.

A sip of coffee warmed my innards as I sat back in contemplation. Sebastian Gray was into magic. Could that be what he was up to every night? Possibly. Could it be what caused his precipitous climb to the top of the corporate ladder? Very likely. *Mr. Gray, you've got my attention*, I thought as I took another sip of coffee. Liz's case went up another notch on the "interesting" scale.

My phone rang.

I pulled the flat rectangle out of my pocket and glanced at the display. It was Ross.

"Good morning, Detective. Two calls in as many days. I'm touched."

"Cut the crap, Kane." Fatigue filtered out of the little speaker, mingled among his words. Our usual banter would have to wait.

"Okay then. What's up?"

"I've got a body at the morgue I'd like you to take a look at."

"I'm not a doctor."

He snorted. "Trust me, you'll want to see this corpse."

"I doubt it, but I'll come anyway."

"Good. I'm at Mass General. I'll be waiting for you. Oh, and that baby skin—we've analyzed it. It's human skin, all right, but the nasty thing wasn't cut off a real kid. The Medical Examiner was flummoxed. We sent it in for a DNA test, but I'm not expecting a hit." He hung up.

Hospitals. I hated them—and still do. Oh, I appreciate what they do for people. It's just that, well, there are things out in the world, like creepies, that feed off misery, which hospitals have in spades. Mass General was big and bound to be full of them. Though I didn't want to go, I couldn't see a way out of it. Ross wouldn't have called me if he didn't need my expertise, and I thought it might have to do with the changeling case. Off I went to the hospital, haven of the sick, the injured, and the creepy.

Chapter 10

Massachusetts General Hospital sat in the heart of Boston, near the Charles River. The sprawling place took up several buildings like a college campus. Nestled in a knuckle-shaped bend in the river, the expansive parking lot was open to icy sea breezes that blew in from the nearby harbor. I parked as far away from the main entrance as possible because I didn't want my Ferrari getting scratched, and I learned my lesson about taking two spaces—it tended to piss people off, and keys could scratch worse than an opening door.

The wind whipped through the lot as I took the long hike to the front door, keeping my head to one side lest the gusts pull the air from my lungs. My coat kept my body safe and warm, but my unprotected cheeks tingled in protest as I hurried along. Soon, the massive building loomed before me, blocking the wind and giving me a chance to catch my breath. On days like this, I often wondered why I stayed in Boston. The only answer I could ever come up with was: it was home.

People shouldered past me as I stood before the hospital's entrance. Once there, I felt a reluctance to enter. I wasn't kidding when I said creepies hung out there. They seemed to take an interest in the ill, and I honestly didn't want to encounter any. But I told Ross I'd be there, and a part of me kicked myself for showing fear. Besides, they stayed near patients in their rooms. As long as I stuck to the hallways and made straight for my destination, I should be fine. With a final deep breath, I plunged through the automatic door and into the lobby.

Private investigators typically didn't go to morgues—at least I never have. Inside the reception area, I looked for a directory. The morgue likely occupied some out-of-the-way corner, not easy to find. The directory seemed to agree with my suspicion. Either they had another name for the place, or they didn't advertise it.

"Simon?" The voice was light with just enough depth to provide a sense of confidence without losing its femininity. It was also familiar.

The woman from the subway stood next to me. She had traded in her heavy coat for blue doctor's scrubs, with her long, brown hair tied into a ponytail. A stethoscope hung from her neck. I once thought no woman could make that outfit work, but she made me take pause. A small name tag read "Dr. Parke."

"Summer, isn't it? Now, this is a surprise."

"Yes, it is. You clean up well."

My smile widened unexpectedly, unrehearsed. Though I typically didn't wear the most expensive clothes, I always bought the best of any given style. People tended to think a shirt was a shirt and pants were pants. That's why I looked better than everyone else, while still fitting in. Fashion was a subtle art that I was accomplished in. The accessories were where I showed off: the cars, the apartment, things like that. And I didn't like suits—they reminded me too much of my father. I sported new blue jeans and a matching shirt—no collar—over which I wore a wool coat. The jacket hung low enough to cover my sidearm, but I had it unzipped to reveal my shirt and provide easy access to the gun at my hip.

"This is how I dress when I'm not undercover."

"It suits you. Are you here for business? An occupational injury, maybe? Or are you stalking me?" Her lips pulled into a wry smile.

"Business. But I would like to take you to dinner."

She raised an eyebrow but kept her cool. "I'm busy. It would have to be tomorrow night or next week."

"Tomorrow's good. I'll pick you up at seven. You'll want to dress up."

"Why don't I meet you there? That would be best since we just met."

"All right, let's meet at L'Espalier at seven o'clock sharp."

Now she looked surprised. "On a PI's salary? Or do you only work for the super-rich?"

"Oh, no. The truth is, I don't make much from my job. The money comes from elsewhere."

Her eyes narrowed, but the wry grin remained. "That sounds mysterious—or suspicious."

"Nothing of the kind. Though I'll leave it for dinner conversation."

"Okay, then. I'll see you at seven o'clock tomorrow

night."

She turned to depart, but I suddenly remembered my current dilemma.

"Wait! Can you direct me to the morgue?"

Like in most TV dramas, the morgue sat in the hospital's basement. Yet those shows never revealed the place would be hidden. Down a long, dark corridor, the gray metal door bore a small window and a label that read simply B13. Anyone who didn't assume the room was a closet might peek through the tiny rectangle of glass and see the lab inside, but I almost walked past it, even though Summer had told me the room number. A slight whoosh of air sounded as I pulled the door open and stepped inside.

The room was a large rectangle, decorated on three walls and the floor by tiles that had once been white but were now yellowing with age. Dull gray metal appliances lined the walls, a desk with a computer, a table with a scale, and several rolling carts loaded with surgical equipment. One wall sported a gridwork of square metallic gray refrigerator doors. Two rows of long fluorescent lights cast the room in a gloomy, antiseptic light. In the center of the room were two metal tables, one empty and one occupied. It was around this table that I found Detective Ross and the Medical Examiner, both turning to regard me as the door closed automatically behind me.

"About time you made it," Ross said irritably. "Did you finally decide to obey the speed limit?"

"I'm a law-abiding citizen," I said, then stopped my

approach suddenly.

A body lay on the table, motionless, and a surge of panic arose in me. Oh, I could handle mutilated animals and terrifying supernatural creatures without any trouble, but put a dead person on a slab, and I got all queasy. It was their faces with their vacant stares and pale skin. They were like human creepies. They wouldn't rise up and attack me—I hoped. But they had the same emotionless expressions that gave me the heebie-jeebies. Also, this was where the Medical Examiner cut the bodies up for autopsy. The thought of seeing a dead man lying there with his insides exposed made me want to puke. This became a day for taking deep breaths, which I had to do before joining the two men at the table. The last thing I wanted was to throw up in front of Ross. *Avoid the body, Simon. You don't need to see it,* I lied to myself. *Focus on the living people in the room.*

My soft-soled shoes made barely a whisper on the smooth floor as I crossed the distance to stand by the detective at the table. Beside him stood a man in his mid-fifties, about average height, with black hair giving way to an onslaught of gray along the edges. His hairline had receded, showing an ample forehead that likely housed a huge scientist's brain. Sure, head size didn't define brain size, but sometimes, you just had to wonder. The rest of his face was a study in dour-ism. Where Liz's art was in emotionless detachment, this man was a master of gloom. He regarded me with eyes that wished me elsewhere and lips that had nothing nice to say. The man dressed in blue scrubs, similar to Summer's, although she wore them far better than he did. And, of course, he had a white apron that tried hard to dye itself red with the corpse's blood.

Avoiding the sight of the cadaver, I extended my hand in greeting to Oscar the Grouch.

"How do you do? I'm Simon Kane."

The ME held up his rubber-gloved hands to show me a handshake was out of the question and said nothing.

"This is Doctor Rosario, the Medical Examiner," Ross said. Then, in a lower tone, "He doesn't like PIs."

"Oh," I said and regarded the man thoughtfully. "Don't worry. I'm better than most."

The doc snorted.

"What do you think?" The detective motioned toward the table in front of us.

With a grimace of determination, I turned my gaze down to the body.

Relief flooded throughout my body. Rosario hadn't cut into it yet. The cadaver was male, approximately five feet, nine inches tall, the pale skin glistening with water. The doctor had rinsed him off.

And he stunk.

The body reeked of mildew and rotting vegetation. Add that to the level of mud and dirt in all its crevasses, and the cause of the odor became clear to me.

"He was found in a swamp."

The detective nodded. "His car was on the side of a road near one. The police over there suspect he saw something in the swamp that got his attention, and he went to investigate."

Feeling better now that its organs were still on

the inside, I made a visual examination of the corpse, carefully avoiding the head—I wasn't ready for those eyes. The skin pruned in places, like the ends of its fingers. The poor guy had been in the cold, stagnant water for some time. A nearby metal table held a pile of clothes. Ah, something to take me away from the body. "May I?"

Ross handed me a pair of rubber gloves, and I put them on and rifled through the dead man's things. He had a suit, a tie, a white shirt. No shoes. The victim had money, but not for long. The newly rich bought expensive clothes but lacked style. The guy probably thought he was hot stuff in that high-priced crap.

"What would convince a businessman to go wading into a swamp, all alone—I assume he was alone."

"Tom Cook, here, went missing while driving home to Winchester two nights ago. They found his car that night, but didn't search for the body until yesterday morning."

"And you only got it now?"

The detective chuckled dryly. "Winchester has its own police department. They held onto the body for a day before sending it to us. My guess is they didn't know what to make of it, so they sent it to us since we were looking for him, too."

Though I was immune to the politics of dealing with other departments, I'd seen him fight it enough times for me to sympathize.

"Did he die of exposure or drowning?"

"You didn't look at his head?" said Ross. "It's why I called you in. Doctor?"

Rosario gave me an excuse to avoid the corpse's head. "So . . . what's up, Doc?"

He ignored my joke. "Cause of death was blunt force trauma to the head." His tone remained even and detached.

Avoidance only managed to delay the inevitable. My gaze dropped from Rosario to poor Tom's noggin, and then looked quickly away. Not because his lifeless eyes stared at me, but because of the condition of the unfortunate guy's skull. The entire right side had caved in, twisting its face into a grotesque caricature.

"Holy crap!" A fresh batch of bile fought to escape, and I forced it down. "How many blows would it take to do that much damage?"

Doc Rosario's voice remained even when he spoke. "This man was killed by *a single* blow to the head. One massive blow."

Cautiously, I moved my attention back to Cook, and thankfully, my stomach stayed intact. Looking at the wreckage on the table, I couldn't argue with his assessment. Only one impact showed on his skull—one hit demolished his head.

"That's not all," Ross said, eying me with interest.

"Yes," Doctor Rosario said. "Though the blow to the head caused his death, he had received several additional wounds. Similar breaks can be found on his left tibia and his right humerus. Three of his ribs were cracked and one broken, here." He pointed to poor Tom Cook's chest, directly opposite his heart. A huge bruise the size of a soccer ball covered much of his ribcage. "Internal bleeding would have killed him. Hitting him in the head put him out of his misery."

Somehow, it didn't look like an act of mercy.

"What could have done this?" My gaze flitted up to the doctor. "A wrecking ball? Was there construction equipment at the scene?"

Ross shook his head. "Show him."

Doc Rosario lifted Cook's left arm. The sharp end of a bone jutted through the skin, just below the elbow. He twisted it slightly, revealing three circular bruises, evenly spaced along his forearm at the break. They looked like finger placements, except the bruises and the spacing between them was way too big to be from fingers. Holding my thumb up, I held it above the smallest print. The mark was at least three sizes bigger. Though they resembled fingerprints—and I couldn't guess what else they could be—they were too big for a human finger.

"I don't suppose there were prints in these bruises." The doctor shook his head gravely.

"But we found a fragment of fingernail," Ross said. "We sent it for DNA testing, but that'll take time. Give me your opinion."

That made me frown. The truth was, I didn't know what could have caused it. All I knew was it had a human-like hand but was not human. Supernatural? Probably. The two watched me, waiting for my suggestion.

"Bigfoot?" It came out with a shrug, and I wasn't joking.

Ross came around the table, ignoring my joke— that's oh and two—and led me to a corner. The doc just stood there, writing notes on a notepad.

"I was thinking it might be one of them," he said in a hushed tone. "You know, one of those *fairy* things."

My laugh came out louder than expected. "You think a fairy did that?" Rosario gave us a curious glance.

"Keep it down!" he hissed. "But couldn't it be? There are different types, right? Could there be a bigger type of fairy?"

"Not every crime has to do with fairies, Detective. Why are you trying to fit them into this one? Is this connected to the Mann case?"

A nod. "Cook is friends with Richard Mann."

"The husband? Really?" Now, that intrigued me. "Then, I want to see where it happened. Let's go to the swamp."

"I can't. Not my jurisdiction."

"That didn't stop you at the Mann's."

"They called for me. It seems I have a reputation for dealing with weird shit."

"Very nice, Ross. A specialization can be an upward career move."

That earned me a sour look.

"I still need to see the crime scene. Where the body was found."

"Good. Then report back to me. Unofficially, of course."

"Then give me directions, and tell me what you know of the place and their investigation."

Chapter 11

The Ferrari's engine rumbled eagerly as I drove across town to Miss Borden's place of business. The talisman was ready, and I needed to drop it off with her. My connection with the artifact fed me more than just its location. The thing was like a living being in my mind, purring at me with barely contained enthusiasm, as though anxious to be put to use. In fact, the device was so life-like I decided to name it. So far, Rocky was worth the ten grand price tag.

Bullfrog Records occupied a unit of a strip mall in Harvard Square. The building didn't resemble the shopping plazas in other parts of the city with its brick walls and Old Boston charm. It was one of the few such places that resisted dumping the "record" from its name even though vinyl was a thing of the past. The picture window beside the front door showcased the day's current performers. Instead of the bright, shiny pop divas that decorated all the other music stores, angry men and women in strange costumes—mostly dark—brooded at me as I pulled my Ferrari to a halt before it. They looked more like horror movie monsters than rock stars.

Inside, the place felt dark, giving the impression you found some hidden trove of underground music. As it turned out, they had vinyl at the store. Apparently, records made a minor comeback so their hesitation at changing their name might have paid off. Liz stood by the register, chatting with one of her coworkers. She stuck out, not because of her black attire—which appeared normal there—but because she was the only member of the staff who lacked facial piercings.

Slipping out from behind the counter, Liz motioned for me to follow, then went off to a dark corner. A poster display loomed beside her, a big print of Kurt Cobain staring at me with unkempt hair and pained expression.

Carefully grabbing the rawhide string that dangled around my neck, I pulled it up over my head. Rocky hummed excitedly in my head, ready to jump into action as I deposited him into Miss Borden's waiting hand.

"Hide this somewhere in his car," I said matter-of-factly, as though there were nothing strange about the request. "And I'll do the rest."

A single raised eyebrow was all it got me. "This is it?"

My head dipped in a deliberate nod. "Not what you expected, I'm sure, but it'll do the job."

"How?"

"Trade secret." Never try to explain magic to the magically uninclined.

The talisman disappeared inside the messenger bag that pretended not to be a purse. "Whatever. He won't get home until late tonight. But it'll be in his car by morning."

"Perfect. There's research to do." With a last glance around the place, I turned to leave.

"Mr. Kane," she said.

I cocked an eye.

"Be careful."

"Of course." She thought Gray was dangerous. After my encounter with him the day before, I was forced to agree.

The drive to Winchester proved uneventful. The town was a bedroom community for well-off businessmen who worked in the city but didn't want to live there. Once I left Boston proper, trees enveloped the street, growing tall and green on both sides, creating a canopy overhead. The road sported more than a few potholes, which made me wince with each one my Ferrari hit. Sometimes it paid to drive something you didn't care about.

After driving in the country for only twenty minutes, the trees opened up on the right, exposing a vast stretch of stagnant water. The shoulder of the road widened, allowing cars to park beside the swamp. Tires crunched on gravel as I parked near the beginning of the opening.

Several acres in size, the marsh consisted mostly of still water covered in a film of pollen and other plant refuse. Lilly pads drifted about, providing refuge for frogs and other small animals. The still water was disturbed by the occasional bug or fish that swam beneath the slime. Dead trees rose at odd angles, their branches broken off, making them appear as tall stumps. They stood as a reminder of the woods that existed before the water came. Being so close to the road, I suspected the swamp of being a byproduct of development.

The mid-afternoon sun struggled to break through the overcast sky and trees, casting barely any light on the scene below. The chilly air still assaulted me, but at least it lacked the biting wind off the harbor. Stepping carefully, I walked around the area, looking for tire tracks that might have been Cook's, but I soon gave up in frustration. The local police made a mess of things. Once they cleared the crime scene, they tramped all over the place. After several minutes of searching, I found where they had towed his car away. My eyes rolled as I stared at the chaos in the dirt. Apparently, the local cops didn't know how to conduct a proper investigation, as I saw dozens of tracks in standard police-issue shoes obscuring any good prints that might have been there.

Then I focused on the swamp. Tom Cook had been pulled from the water. There were no rocks, logs, or islands to help him cross the expanse. To enter it willingly, he would have to either row a boat or wade. The water depth was impossible to tell with all the crap floating on the surface. It was all dark and forbidding.

He wouldn't have walked in there. Not in those clothes, and not in this weather. Someone must have dumped the body.

With some searching, I found a spot where the brush had been pushed aside. Footprints led through, right to the edge of the water. With one hand pushing the branches away, I knelt down and examined the prints. A man had walked through the bushes and into the freezing cold, stagnant water while wearing dress shoes. They would have been a match for the suit Cook wore. There appeared to be no hesitation showing in the tracks. He just left his car and strode right in. That was odd.

This wasn't a body dump, after all, I thought, scratching my head absently. *That meant he was killed out in the swamp by something big, nasty, and probably supernatural. But what? And why on earth would he ever go in there in the first place?*

My eyes traced a line across the expanse of water toward the other side. Maybe if I spotted what caught Cook's attention, I could return with a boat and investigate. At first, I stared at the water with its logs, dead trees, and reeds. Then at the woods in the distance. Yet it was just an ordinary swamp.

Nothing about this made any sense. Why would a successful man in expensive clothes go wading into a freezing cold marsh? The answer was clear: he wouldn't.

A quick flash of light came and went near the center of the expanse before me. I strained my eyes and at first, saw nothing. Then it happened again. A flash, as of sunlight glinting off a mirror or a shiny piece of metal. Could that have been what he saw? Whatever it was, it came from the general direction of Cook's path. The glare flashed more now, becoming almost continuous, but varying slightly in brightness. I stared, trying to identify what it could be. It seemed so familiar, but I couldn't quite place it. If only I were a little closer . . .

Chapter 12

I came to with a start. Darkness enveloped me, the sun gone as if in the space of a heartbeat. But it hadn't been a heartbeat. A shiver surged through my body, causing my teeth to chatter, and I realized with sudden alarm that I was no longer on the side of the road. Somehow, I stood waist-deep in the middle of the swamp, shaking from the frigid water that surrounded me. My entire body was drenched, as though at one point, I had fallen in. Straining my eyes, I scanned the horizon, but couldn't see the shore in any direction with the clouds covering the night sky.

Tom Cook's fate came to me with startling clarity. The poor man had been lured out there, entranced by a fairy's will-o'-the-wisp. And remembering the body on the slab in the morgue, I knew what would happen to me if I stuck around.

Now was not the time to think about why the wisp targeted me. It had, and I was a goner if I didn't get out. The glow of the moon cast a silvery sheen over the still water as it emerged from behind a cloud, but the scant light didn't help in finding my way out. Each direction looked the same: stagnant water stretching out toward a line of trees. Every shore looked indistinct and horribly unidentifiable.

My hands shook as I drew my keys from my pocket and pressed the panic button on the car's remote. No sound came, which told me either the car was too far away, or the waterlogged remote didn't work. There must be another way to find the right shore.

The talisman! Liz—and Rocky—were in Boston. By then, she would be home, but still off in that direction, which would be east of the swamp. Closing my eyes, I concentrated on the small, stone device. The engraved writing on its smooth surface came to my mind, and I could picture the strange letters glowing red. Then I called to it. *Rocky! Show me where you are!* The direction of my new little friend's location came to me right away. If I went in a straight line off to my left, I would eventually find it. *Okay, left is east*, I thought, my mind working too slow for my liking. The swamp had been to my right when I parked, so that would put the road somewhere in front of me.

A section of the woods must jut into the water, like a tiny peninsula, obscuring my sight of the street. I made straight for it.

The task proved almost impossible. Each step took a lot out of me for only a little progress. Sloshing in waist-high in freezing cold, April water was hard on its own. But the mystery of Cook's missing footwear became clear to me every time I lifted a foot. The muck at the bottom sucked at my feet, and my shoes were quick casualties in my struggle against the swamp.

Something the size of a soccer ball struck the water right in front of me. The splash it caused soaked my face, betraying its considerable weight. My head whipped around to see a lone figure standing in the water thirty feet off to my right. A humanoid of immense proportion, the newcomer couldn't be human. My earlier joke about Bigfoot came to mind. A moment's fumbling in my jacket pocket produced a flashlight, and its beam I aimed at the creature.

Insatiable curiosity had always been one of my faults. It was likely to get me killed one day. This might have been that day. At least eight feet in height with broad shoulders, the beast was hairy, but not like an ape. A tangle of hair covered the top of its head, and more of the stuff grew on its chest. Its tree trunk arms stretched far down the length of its body in a weirdly inhuman fashion.

But it was the face that froze my blood. Dispro-portionately large and elongated, its maw dangled in front of its neck. The monster's big eyes reflected the light of my flashlight, giving off an eerie glow. Its mouth hung low and open, revealing uneven, sharp teeth, with two fangs protruding like sabers from its upper jaw.

An ogre. A fucking ogre. And it held a rock nearly the size of its enormous skull above its head. The monster bellowed at me as I flashed the light on it.

I ran, or that is, I trudged as fast as I could toward the trees. My only chance of survival was on solid ground, so I struggled as best I could in the water and muck.

The rock struck my left shoulder, and I fell forward

into the freezing water. Pain shot through me, but that was the least of my worries. Exposure, which had already been a problem when I woke from my trance, and of course, the ogre were my primary concerns. Half shoving with my feet, half swimming, I came up from the bottom and burst from the water, sputtering.

The ogre now tromped through the water toward me, a tree trunk it clearly considered a club waving in its right hand. Although it had difficulty with the muck, the monster still moved a lot quicker than I could. Two options lay before me: shoot or swim. There was no guarantee that my .45 would stop an ogre, and I didn't relish the idea of fighting it hand to hand in the water. So, I dove.

The downside to swimming became clear right away. My waterlogged clothes dragged with every stroke and threatened to pull me under. The frigid water froze my joints, making the task impossibly painful. I tried not to focus on the cold and concentrated on the shore that seemed too far away. My feet pushed off from the bottom, much like when I fell in, but in the direction of the trees. That put some distance between the monster and me. Desperately, I focused on my strokes, first my left, then my right, then my left again. My shoulder burned from the injury and my joints grew stiff from the cold, but I kept going. Stroke after stroke and the shore approached. The ogre was behind me somewhere, but there was no time to worry about it. Only the water and my strokes existed in this world. Left. Right. Left. Right.

My hand dug into the peat. I had reached the shore!

Hope sprung to life in my head as I dashed a few feet inland and spun around. Almost falling, my legs, numb from the cold, wavered as I steadied myself. Hunched over in the edge of the woods, I caught my breath and shivered from head to toe. The frigid water had taken its toll. Exhaustion overwhelmed me, and every inch of my body and mind screamed for sleep. That was perhaps the hardest battle I fought that night.

After a small eternity, I looked up toward the swamp I had just left. The ogre climbed out of the water, looking a lot less winded, and far more terrible than before. It snarled, and I felt the deep bass of it in my shoeless feet. The monster stood no more than ten feet from me and took the time to consider me before bashing my brains in. How nice of it.

My brain shouted at my arm to draw my beautiful, tricked out handgun, and when I saw it rise to aim at the beast, I squeezed the trigger.

The gun fired, as it had at the changeling. The bullet ripped into its right shoulder, opening a deep hole from which blood sprayed.

The creature jerked, that hideous face twisting into a frown. The massive head turned to look at the wound, as though it was hit by a golf ball. One gigantic finger touched the injury, and the ogre winced.

I should have shot the fucker while its head was turned. Even in my condition, I could have hit its temple, turned its brain to mush. Yet I didn't. Like a victim in a cheap horror flick, I just stood there dumbly. The pain in my shoulder, the unbearable cold, and the shock that comes from realizing I was out of my league kept me rooted where I was, unable to act.

The ogre, however, could. With only a moment's pause, it charged, crossing the ten-foot distance in one enormous stride, its tree-trunk club arcing toward my head.

My paralysis broke, and I dove out of the way, the whoosh of swinging death loud in my ears as it passed overhead. The dive sent me sprawling to the ground off to one side, and at first, the monster hesitated, as though wondering where I went. Then once again, it loped with surprising speed toward me as I brought my gun up for another shot.

There was no time to aim for its head—center mass was my best bet. Two rounds fired, minor explosions reverberating in my ears as both struck near its heart. The bastard didn't slow down, but the shots forced a howl of rage as the monster swung the club downward in a crushing blow toward my chest.

The wounds must have had some effect, because it missed, failing to squash my head like a melon. However, it did hit my right arm. This time I heard the bone snap, and I screamed in agony. *Run, run, RUN*, my brain wailed at me, forcing my body into action. Using my less injured left arm, I squirmed to my feet and ran. My gun lay on the ground, having dropped from my useless hand.

I ducked behind a tree, the ogre thundering behind me. Instead of following me around it, the big dummy swung the club at it, connecting with the trunk with an ear-splitting crash. But for all its massive size, the young, healthy wood was too much for the makeshift bat. The improvised weapon shattered into splinters.

The ogre's momentary confusion gave me time to dash to the safety of a tall pine. The broken remains of its bludgeon dropped forgotten to the dirt, and it gave chase, a howl of rage ensuring that no animals were left within a one-mile radius.

This one wasn't as thick as the last, but it still provided some cover. The ogre reached around the trunk, first one way and then the other, trying to grab me, but I was too fast. The beast changed its tactic and, grasping the tree in both hands, pulled with all its might. The wood creaked and groaned, and finally started to crack.

Yup. The fucking monster was going to pull the tree from the ground or break it in two.

As it struggled, I shot off again. Running was out of the question, as my frozen legs began to seize up, and I almost fell. My arm and shoulder sent charges of searing pain through me as I stumbled forward. Yet if I timed things right, I wouldn't need to continue for long.

Every tree I ran to brought me closer to my forsaken gun. Nothing else would kill the thing—and even then, I needed a headshot. The ogre gave up on its attempt to uproot the pine and came after me, each footfall thundering and sending tremors up my legs.

My arm was yanked suddenly backward, and I was spun around to face my assailant. The beast glowered over me, holding me in place. I couldn't fight the thing, even in prime condition—which I wasn't. This close, I could feel its hot breath, reeking of death. One free hand struck me across the face, and I heard something pop in the vicinity of my jaw. Stars bounced in my vision, and I knew I was going to die.

Instead of crushing my skull, like poor Cook, the ogre tossed me. My body flew like a rag doll to land heavily on my chest a good ten feet away. Rolling onto my back, I glanced up at the monster. The grin it flashed me almost made me vomit. The bastard was toying with me, like a cat playing with a mortally wounded mouse. It let me go, only to catch and hurt me more. This game never ended well for the mouse. Unable to stand in my condition, I looked around wildly for anything that could save me.

My gun lay no more than two feet from my left hand. An armed mouse had a chance.

With one deep breath to brace for the pain, I shoved my arm toward the weapon. The ogre must have seen what I was doing because it grunted and started forward.

Good. The closer it was when I shot, the better.

My hand closed around the gun's grip just as the monster grabbed me by the neck. It lifted me off the ground and snarled triumphantly at me. Then, its eyes widened when I put the barrel between its bloodshot eyes and squeezed the trigger.

The recoil sent another surge of pain through my shoulder. Hot blood splattered my face. But the monstrous hand opened, and I dropped with a *thud* at its feet. The ogre stood there, wobbling a little on its massive legs, its face bearing a look of mingled surprise and fear. Two more rounds tore at the thing's head. A third missed, but it didn't matter. There wasn't much head left at that point. The ogre stumbled backward, flailing, and fell to the ground with a minor earthquake. It took no more than ten seconds for the arms to realize their master was dead and drop to its sides.

The gun hit the dirt with a dull *thunk* as I rolled over onto my stomach and threw up.

Chapter 13

All concept of time escaped me as I lay where the monster had dropped me, going in and out of consciousness. Eventually, I became aware that I was cold, terribly cold, and it could kill me if I didn't warm up. My right arm was broken, and my left shoulder hurt like a son of a bitch, but my arm still moved some, so it couldn't be too bad. My jaw taught me new lessons in pain, and my new skin color was black and blue. Yet somehow, my head survived, and my legs. I could walk and think, and between the two, I had a fair chance of survival.

The ogre's carcass still lay on the ground nearby. Though I yearned to examine the body, I had only one plan at the moment: get to my car. Working slowly, to cause as little pain as possible—an impossible feat—I holstered my gun and tried to stand. That proved harder than expected with a broken arm. The adrenaline from the fight abated and left me at the mercy of my pain. However, after a lot of squirming and struggling, I managed to rise and hobble through the woods towards where I imagined my car to be. My frozen limbs didn't want to support my weight, much less carry me out of the swamp, but I proved more stubborn than them.

The journey took forever as I made an excellent impression of a zombie. The darkness closed in, the occasional clouds blocking out the silvery glow of the moon. Every couple of minutes, I pressed the panic button on my car remote and was ecstatic when my car's lights flashed, and the horn honked. The door responded with its satisfying click, and I climbed in. The car came to life with the purr of a lion waiting to pounce. A moan escaped my lips when the heat came in to warm my body. Though my car begged to be driven, I was not that stupid. Sometimes—just sometimes—I knew when to call for help.

My concerns about exposure were exaggerated. Though I was thoroughly frozen, and I could have died had I stayed in the swamp much longer, the car's heater took away the chill, and I felt much better.

My phone turned on when I plugged it into the charger on the dash, and I told it to call Ross.

The detective's voice came over the stereo's speakers after three rings.

"What did you find?" was all he said in greeting.

For once, I was in no mood to chide him. "I'm hurt." My eyes widened in surprise. The damage to my jaw made me almost unintelligible.

"Christ, Kane! You sound like shit."

"Thankth. I can't drive. Come get me."

"You still at the swamp?" he sounded concerned now.

"Yeth."

"I'll call an ambulance."

"No! No hothpitalth."

"But you need one. Don't be stupid."

"Jutht get your ath over here, or I'll drive mythelf."

Ross paused as he considered my request. "Okay. But I'm bringing someone who can help."

"Good. Pleathe hurry."

The thought of waking up in a hospital bed with a creepie bending over me sent a shudder through my body. They scared me more than most supies because I didn't know how to fight them. Usually, supernatural beings could be hurt by some kind of physical attack, but I suspected creepies couldn't. Nope. No hospitals for me.

Besides, I was resilient. One of my "special abilities" was I tended to heal better than other people—it was why I didn't succumb to exposure. This may have been the worst beating I ever endured, but I knew I'd do all right without staying at a hospital.

Ross was easily an hour away since he had to round up his friend. There was time to think. Ogres didn't usually live in our world. At least, not this close to civilization. And will-o'-the-wisps were classic fairy tricks. This was a trap, carefully planned by fairies, to lure people out into the swamp and kill them—and in the most excruciating way possible. But not just any people. Only the poor man on the slab and myself. Now, I understood why they wanted me—I shot the changeling. That couldn't have made them happy. Fine. Yet I wasn't the primary target, only a lucky coincidence. So, why Cook?

Ross said the guy was a friend of Mr. Mann, and both were targeted. They must have been involved in something that angered the fairies—enough to kill. I needed to find out what the two men were doing. That required research and some PI work. Mann should be easier to tail than Sebastian Gray.

A car pulled off the road and came to a halt forty minutes after I hung up the phone. Two plainclothes cops emerged. One was Ross, the other new to me.

Detective Bill Kravitz was in his mid-forties with a square jaw and brown eyes. The standard suit and tie he wore screamed cop, but his strongly built arms and chest made him look uncomfortable in the getup. Yet for all that, Kravits had a softer demeanor than most detectives I'd met. A medical kit dangled from one hand as he and Ross approached my car.

A blast of cold air assaulted me as I opened the door and turned to sit sideways, my feet just touching the ground. The half-hour of rest caused all my joints to stiffen, and I winced as my broken arm nudged the steering wheel.

"Holy shit, Kane!" Ross gaped when he came to the open door and saw me in all my glory. "You look a lot like the guy in the morgue."

Detective Kravitz pushed past his superior and knelt in front of me. First, he inspected my jaw, frowning. "It's not broken, just displaced." Without another word, he opened his medical kit and got to work. First, he doped me up something to deaden the pain. Then he applied pressure to my jaw, downward and to one side, to snap it back into place. The thick rubber gloves he wore had extra padding on his thumb, which made sense once he stuck it into my mouth to do the procedure. My jaw snapped closed with great force when it popped into place. Kravitz just winced and removed his hand from my mouth. He finished the job by fastening a cloth strip over my head, toothache-style, to keep my jaw from dislocating itself again. "Keep this on for a couple of days until the muscles heal."

"Thanks, doc. Now if you can check my arm—it's broken." My head tilted toward my right arm that hung limply at my side.

Kravitz nodded grimly and got to work examining and bandaging it. No bedside manner. All business. Probably military trained.

"What happened?" Ross asked.

Another head tilt, this time toward Kravitz, preceded a knowing glance at Ross. "I had a run-in with Cook's killer."

"You did?" he said excitedly. "Can you give a description?"

"Better yet, I can give you its body."

The lead detective opened his mouth to speak, and then hesitated. He noticed I said *it*. The deadpan expression he gave me said, "later." Nobody else would have caught it, but given the context we both shared, the message was loud and clear.

"Where is it?" His voice held its customary curtness.

I told him, and he went off at a jog, retracing my steps to the scene of the fight, leaving me alone with the doc.

The doctor was not a talker. He hardly said anything

while he worked on me, except to ask questions relating
to my injuries. And he made no attempt to identify the
cause, just to treat. The silence helped, and I wondered
if he knew that. In the end, my right arm was in an
aluminum splint, my left in a wrist sling to prevent me
from moving my shoulder, and I had bandages over
various cuts and abrasions, which stung.

Ross returned shortly after the doc had finished. He
stopped talking on his cell phone and put it away as he
approached.

"How is he?" he said to Kravitz.

The doctor shrugged. "He needs a hospital, but
he'll live."

The detective glanced at me, and I shook my head.
"Stay here and wait for the Winchester Police to show
up. I'll drive Simon home." Kravitz nodded, and Ross
motioned with his thumb for me to move. For once,
I didn't feel like driving, so I hobbled like an old man
around to the passenger side. The Good Doctor helped
me.

It took some effort for Ross to get used to the
Ferrari. The car was too responsive and too fast. But,
after some jerks and tire screeches that made me wince
in sympathy for the poor car, he got the hang of it, and
we were on our way back to Boston.

"So," Ross said as he drove, his eyes glued to the
road ahead. "What was it? What killed Cook and made
you look like the walking dead?"

"You saw it. What do you think it was?"

"I didn't find the body. Your footprints were all over
the place, as were some huge ones. There was a giant

pool of blood and the signs that something dragged itself back into the water."

"What?" I said, shocked. "I blew its head apart. There's no way it could have crawled anywhere."

"Then, maybe something *pulled* it into the water."

A frown creased my face, which hurt. The fairies would want to clean up after themselves. They wouldn't leave proof of their kind lying around.

"That could be the case," I said.

"What was it?"

"An ogre."

"No shit?" he threw me a quick glance, as though to see if I was joking.

"Dead serious."

"Is it a type of fairy?"

"Maybe. But they summoned it." I told him the entire story, beginning with getting duped by the will-o'-the-wisp, to the point where I hobbled back to my car. I left nothing out, except for my use of Rocky. He didn't need to know about that since it was for a different case. Ross sat quietly and drove, occasionally nodding or grunting at certain points. He didn't speak right away when I had finished.

"They're mad at Richard Mann and his friend Tom Cook," Ross said. "They killed Cook, and the changeling is done, thanks to you. They might try to kill Mann. I should talk to him and put him and his family in protective custody."

"I'm not convinced Mann and Cook are simple victims," I said. "Those two men did something to anger the fairies, and that's not easy to do. Though they can be ruthless when angered, fairies don't go around hurting humans every day. I suspect the men were doing something out of the ordinary—something supernatural. And I'll bet it's not wholesome either. Or legal. I'm going to investigate them and see what I can dig up."

Ross shook his head. "You're in no condition for that. The doc said you need a hospital, but if you refuse to do that, then you're at least not going to work. Stay home and rest."

"Yes, mother," I said, and he flashed me a sharp look.

"You and I don't always get along, and you can be a real pain in the ass. But I don't want you to end up on a slab. This case is obviously too much for you."

"Don't go there, Ross," I warned. "I'm not leaving this case. This is precisely the kind I went into business for. If fairies are involved, there is no way you can stop me from investigating. No way."

The detective paused before speaking. "Fine. You're still on the case, but not on active duty. Do your research. Don't go out and snoop around. Not until you've healed up."

"Okay. No physical stuff until I'm feeling better. Got it."

He cast me a sidelong glance, brimming with suspicion. "I'm not joking. I can make things difficult for you."

"Detective Ross," I said in my best placating tone. "I fully respect your authority. You're in charge. If you want me healed up before I do anything physical with the case, then so be it."

He gave me that look again. "Why do I have the feeling you're not going to do as I say?"

"I have no idea," and I smiled when I said it—which hurt like hell.

Chapter 14

I took a shower as soon as I got home. Though I was practically a zombie from exhaustion, the stink of the swamp, the mud, and the ogre's blood had to come off. And the cold still clung to me like a leech. Hypothermia or not, the cold wouldn't go away. Forty-five minutes in a hot shower did the trick.

My bed beckoned when I emerged from the bathroom, and I went to it gratefully. My exhausted body thanked me when I lay down and closed my eyes. The dreams that invaded my mind were full of ogres, mysterious lights, and swamps—hardly restful. Though considering I awoke at noon, I was as rested as possible.

After fumbling unsuccessfully in the kitchen, I decided to take Ross' advice and stay out of action until I felt better. Nothing was easy with one arm out of commission and the other impaired. Besides, twenty-four hours should leave me completely healed. That's how resilient I am. Giving up making breakfast, I ordered some delivery and got down to work.

One call to Ross with the promise of sitting tight and doing research resulted in access to the files on Richard

Mann and Tom Cook. Taking a seat at my dining room table, I dug into the lives of the two victims.

Richard Mann was an entrepreneur. That is, he *tried* to be one. He started three different dot-coms, and each one failed miserably. I pitied the man as I read his file. They all had marketable concepts, but he could never make them take off. The endeavors were an excellent way to go broke. After the third business went under, he began having trouble with the law. The poor guy got arrested twice for shoplifting and once for petty theft.

Then his luck changed. Two years ago, he started a fourth company, AddictedHot.com, which did remarkably well. This didn't make sense because his prior business ideas were much better. The startup grew big overnight and was now working toward an IPO. He married his wife shortly after founding AddictedHot, and she got pregnant soon after. Just when life had hit rock bottom, he bounced back and achieved the American Dream in record time.

Tom Cook's file told a similar rags-to-riches story. After taking six years to graduate from college with an English degree, he jumped around from job to job, making little more than minimum wage. Then, two years ago, he wrote a book—a novel about vampires and werewolves in modern day New York City. It took off, becoming a bestseller virtually overnight. Now it had a movie deal and sequels on the way.

My curiosity piqued, I purchased the eBook of *Darkness Strikes* and read a few chapters. It stunk. The plot was derivative and poorly paced, the characters bland and lifeless. And I couldn't stand the writing.

Some stinkers managed to become best sellers, but there was always something about the books that would redeem them. A clever idea, romance, or an understanding of its audience. Cook's masterpiece failed across the board. The book's popularity was as much a mystery as AddictedHot.com.

Both victims had seen recent success, enough to raise them from poor to wealthy practically overnight. Suspicious, but it didn't explain why fairies would want to hurt them. I needed more.

The Internet provided little more regarding Mann. An article or two discussed the rise of his new company and the fall of the rest, but I found no revelation. His first companies went under due to a lack of business acumen and managerial ability. They were *his* failures, not those of the market, the economy, or his employees. *He* had failed. Though he held the reins of his new venture, there appeared to be no sign of his prior inabilities. At some point, while stealing from convenience stores and snatching purses, he managed to become a business genius. I didn't buy it. There must have been some secret to his success I couldn't find. Perhaps some colleague working behind the scenes was calling the shots.

Research on Cook, however, hit pay dirt. First, every review of his horrible book raved about it. Every. Single. One. Magazine reviews, blog reviews, newspaper articles, even user feedback on online retailer sites sung the praises of *Darkness Strikes*. Impossible. Even superstars like Stephen King got random one-star user reviews. And that was for King's best. Yet one of the worst books ever written got nothing below five stars.

No way!

Two friends, both of them losers in their own right, suddenly strike it rich at the same time. Oh, yeah. My supernatural radar beeped loudly in my head. Cook possessed no innate abilities, or I would have detected residual magic at the morgue. Mann's earlier experiences ruled out the same for him.

Ritual magic. It had to be.

That didn't explain how they'd angered the fairies, but I finally had a lead. Of course, I couldn't question Tom Cook, so it was time to talk to Richard Mann. The promise I made came back to me. No field work while I recovered. After all, I did feel like shit. Since I still expected to be ready for action the next day, I decided not to push things. Especially with the ridiculous cloth around my head. That gave me the night off.

The date!

It came to me in a flash when my mind wandered to dinner. A glance at my watch showed just past four. With less than three hours to get ready, I would be a total wreck. Hell, five hours couldn't give me the makeover I needed. No way was I going to show up at L'Espalier with this headgear. I had to cancel.

She never gave me her phone number, so I called the hospital. Pressing zero on their menu and asking the operator for Dr. Summer Parke ended with me sitting on hold for five minutes.

"Hello?" Summer's familiar voice replaced the bland pop music that droned on during my wait.

"Hello, Summer. It's Simon."

"Oh! Hi. To what do I owe the pleasure? You're not

canceling, are you?" she added jovially, but with a hint of suspicion around the edges of her words.

"I'm afraid so."

A moment of silence followed my statement, making it seem hollow. When she spoke, her tone was harder. "Why?"

My father once tried to teach me all he knew about women. "Son," he had said. "Women aren't like men. They don't want to hear the truth like we do. Tell a woman you love her, and she'll stay with you for as long as you want her. She'll be happy if she thinks everything's rosy, so always sugar coat your bad news. It'll save you a lifetime of headaches." I should have realized the one piece of fatherly advice he ever gave me was a crock of shit. But I burned through woman after woman before I learned that valuable lesson.

"I got hurt last night," I said, ignoring my father's advice and thus giving myself a chance with Summer. "A work-related accident."

"Hmm . . ." She sounded suspicious. A common excuse, perhaps? "What kind of accident can a PI have? Some guy catch you taking pictures of him? I don't mind a black eye."

"An animal attacked me in a swamp near Winchester."

A moment passed as she processed what I said. "What were you doing in a swamp?"

"It's a case. I can't tell you much about it. Someone died there, and I went to investigate."

"That's why you went to the morgue."

"It is. Now, I do want to take you to dinner. Just

not tonight. I'm still recovering."

"How bad is it?" Her tone was still hard but lost some of its ice. Being a doctor, she would undoubtedly know if I made anything up, so once again, the truth was my wingman.

"I have a splint on one arm, my other's bandaged, and another bandage is holding my jaw in place."

"Why aren't you in a hospital?"

"I don't like them."

The look she flashed me was full of *I've heard that one before.* "That's not a good reason."

"It is for me."

"What are you going to do while you recover?"

"Stay home and watch movies," I said.

"Sounds boring."

"Yeah, but I need my rest."

"You know that means you won't see me until next week?" she said.

"It's regrettable, but I can't see a way around it."

Another pause. "Well, it's your loss."

"Too true. But if you give me your number, I can call to reschedule."

Another moment to consider the request, then she gave it to me.

"Well, good night, Simon Kane. I hope you recover quickly, although you would in a hospital."

That conversation didn't go as bad as I thought it would. Had I found a woman worth dating? Maybe. Could it be I finally learned how to talk to a woman? I seriously doubted it.

Chapter 15

Taking the night off shouldn't be that bad. After all, I owned an expensive home theater that I hardly ever used. I ordered pizza and settled in for a night of recuperation.

The truth was, I didn't know how long it would take me to recover from my injuries. To my knowledge, I never broke a limb before, and the jaw injury was new to me. In fact, aside from the bruises, scrapes, and cuts, I had entered uncharted territory. For all I knew, my healing ability might only work on superficial injuries— which had already gone. The medication had worn off, and my shoulder still ached. Kravitz did a bang-up job on the splint, which I tried to keep intact overnight, so my arm felt okay until I tested it. Nope. Not healed yet.

Seven o'clock came, and the doorbell rang. Dinner time! But when I opened the door, Summer Parke stood in the hallway, holding my pizza in one hand and a bottle of wine in the other. She dressed casually in an oversized Boston University sweatshirt and blue jeans that were tight enough to hint at the curves they covered. Her long brown hair cascaded in waves down her back, which was an improvement from the ponytails I had seen so far. I realized at that moment how striking she looked. The milk chocolate eyes that greeted me were warm and gentle, yet failed to conceal the fire that smoldered behind them. Her smile was genuine and disarming.

And I stood in old sweats with one arm in a sling and a bandage around my head, its knot resting stupidly on top.

The smile faltered for a second when she saw the bandages. A hint of relief flashed across her face. My comical appearance laid her fears to rest—I really was hurt. "Your pizza is here."

I blinked, taken off guard, and I smiled. "They're hiring better delivery people."

Chuckling at my joke, she motioned to the box with her head. "It's getting cold."

"Of course! Come on in." A grin spread across my face as I opened the door wide.

Summer entered and looked around. "The PI business must be a cash cow."

"Nah." The door clicked closed behind her. "Family money."

"I know. I did my homework."

"Smart woman."

She set the pizza and bottle on the coffee table by the couch while I fetched glasses, plates, and silverware. A moment later, she appeared by my side and took everything from my hands.

"Go sit down. Doctor's orders."

Her tone was just firm enough to tell me not to

push it. I carried the glasses and bottle opener to the couch and went to work on the wine. The act of opening a wine bottle proved harder on my arm than expected. Summer sat beside me and once again took it all away from me.

She popped the cork as I served the pizza—a job that was thankfully not beyond me. As we sipped and ate, she regarded me curiously. Then, after eating one slice, she set her glass on the table and turned to me.

"Let me see." Summer gently examined my jaw, touching and prodding the muscles and ligaments. Her gentle touch caused no pain.

"Does this hurt?" She applied pressure with her thumb to a series of muscles on each side of my mouth.

"No." I felt sure at that moment it had completely healed.

"It doesn't look bad. When did this get set?"

"At about two or three this morning."

A frown creased her forehead and her nose scrunched up in a way that made me smile. "That can't be. Or at least, I don't think so. It should take a long time for the muscles to heal."

"You're a student," I said. "Maybe it's harder to diagnose in real life."

That won me a wry smile with a hint of *watch it, buster.* "I'm an *intern.* My brother had his jaw dislocated once. I fixed it myself. It took a lot longer to for him than you did."

"Yet I'm not wearing this fashionable bit of headwear for nothing."

"And I believe you. Did you fix it yourself?"

"No. The doc did this morning."

"You *did* see a doctor."

"The detective I'm working with came and got me. He brought a cop medic with him."

Summer considered that for a minute, then moved on to my arm. Once again in her element, she inspected the splint and injured arm, and I winced only once as she tested the break. This was fun for her. At some point, I came to that realization. Just like hair stylists enjoy practicing on all their friends, Summer had a great time diagnosing people whenever she got the chance.

"Now, what's wrong with your left arm?" Her distrust was now gone after seeing my broken arm.

"I don't know. The doc never said. It's my shoulder blade. A big rock fell on it."

"Okay. Off with your shirt." Her terse commands were part of her professional doctor's manner. Summer was in her element.

For some reason, I found myself reluctant to remove my shirt. Now, I had been with women before—plenty of them. And I was not shy. There was something intimate about the situation that made me nervous. Yet I couldn't refuse at this point. I pulled it over my head and turned my back to her. The bruises that had colored my chest after the fight were gone now. Only the serious injuries remained.

Summer examined my shoulder gently for a minute before telling me I could put my shirt back on. Once I had safely dressed again, I turned to face her.

"What's the verdict?" I asked.

"Well," she started, as though still considering the

evidence. "You are hurt. The arm's clearly broken, and the doctor did a good job setting it. Your shoulder blade is badly bruised, but it's healing. Your jaw seems to be totally healed, which doesn't make sense. Still, you should keep the bandage on until at least tomorrow, just in case I'm wrong. I *should* be wrong."

"Thanks, doc," I said with a smile and toasted her with my wine. She smiled, and we sipped and ate in silence for a while.

"Why did you decide to stop over?" I asked between slices. "Couldn't wait a week to see me?"

She chuckled. "Part of me wanted to see if you were telling the truth. The other part figured I could help if you were."

"So, you decided to track me down and show up unannounced?"

"It doesn't take a private investigator to look someone up. Especially someone as well-known as you."

"And? Are you convinced?"

Summer nodded. "I think your jaw is fine now, but don't trust me. By all rights, it shouldn't be. But your arm is broken, and your shoulder shows signs of damage, although the bruising is nearly gone. If I hadn't seen you yesterday, I would have said this all happened a week or two ago."

"Just a quick healer, I guess."

"It would seem," Summer said. The young doctor was still stewing on my speedy recovery. At least she believed me.

She poured herself another glass. "What are we watching?"

Eyebrows raised as my mind was ripped away from thoughts of Summer. My gaze went to the television that hung cold and dark on the wall.

"Oh, yes!" I said, recovering. "We could watch something new, or perhaps a classic. Which do you prefer?"

"A classic sounds nice. How about *The Big Sleep*?"

"Bogart?" A grin pulled at the corner of my mouth.

"Sure. I'd like to see what you do for a living." Her smile, even in jest, was genuine.

My laugh was, too. "Bogart it is. Though my job is a lot more exciting."

"I'm sure."

We watched the film and finished the pizza. At last, Summer rose and stretched as the credits scrolled across the screen.

"It's been a fun evening," she said. "But I have work tomorrow, and I think you need the rest."

We walked to the door, then she turned to face me.

"I had a good time."

"I'm glad you dropped by. It was a good alternative to L'Espalier."

She waved dismissively. "It's not the food that matters. It's the company. In my opinion, this was a far better date than it would have been there."

"You might be right. But I'll still order a nicer meal next time."

"Assuming there *is* a 'next time.'" Summer grinned

mischievously, then kissed me quickly on the cheek and padded off down the hallway.

"Goodbye," I called after her.

"Ciao!"

Chapter 16

At ten the next morning, I found myself once again parking on the road in front of Richard Mann's home in Brookline. I felt much better after a good night's sleep. My jaw was indeed fully healed, and I no longer needed the sling. The shoulder was a little sore but didn't hurt when I moved it. But my right arm was still broken and remained in the splint. With only the one injury remaining, I was ready to get back to work.

The door opened two minutes after I rang the doorbell. Mrs. Mann stood before me, trying hard to appear as though nothing was wrong, but her face betrayed the facade. Her red eyes had bags that showed she hadn't slept much since last we met. She perked up when she saw me standing before her.

"Have you found him?" It came almost as a whisper, but the hope it carried echoed loudly in my head.

"Not yet, ma'am," I said carefully.

The woman deflated like a balloon with its knot untied. The mother seemed to age ten years in those few seconds.

"Is your husband home? There are questions I'd like

to ask him."

The woman's head shook slowly like an automaton.

"Could I find him at work, then?" Life seemed to seep back into her eyes, and she stopped acting like the living dead.

"No," she said, recovering quickly. "He's taking a leave of absence while we look for Jacob."

"May I come in, then? Maybe you can help with my questions."

Mrs. Mann nodded and stepped aside to let me in. The familiar foyer appeared bigger now that all the cops had gone. It was cleaner than before. Busy work. Bastion of the grieving.

A pleasant smile forced its way onto my hostess' face as she led me into the living room and I took a seat on the couch. She lowered herself into an easy chair across from me. Behind her, the spot where the playpen had been was empty, and the room bore an antiseptic odor. The remains of the changeling likely made a mess of her nice carpeted floor.

"Mrs. Mann," I began, bringing my attention back to her. "How does your husband know Tom Cook?"

The surprise on her face showed no sign of guilt. Though she didn't expect my question, she also didn't think she had anything to hide.

"They're old school friends. Why do you ask?"

"Just gathering information. I'm trying to figure out what made the fairies mad at your family. To do that, I need to know what each of you has been doing lately."

"And you think Tom is involved?"

"I suspect it may have something to do with his death."

The pained expression that marred her delicate features told me I should have been more careful. This happened to me more often than it should, given my profession. My bedside manner rarely worked with ordinary people, so I got these faces a lot.

Mrs. Mann stared blankly at a point two feet to my right as she processed the news. After a deep breath, she met my gaze.

"How did it happen?"

"I can't say. It's part of a police investigation."

"But you think it has to do with—with what happened to Jacob." It was not a question.

A single nod, slow and deliberate. Sometimes it was best not to speak in sensitive situations like this.

"They're close friends. They go out a lot, in the evenings."

"Do you know where they go, or what they do?"

The shake of her head had all the emotion of a robot. The poor woman was trying hard to stay calm. I wondered how long she could keep it up. "Do you think they're into something bad?"

Yes. Though I wasn't going to say that. "I'm still gathering data."

"But it's possible . . ."

"Anything is possible, at this point."

Keep her talking. It would take her mind off her dark thoughts. Help her stay her calm. "You said they are old school friends. From college?"

"Yes. They met at Boston University. Tom was

Richard's roommate during their freshman year."

"They've been close ever since?"

"As long as we've been together, but I think they'd been out of touch for a while after they graduated."

"Can you tell me when they reconnected?"

A shrug. Tiny. Nearly imperceptible. "A couple of years ago."

Bingo.

"Have they been going out a lot the whole time you've known Richard?"

"Yes."

The excitement that prickled in my mind remained hidden as I rose. "That's all I've got, for now, Mrs. Mann. I'd like to talk to your husband sometime. Soon."

The evil magician's wife stood and walked me to the door. "Do you think he's in danger?"

"I think you both are. That's why I need to speak with him."

"He won't believe you about the fairies."

"Did you tell him what happened the other day?"

"Not about your fairy theory," she said.

"It's not a theory. But that's probably a good idea. Have him call me as soon as he can."

"I will." She opened the door. A man stood in the doorway, wearing a modest business suit. Another man was at his side, dressed far better. I recognized the second man right away.

Sebastian Gray's eyebrow raised at the same time mine did.

Chapter 17

Gray blinked at me in surprise, his cool countenance never breaking for a second. Richard Mann, on the other hand, glowered, his gaze flitting from me to his wife, then back again.

"Who the hell are you?" he barked. He was no Schwarzenegger but his muscle-bound arms pushed tightly against the sleeves of his suit jacket, and I didn't want a fight in my condition.

Gray smiled, the cold eyes that matched his name locked onto my face. "Why, this is Simon Kane, the private investigator that's been following me around."

A big hand grabbed my shirt by the collar before I could flinch. The brute's other fist went back in preparation for a collision with my face.

Not again, I thought, picturing the bigger, uglier ogre of two nights ago. Gray stood there, smiling smugly, appearing far too satisfied with the turn of events.

Mrs. Mann came to my rescue. Grabbing her husband's arm, she put her face in front of mine.

"Stop it!" she screamed. "He's here to *help* us!"

That made Richard hesitate. Even Gray raised an

eyebrow with the revelation.

"Becca?" The owner of AddictedHot frowned at his wife, his fist still poised like a battering ram waiting to crush the castle door.

"The police hired him to help find Jacob," she said.

The mini-monster's glare deepened into a frown. "This true?"

"It's my job."

The brute glowered at me for a moment longer, then lowered his fist. The vice-like hand released my shirt, and I afforded him a pleasant smile.

"Why were you following Seb? You think he took my son?" Some men hid behind their anger, as though by keeping their faces red, they could put their enemy on the defensive. Well, I saw through his ruse, and the sudden presence of Gray intrigued me. With a little luck, I might learn his connection to Gray—and keep my face intact.

"Why don't we sit down and talk," I said. "After all, I had really come here to speak to you."

This made him frown more—if that was possible—but he relented. We adjourned to the living room where I resumed my place on the couch. The business suit (another rich man with middle-class style) tightened on his body as Mann settled into the chair his wife had occupied earlier. The object of my other case wandered casually around the room as if to imply he didn't care what we talked about. Right. Rebecca hovered near her husband, as though not yet convinced that he wouldn't haul off and deck me. I was glad for that.

"Nice car," Gray said, gazing out the window at my

Ferrari. "Much better than the one you had the other night."

"That was my work car."

"Smart. You wouldn't want to lose this one." Something in his tone betrayed knowledge of the accident that claimed my Ford. There was something more hidden in those words. A hint of satisfaction that shouldn't have been there. Could he have had something to do with it?

"All right," Mann said, changing the subject. "Talk."

Bad manners to show the guy looking for his baby. But I let that slide and did as instructed.

"The Boston Police Department hired me as a consultant on the case of your missing son."

"Why?"

"Because of the, shall we say, strange circumstances surrounding his disappearance."

"And what circumstances would that be?"

Right. His wife hadn't told him about the fairies.

"Mr. Mann, what do you know about the events of three days ago?"

The man's eyes narrowed as he thought back. "Becca called the police because Jacob was acting weird. They said it wasn't our baby—that it was some kind of impostor. The detective said they don't know who has our son."

Now for the tricky part; finding out what he knew about fairies without sounding crazy.

"Did you see Jacob that morning?"

"Of course I did," he growled. "I'm a *good* father." Genuine. Not bad. Brownie point for Richard Mann.

"Did you think he was your son at the time?"

He stewed on my words for a moment before nodding slowly.

"Isn't it highly unlikely someone could replace your child with an impostor so perfect, it would fool even his own father?"

"Are you accusing me of something?" The snarl threatened the return of the anger and the fists.

"Of course not," I replied calmly. "The police call me in for cases that involve strange events. I'm sort of an expert on the subject."

The big man sat back and considered my explanation. All things considered—being alone with his wife and tailing his friend—he had no desire to trust me, but I had him hooked. The good father was afraid for his kid.

"How did they do it?"

My gaze flitted to Gray for a moment. The cool bastard stood by the fireplace, inspecting family pictures. But he listened intently to our conversation, and his expression betrayed his interest.

"In ancient Ireland, fairies would replace a baby with a changeling." Liz's stepdad paused and then glanced at me quizzically. Mann shot a quick peek at his friend. I hit a nerve. "This fairy would look just like the original child but would be different. The imposter would misbehave, either by feigning illness or by behaving in ways that would torture the child's parents."

He shifted uneasily in his tight suit. "You think fairies are after me?" The statement was meant to sound ridiculous, but he failed to pull it off.

Rebecca turned to her husband, frowning. "You know something about this," she accused. "What are you doing? What are you *two* doing?" The woman's blue eyes cast an icy glare at Gray, who merely smiled and shrugged.

"Come on, Becca," Mann said, recovering from his initial shock. "You don't believe any of this crap."

"Oh, yes I do!" Her voice rose with mounting hysteria. "And I think you do, too."

The irate husband opened his mouth to retort, but his friend cut him off.

"Mr. Kane, you think fairies replaced poor Jacob with a changeling?" None of the contempt and ridicule there should have been was in his tone. Either he was playing along with me, or he believed I could be right. I'd bet money on the latter.

Sebastian Gray had forsaken the pictures on the mantel and stood facing me, his gray eyes locking with mine. This was a man of confidence, used to being in control. I returned his gaze without flinching. So was I.

"I do."

"You don't look the type to believe in fairy tales."

"I believe in a lot of things."

"Apparently, I was wrong. You are indeed a man of some intelligence."

"Why do you suppose a fairy would go to the trouble to replace Jacob Mann with a changeling?" I asked Gray.

"Of course, I have no idea. What do you think, Rich? Are you doing something to upset fairies?"

The burly man chuckled. "Hey, private *dick*. How

does someone go about making fairies mad?"

My gaze returned to him once more. The brute finally gained some composure. He no longer looked angry. In fact, he acquired the appearance of a high school jock engaged in some spirited fun with a forty-pound weakling. A look he wore a lot as a kid, I would imagine.

"Now we come to my reason for visiting. You and your family are in danger. Somehow, you managed to piss off some pretty powerful supernatural beings, and they're out for blood."

The teasing grin dropped from his face. "Are you saying they killed Jacob?" More genuine concern.

Amazing. Neither man was toying with me. Both believed in fairies and seriously entertained the possibility they were involved in the disappearance of the little boy.

"No. Though they murdered your buddy, Tom."

The man's red face went ashen. Then, he glanced meaningfully up at Gray.

Paydirt.

My eyes followed his gaze. Gray looked surprised. Not upset, mind you. Just surprised.

"How?" was all he said.

"Sorry. The police are investigating, so I can't say. Only that you managed to make enemies of powerful creatures with powerful friends."

"And you came to warn us?"

"I came to warn *them.*"

"Hmm. Well, it was nice of you to drop by with your warning, but now that you have . . ." Gray trailed off.

"It's time you leave," Mann finished for him.

"You're right, I should be going." Without another word, I went to the door. Rebecca followed me.

"Thank you for your hospitality," I said quietly to her as she opened the door.

"I'm sorry," was all she could say.

"No need. *You* were quite gracious."

Chapter 18

The road passed by in a gray blur as I steered the car up and down random streets. Driving often helped me think, and I needed to sort through all I learned at the interview. When it began to rain, I decided to stop for lunch.

A proverbial hole-in-the-wall, Antonio's took up one slot in an old brick building. A neon sign read "pizza" beside bigger signs advertising beer. Inside, the narrow place ran deep into the heart of the structure, with the front end taken up by a bar. Blue collar workers sat on the stools, drinking their beers and talking about The Patriots as they watched clips from last year's game on the TV that hung from the wall. The haze of cigarette smoke was conspicuously absent, thanks to state laws. Tables lined the area beyond the bar, where people came to eat. The place didn't fit in with my usual tastes, but as this was the best pizza in Boston—and that was saying something—I was willing to slum it on occasion. Though busy, I found a cozy booth in a back corner where I could eat in peace and mull things over.

Though I loved extravagant foods, pizza was meant

to be simple, and I went all the way to carnivore. The waitress came, and I ordered my meat-lover's pie and a beer, and then sat back, closed my eyes, and considered the sudden turn of events.

Sebastian Gray was involved with Mann and Cook. He was a big-wig at Dynamo—their COO—but two years back, he was just a grunt programmer. I should have noticed the pattern before. What were they into, and how could it have pissed off the fairies? They all had big dreams but were unable to make them come true. Until at some point two years ago, when all of a sudden they got everything they wanted. All three got tremendously lucky at the same time.

Luck!

Of course. Gray was studying magic—*real* magic. Presumably, they all were. All three of them used it to give themselves extraordinary luck in their careers and personal lives. You see, most magic wasn't like in games and movies—at least not the type humans couldn't do. You couldn't do anything crazy like shoot fireballs from your hand or whip up a blinding blizzard in a room. It was all subtle. Magic manipulated our world through probability. You couldn't cast a spell to force a woman to love you, but you could perform a ritual to increase the chances of meeting a woman who will fall for you. In the end, you couldn't tell if your new romance was due to your spell, or just coincidence.

The three amigos' sudden rise to fame was not subtle at all. Sure, most people wouldn't have noticed. Yet I did. That meant they had some heavy duty power behind their spellcasting. Something that broke the natural laws—something that angered fairies.

I opened my eyes and saw two things. My beer had arrived while I was lost in thought.

And a man sat across the table from me in my booth.

The second of the two made me frown.

He was of average height, with straight brown hair, and a face his own mother would forget. A black shirt was visible under a gray fleece jacket. His face sported a warm smile as he removed his sunglasses and fixed me with a gaze that gave me the willies.

His mother would remember the eyes. They were shaped like a human's, but there the similarity ended. Yellow and cat-like, I first thought he wore a pair of those specialty contacts geeks like to wear at anime conventions, yet I had the distinct impression they were real. This man wasn't a normal human. If you recall, I could see supernatural things for what they were, and this guy radiated like some kind of human-supey hybrid, like me.

One thing was certain: I didn't trust him. He tingled with magic, so I had to expect the worst. My initial frown forced its way into a smile. A professional one like I would give to a client. Under the table, I slid my hand to the holster on my hip.

"Can I help you?" My voice was steady, neither friendly nor confrontational.

He continued to smile, and something about it made me want to put a fist in it. "Perhaps *I* can help *you*. You're a special man, Simon Kane. I represent an organization made up of *special* people, like yourself.

I'm here to offer you the opportunity to join us. You can learn a lot from us."

My eyes never left his face as I paused for a moment to consider what he said. First, he knew who I was. Second, he knew *what* I was—or at least he had an idea. My hand hovered by the grip of my handgun, but I didn't grab it. Though I didn't expect to shoot this man, he gave me the heebie-jeebies and that warranted caution.

"You're a recruiter?"

The man chuckled. "I suppose you could say that. Are you interested in learning more about our group?"

Playing dumb about his meaning of "special" was unnecessary, given the circumstances. "It depends. What do you do? Use magic to help old ladies cross the street? Or are you trying to rule the world?"

"Nothing so trivial as the former, nor as grandiose as the latter. We help each other learn about our gifts and strive to utilize these gifts to the benefit of mankind."

"Sounds nifty." I had a problem with organizations. When people built an organization around something important, it was usually just to take control over that thing. I had nothing against God, but I didn't like religion. They used God to make people do what they wanted, and they wielded that power like a weapon. History was full of it. Some had better intentions than others, but it was always the same thing. My gut told me this guy's goals were less than altruistic. "Why do you want me?"

"I think you know the answer to that, Simon." The strange man kept his smile, but I wished he didn't. He seemed creepier the longer he held it. People didn't smile constantly, except when they were hiding something.

The breath I released was long and intentional—for his benefit. "I appreciate the invite, but I'm not interested in joining your club."

His smile didn't waver, but my refusal did earn a raised eyebrow.

"No offense, but I don't think you understand what our organization can do for you."

"Oh, I'm sure you could do things for me, and recruiting me into your club could make you look good to your superiors. But I'm simply not interested."

That did it. His smile faded instantly, replaced with an expression of concern mingled with a hint of anger. I liked that better. It was more human.

"We are not a *club*, Mr. Kane." He said it slowly, so he could stuff it chock-full of implications. "We are also not to be trifled with."

"I have no intention of trifling with your club. In fact, I have every intention of leaving you and your group alone." That response was perhaps a little glib, and it sounded too confrontational for my liking. I softened my tone.

"Sorry," I began. "Look, I mean no disrespect to you or your organization. I'm not what you'd call a team player. Joining groups, or clubs, or organizations is not for me. I work alone."

My tablemate sat for a minute, considering me. Eventually, his smile reappeared. Damn.

"I owe you an apology, Mr. Kane. I'm afraid I handled this interview badly and would greatly like an opportunity to make it up to you." He extended his hand across the counter toward me, and I moved my thumb to the safety of my gun, and my index finger to hover by the trigger guard. But then he withdrew his hand, leaving a business card lying on the table before me.

The odd man rose from his seat and bowed his head slightly. "Please consider my offer, and call me when you are ready to talk. Good day."

His sunglasses once again covering those cat eyes, he turned and left the restaurant just as my pizza arrived. The breath I had been holding released then, and I looked at the card he had placed on the table. On it was a strange symbol, I took to be magical in nature, followed by a name and phone number.

The name read, "Aleister Crowley."

Chapter 19

The Ferrari roared to life, and I shook my head at the thought of my mysterious meeting. Aleister Crowley—*the* Aleister Crowley—was said to be the greatest practitioner of magic the western world ever knew. He was also dead. The master of the Thelemic Tradition died in the 1940s. The strange recruiter with the cat eyes was fully alive. Sure, the real Crowley might have survived death—the paranormal offered many such options. Yet I didn't want to jump to a wild conclusion when a mundane one presented itself. My weird new friend chose the name of the most famous magician in the hopes he would gain some of Crowley's greatness.

This cemented my determination not to join their little sorcerer's club. Taking a name like that was a sign of ego, and I got enough of that to last a lifetime with my family. Besides, he never told me the name of the group. Was it so secret that I wasn't allowed to know its name until after I joined?

Son of a bitch!

My foot slammed on the gas pedal, and I shot down

the street like an Indy car on race day. This annoying incident only served to derail my thoughts about my interview with the Manns. Mr. Crowley with his creepy eyes and the even creepier smile would have to wait.

Sebastian Gray, Richard Mann, and the late Tom Cook were all practicing magic to boost their luck and make themselves rich and famous. That by itself was not evil. It was all about the details, so they say. The details, in this case, was the speed in which they all rose to riches and the specific magic they used to do so. All three of them were normal humans, as far as I could tell, and humans typically can't cast spells with that level of intensity. I needed to learn what kind of magic they did, and how they did it. That required investigation. With Cook dead and Mann clearly not the evil mastermind type, Gray became my most likely target. Now Liz's case was the course of action. Rocky was in place in her stepfather's car, so the time had come to put it to use.

The talisman I bought from Nick was a curious device. Being a small, smooth stone, it looked simple enough. Yet once I had performed the binding ritual, I was linked to it. If I concentrated on its whereabouts, I would know the direction in which it lay. But it also communicated with me. For instance, I would get a sudden feeling whenever it was on the move, and I would know when it stopped. The BMW was left behind at Dynamo when Gray went with Mann today. The plan was to follow Rocky's cues and show up wherever it went. This would be much easier now that I no longer needed to tail him. It promised to be the best three grand I ever spent.

My apartment beckoned to me, so I went home and rested for a while. There was nothing to do until five o'clock when Gray would get in his car and go to his nightly rendezvous.

The phone rang, and I almost fell off the couch. I hadn't meant to fall asleep, but the events of the past few days had caught up with me. A glance at the clock showed 3:20 pm. Good.

"Hello?" I said, trying not to sound groggy.

"Surprise!" came the cheerful reply over the line. Summer's voice was like a splash of cold water on my face, bringing me to full wakefulness in seconds.

"Are you calling from the hospital?"

"We were overbooked, so my boss offered me the night off."

"And you thought of me? I'm touched."

"Everyone else was busy." Summer smiled across the line.

"Hmm. That figures. I have to work tonight."

"Aww," she pouted. "Can't you call in sick?"

"If only I could, but I'm afraid it's important."

"What is it? Snapping pictures of adulteresses in action?"

A chuckle forced its way out of me. "Not this time. Just a stakeout."

"Ooh, that sounds fun! Can I come along?"

Another laugh, but a bit bigger this time.

"I'm serious," she said. "I'd love to come. I'm interested in seeing what you do."

That took the humor out of me. Gray was a dangerous man, and I didn't want her to get involved. Then again, my plan for tonight was only to watch. No confrontations.

"Okay. It's a date. I'll pick you up at 4:30, and dinner will be anything with a drive-thru."

"Mmm. Junk food. Nice! I'll be ready." She gave me her address. An apartment near the Museum of Fine Arts.

"I'll see you then."

Summer lived in an old brick complex within walking distance of several colleges. She came down the broad concrete steps as I pulled up, a rather large handbag on her shoulder.

She climbed in and looked around the interior as I put the car in gear and drove off.

"I must admit, I expected something a bit more extravagant," she said.

"We're undercover tonight."

"Yeah, but a Toyota Camry?"

My smile showed genuine affection as I patted the dashboard. "With a 358 NASCAR engine. She'll out-perform anything on the road." When she gave me a quizzical look, I added, "I have a car guy."

"You hired someone just to trick up cars for you?"

"He doesn't *just* work for me, but he'll do jobs when I need him. I needed a sleeper—something that looks ordinary but is actually high performance."

"I'm impressed."

"You should be."

She gave me a strange look but said nothing.

We stopped for burgers and sat in the car, eating

while we waited for Gray's BMW to start moving.

"You really slum it when you're on duty," she said. "The fast food, the blue jeans."

I glanced at my get-up. The faded jeans and a light jacket I bought off the rack at Walmart were my undercover clothes for the day. "It's important not to turn heads. Your presence puts a crimp in that plan."

"Hah! Good one. And I thought you'd be above cheap lines."

"The truth isn't cheap. Someone like you is likely to get people's attention."

Still smiling, Summer fished around in the car and found a baseball cap I sometimes used for disguise. She put it on, pulling the visor low over her face.

"There," she said.

I laughed, and she joined me.

We didn't have long to wait. As we sat, enjoying our French fries, I got the unmistakable feeling that Rocky was on the move. It came as a subtle tug in the back of my mind, like a hunch, but a little bit more. We were parked deep in the heart of the Boston, through which Gray had driven the other day. Since I felt he was not likely to stray far from the city, I decided to wait until the talisman stopped before tracking it down. He saw me somehow when I tailed him before, and I wasn't going to let that happen again.

". . . but another intern took my night. So, here I am." Summer continued to talk, but I smiled and kept concentrating on the artifact. Without giving it my full attention, I might miss when it stopped moving.

"Are you okay?"

"Hmm?" My head turned of its own accord, as though coming out of a trance. I had no idea how long I hadn't been listening, but by her expression, it had been a while. Yet instead of anger, concern creased the smooth skin of her forehead, and her eyes were deep with care.

"You seemed a little dazed. Are your injuries flaring up?"

"Oh, no. Nothing like that." It was the last thing I wanted to talk about since they had mostly vanished. "I was lost in thought. The case—it's a tough one to crack."

"Explain it to me, then. Sometimes talking about it will help you catch things you normally wouldn't."

"True. Though some of it's related to a police investigation. The rest is—well, the rest is hard to swallow."

"I work in the emergency room. I've seen a lot of strange stuff."

"Not like this."

"Like what?"

Rocky spared me the need to answer by telling me it stopped moving. It paused several times during its trip, but this time it sent me a confident impression of destination.

The clock on my stereo read 5:58 pm, but I glanced at my watch anyway and raised an eyebrow. Summer couldn't feel the talisman's message, so I had to give a reason for jumping into action.

"Time to go." The engine growled like a lion

stalking its prey, low and powerful, as we pulled out of the parking lot.

"Awesome!" She perked up and looked about, as though searching for a suspicious vehicle in the traffic around us. Her head tilted back so she could see past the visor that still obscured her face. "Where's the stakeout?"

"We'll see when we get there," I said, my eyes glued the road.

"Are you trying to be mysterious, or is it just working out that way?" Summer clearly enjoyed the mystery.

"There are some things I can't tell you. Some due to client confidentiality, some because I don't know them yet. Just be patient. We'll be there shortly. Right now, I need to concentrate. I have some thinking to do about the case."

She seemed satisfied with that and nodded.

The talisman could easily tell me in what direction it lay, as it had back at the swamp. That was of little use to me now, as I was at the whim of the maze of city streets that wound between skyscrapers and highway overpasses. Still, Rocky wanted me to find it, and I knew it would guide me and bring me eventually to my quarry. All I needed to do was open my mind to it and drive.

The route I expected to take would send me toward Government Center, as Gray had gone the day I tailed him. Instead, Rocky led me inexorably toward Charlestown, an old Irish borough. I had hoped we would end up at the site of Gray and company's magical rituals, but I had a sinking feeling it would not happen tonight. As we drove, businesses gave way to restaurants and gas stations, which were then replaced by residences. At last, I pulled the car to a stop in one of the oldest neighborhoods in Charlestown. Judging by the old houses and big, boaty cars, I doubted any of the residents there had never received a Social Security check.

Sebastian Gray's BMW sat on the side of the road in front of a blue cape. A yellow Volkswagen Beetle was in the driveway. Lights showed through the curtained windows on the first floor. A warm golden light glowed from a room upstairs, and I thought I saw a shadow move past as I pulled in behind a car one house down and across the street. With a turn of the key, the purring engine went silent. "We're here."

"Is it that one?" Summer motioned toward the blue cape.

"How did you know?" I asked as I scanned the windows and yard, looking for signs of activity.

Her ponytail bobbed out the back of the hat as she shrugged. "You'd get a clearer view of the house in question from across the street. Its lights are on, and an expensive car is parked conspicuously in front," she said smugly. "And, you were staring at it before you even stopped the car."

"You may have missed your calling."

"Oh, I'm a better doctor. Trust me."

"I have no doubts."

Summer sipped her Coke with its straw. "What are we looking for?"

"Anything," I said. In truth, I had no idea what to

expect, considering I didn't believe Gray came here to cast spells.

"You're interested in the owner of the BMW." It was not a question. "But you don't know why he's here."

"That's right," I said.

"Whose house is it?"

My gaze turned to her. "You're absolutely right. Sometimes you *do* learn from talking. Please, keep your eyes on the house and tell me if you see anything."

"Will do."

After a brief shuffling in my duffel bag, I pulled out my tablet computer and brought up the app I used to look up addresses. My fingers flew on the on-screen keyboard as I entered the address and tapped "Search." A few seconds later, the latest in modern marvels displayed the information I desired.

"Owen Donnell," I read aloud.

"Excuse me?" Summer said, looking at me. I pointed at the house, and she quickly turned back to it. "Did you say, 'Owen Donnell?' *Doctor* Owen Donnell?"

"You know him? Does he work at the hospital?"

She laughed. "Not that kind of doctor. He has a Ph.D. in Anthropology. He used to teach at Harvard. I think he's retired now."

"Really?" Perhaps this night might pay off after all.

"Yeah, I learned about him in school. Read a couple of his papers. He traveled all over the world, studying primitive cultures and working on archaeological digs. He started teaching when he got older."

Setting the tablet down, I resumed my vigil on the good doctor's house. "If someone had questions about, say, the occult, this Dr. Donnell would be the one to talk to?"

Summer flashed me a curious look. "The occult, eh? I suppose he'd be the expert—in Boston, anyway. It comes from ancient and primitive cultures so he might know a lot about it."

I doubted the old professor would be involved in Gray's evildoings, but I'd bet Liz's stepdad could be very convincing. He was probably duping the old man into giving away valuable information under the guise of academic interest. What could the professor know that Gray would want, I wondered? Yeah, Doctor Donnell just became interesting.

"How did you come to be investigating a case involving the occult?" Summer asked without taking her eyes off the house.

"It's a long story," I said. "But it's kind of my expertise."

"Yet you didn't know who Owen Donnell was. What would you do without me?"

"Apparently, a lot more research. I'm glad you came along."

She flashed me a smile, and I thought then of kissing her. But her face clouded suddenly, and she nodded toward the house.

The front door had opened, and Sebastian Gray exited. He turned to say goodbye to his host, and I was surprised to see not an old man, but a young woman. She looked to be in her twenties, with long, blond hair tied in a ponytail. They had a few words, and then they hugged. Perhaps this woman was a daughter or niece of

Dr. Donnell who took care of him in his old age. In that case, she was the target of Gray's manipulation.

My suspect turned and strode down the cement walk toward the road, pulling his keys out and unlocking his car as he did so. I reached for the ignition, but then stopped.

Darting out of the house, like a bird freed from a cage, flew a fairy.

Chapter 20

I grabbed my binoculars to get a better look at the scene. The fairy regarded Sebastian Gray with an expression akin to a Jew meeting Hitler. The intense hatred mingled with fear showed clear on the tiny face, and its miniature hands spasmed between fists and claws, as though it couldn't decide whether to strangle Gray or claw his eyes out. But it did nothing. It buzzed angrily around my quarry from a safe distance, as though terrified of him.

Gray took no notice of the fairy as he strode to his car and climbed in. The BMW roared to life and pulled out, shooting down the street at a speed designed to show off its power. The tiny being hovered by the curb the car had just vacated, staring after taillights that even now reached the end of the road.

Setting down the binoculars, I got out of the car and strode purposefully toward the fairy. Gray's car disappeared around the corner, but I didn't care. The fairy hung in the air, its tiny body drifting slightly in the breeze. There was no precedent for fairies allowing an interview, but I had to try. The wet slap of my footsteps on the pavement pulled it from its impotent glaring after the vanishing BMW, and it whirled around to face me.

The fairy resembled a human being, but of minute size. No more than six inches tall and with no wings, it floated in mid-air, looking like a Ken doll come to life. Young-looking and healthy, its tiny six-pack was visible on its bare chest. Only his bitty loins were hidden, covered by some kind of cloth or leaf or something.

Recognition contorted his face, and he pointed an accusing finger at me. Stopping in the middle of the road, I smiled back and waved at the little guy, wiggling my fingers in the air.

"I'd like to talk to you," I said politely.

The little bastard gave me the raspberry.

"What's your interest in that man?" I asked, gesturing toward the car that had already disappeared around the corner.

He sneered and silently mimicked my words. Mr. Fairy obviously didn't fear me like he did Gray.

"I'm after Sebastian Gray, too," I said. "Let's work together."

The fairy frowned and gave me the finger. Then, he shot off down the street, almost as fast as the BMW had gone.

Perhaps shooting the changeling had been a mistake.

Back in the car, I sat in the driver's seat, stewing over what just happened. Summer stared at me, as though I had suddenly spoken in tongues.

"What was all that about?"

"What was *what* about?" I replied, still partially lost in thought.

"All that," she said, gesturing out the windshield. "Getting out of the car and talking to yourself."

"Oh!" I said, finally bringing my attention back to her. "Well, it's hard to explain."

"Try me."

"You're not ready, though I think you might be in time."

"Now you're talking in riddles."

"No. I'm being vague. Unfortunately, I must keep it that way until you're ready to accept my explanation."

She studied my face for a moment. "Whatever. I'm a lot more understanding than you think I am."

"I'm sure you are. But I routinely deal with things that everyone else refuses to believe in and often scoffs at. I'll tell you soon, but not right now. Now, please let me think for a minute."

That fairy wanted to kill Gray, which made sense since he seemed to be the ringleader of the little occult group. I'd seen fairies before, and it took a lot to make them mad, and even more to make them afraid. Sebastian Gray managed both with one trip to Dr. Donnell's house. They would go after his family next.

His family.

My cell phone came to life, and I hit Liz's contact. It rang for a long time before answering.

"This is Liz Borden," came her disaffected voice over the line. "Leave a message."

With a frustrated grunt, I tossed my phone onto the dash and turned the key in the ignition. If I left a message, it would only put Liz in more danger, since Gray could see her phone.

"Buckle up," I said as I pulled out of my space and took off down the road, leaving a lot of tire on the pavement behind, and putting the Beemer's departure to shame.

"What's wrong?" Summer asked.

"My client's in danger."

"Life or death?"

One curt nod.

She considered for a moment, her face serious as though she was examining a gunshot victim in the ER.

"May I ask what made you realize it? Because I saw nothing—just a man getting into his car and driving off."

"There was something else. Something you didn't see."

"One of those secret things?"

"Yes."

She said no more but stared ahead, her expression grim. There was no suspicion on her face, only determination. Summer believed me and prepared herself for whatever trouble we raced toward. If only I could tell her what to expect. If only I knew.

The Camry wove a pattern around the cars on the road, and I put all my skills to the test. Dodging traffic, shooting down less busy streets, and avoiding police cruisers was hard enough. Doing it while maintaining speed at least ten miles over the limit was harder. It would be too much for almost anyone. But I wasn't just anyone. I was Simon Kane, and I didn't wait for anything when I was in a hurry.

"Where are we going?" Summer made a valiant attempt at not freaking out at my driving, but she had long since stopped looking out the window, and her voice shook just a little as she spoke.

"A music store in Cambridge."

"And your client's there?"

"She didn't answer her phone. It's either her work or her home—and that's out of the question."

She opened her mouth to speak, but then closed it again.

The neon "Open" sign on Bullfrog Records' glass display window still glowed brightly when we arrived at seven o'clock. As we entered the building, I felt a strange sensation, like the one I got in the garage before my car got crushed. A shiver went up my back and shot through my entire body. Something terrible was going to happen here, but I didn't know what, and I didn't know why I knew. I had no precognitive powers.

Liz wasn't at the counter. Quickly walking past the aisles, I found her halfway down aisle three, a stack of CDs in her hands. Without hesitation, I rushed toward her, Summer following closely.

Liz frowned when I approached. She opened her mouth to speak, but I cut her off.

"There's no time. You're in danger. We have to—"

The sound of a revving engine came from outside, and that strange feeling returned, only stronger. My hand seized Summer by the wrist, and I ran, forcing Liz back as we went.

The sudden crash of broken glass and smashing

wood confirmed my fears. I flung Summer forward, and dove into them, the three of us toppling to the ground at the back wall of the store. My face went flat against the carpeted floor, as the unmistakable sound of a car plowing its way through the building roared all around us. Glass and bits of splintered wood and CDs fell over and around us. A chaos of noise enveloped me, and I think I screamed as it all came inexorably toward me.

Then it stopped. The engine went dead, and the vehicle crunched to a halt. The tinkling of glass filled the otherwise silent building. With a single gulp of saliva, I raised my head and looked behind me.

Half a foot from my face was the hot grill of an old Pontiac LTD.

Chapter 21

The car was parked unceremoniously in the center of Bullfrog Records, sitting on the remains of two aisles. Most of my body lay underneath the car, safely between the two front wheels.

CD cases shattered under my hands and feet as I scrambled out from under the monstrosity. An old man sat behind the wheel, an expression of confusion mingled with terror on his face.

"Are you okay?" I said to the women as they stared incredulously at the car.

Liz nodded, clearly in shock. Summer answered in the affirmative.

That strange tingling feeling still ran along my spine. The attack wasn't over. The sensation of magic clung heavy in the air.

"We have to go. Now!"

"But we can't leave the scene of an accident," Summer said. Dumbstruck, Liz stared past me at the car that failed to kill her but assuredly murdered her job.

"This'll happen again if we stay."

"I don't understand. How could . . ."

"Just trust me," I cut in.

Without waiting for her response, I turned to Liz.

"Is there a back entrance?" The poor girl was having trouble coping with the calamity and continued to stare at the wreckage. With her head in both my hands, I forced her to look at me. "We have to leave. *Is there a back entrance?*"

Precious seconds clicked loudly in my head before she suddenly blinked, as though breaking from a trance. The facade she used as a shield fell into place, and she turned away. "Follow me."

Summer and I went single file behind her, and we made our way along the rear wall to a door in the back corner. Beyond was a short hallway with two doors that probably led to a storeroom and maybe an office. At the far end, a metal door stood in solemn defense, a lit neon sign above it reading, "Exit." Striding purposefully down the passage, Liz muttered, "This sucks! Out of a job for at least a month!" The bar across the door rattled as it opened and the chill spring air hit us as we ducked out of the building.

The rear lot was empty, save for two cars parked in spaces. The tingling still filled me with a nameless dread, but I needed time to think. The same sensation visited me right before my Ford Focus got squashed by a collapsing garage. Now, a car careened into the store, missing me only because of that tingle. Someone, or something, was using magic to try to kill me. The fairies didn't like me for shooting the changeling. That's why the ogre went after me and why that fairy reacted the way it had tonight.

Gray was a possibility. If he and his buddies were into occult magic, they might want to silence me. This kind of thing didn't fit the fairies' MO. The amount of power required to make this happen would be huge, and I doubted Gray and company had the magical muscle to do that.

Home. That was where we had to go. The entire apartment had been blessed, and I had placed some artifacts I bought—at great cost—from Nick Ibori, designed to keep negative energies away. And I needed to bring Liz there because this attack might as easily have been for her.

"We have to get to my apartment," I said.

Once we had left the building, Liz slammed the door. "I need to go home."

"Out of the question. That's the last place you should go."

"Why not?"

"Because your father is into some seriously bad shit and has pissed off something that wants to hurt him— and his family."

A frown creased her young face, and she shot a glance back at the building. Sirens wailed in the distance, coming closer.

"Do you mean that wasn't an accident? That someone's trying to *kill* me?"

Two quick nods of my head were all I afforded her. Two nods that screamed *shut up and do as I say*. "Your house isn't safe, but mine is."

"Then I need to warn my mother."

"Once we're at my place," I said. "And we have to

hurry. They're not done with us yet."

Fear showed on her face. Not just shock, like before, but *real* fear. She nodded.

"Good. Now, I'm not driving. Too many ways for them to get us. Walking is out too, for the same reason."

"The subway," Summer said.

Jesus Christ. "Where's the nearest T stop from here?"

Liz tilted her head down the road. "About two blocks that way, across the street."

Of course. Travel in the city was never easy, and nothing was right nearby. "Then let's go. But pay attention to everything. We have no idea where the next 'accident' will come from."

The three of us half walked, half ran the two blocks, looking nervously this way and that. Several people gave us weird looks. Whatever. At that moment, I couldn't care less. Only a few minutes went by, and we stood directly across from the T station. A ladder-shaped stretch of white paint was the only thing to protect us when crossing the road. Every day, people walked out into traffic, placing their lives in the hands of a gallon of paint. Today, that white bastion of salvation seemed woefully inadequate.

Yet there was one ray of hope: it was a divided street with a concrete island running lengthwise between them. Only one lane to deal with at a time. However, the creepy sensation grew stronger the longer we waited.

"Go!" Summer cried, and we rushed across, reaching the island without incident. She flashed a weak smile, as though assuring that all was good.

Waiting for the next break in traffic took an eternity

that I'm sure was only a matter of seconds, but finally, we crossed. Fewer cars drove along this stretch, so we breathed easier as we went. In a few moments, we stood gratefully by the entrance to the subway station.

"We made it," Liz said.

Summer grinned in response, but the words of caution froze in my mouth when a sudden squeal tore through the air.

A car lost control in the first lane of traffic, careened over the island, and bore down on us as we stood, recovering from our crossing.

"Shit!" With both hands, I shoved the two women forward and plunged headlong into the dimly lit cavern of the T station.

Wide, concrete steps made their way steeply down inside the entrance, which I took two at a time, the girls stumbling after me. A loud, metallic crash mixed with broken glass followed us down the passage, but the car remained on the sidewalk, blocking the entrance we had just vacated.

The station opened up before us as we stumbled in, then stood, panting. The sensation still tingled and turned up the hairs on my skin, but it was far diminished. Whoever was causing this was running out of steam.

Determined to take advantage of our unseen enemy's momentary lapse, I led the way quickly past the turnstiles and out onto the platform.

"I have a question," Liz said as we waited for the train. Creepies were already congregating inside the pit, so I leaned against the back wall, and the women joined me. "Why would someone try to kill us by crashing cars at us? It doesn't make sense. Shooting us would be easier."

"It worked on 9/11," Summer suggested.

"But buildings can't get out of the way," Liz persisted. "So, what's *really* going on, Mr. Kane? This has something to do with my stepfather—you said that yourself. What is it?"

I wondered if I had time to tell her. "Once we're safe inside my apartment. This place is too public."

Liz looked around. About a dozen people stood on the platform, and the cavernous acoustics carried every word we spoke.

"Okay, but no later." She had recovered from her fear and shock and was once again the apathetic goth-girl she pretended to be.

Only a few minutes went by when the dreaded sensation once again tingled up my spine. This time, the magical energy rippled through me, and I shook noticeably. This was worse than before and worse even than when my car was demolished. Another attack was coming, and they weren't fooling around. They wanted us dead, and this was to be their masterstroke.

My head spun in all directions as I scanned the platform for any means of escape. A dull rumble was followed by a fall of dust from the ceiling. Only a couple of people looked up before shrugging and returning to their phones.

Summer grabbed my arm. "What's wrong?" she whispered.

"It's coming again," I hissed. "Only worse!"

"The entrance is blocked," Liz said.

"There's only one way," Summer said and stared out at the empty train tunnel.

Running to the edge, I looked in. The creepies were gone. They felt it too.

"Kane," Liz said. "How sure are you? I don't want to go in there?"

"If we don't, we'll die. Guaranteed!"

Without another word, I jumped.

I'm a decent jumper. In my line of work, it went with the territory. I stuck the landing, letting my legs collapse under me to lessen the shock, then rose and held up my arms to catch Liz.

People were chattering now. Some had come to the edge and yelled at me, telling me to get back up.

"Come on!" I shouted, and she leaped. One woman tried to grab her but was too late. She landed right in front of me, and I caught her on her way down, cushioning the impact.

Summer thumped down beside me after Liz.

"Run! Everyone run!" Summer yelled up at the people on the platform, but they just stood there, staring dumbly at her. Someone called her a bitch.

"Let's go!" My shoes crunched on the gravel floor of the tunnel as I ran in the direction opposite where the train would come. Near total darkness engulfed once we left the lights of the stop.

The roof caved in with a suddenness that made me jump even though I knew it was coming.

Chapter 22

Have you ever seen those actions movies where the protagonist outruns an explosion? Well, it felt like I was in one of those. The ground rumbled, threatening to throw me off my feet as dust and small chunks of concrete and rock rained down around us. My back was pelted with bits of debris, some of which made me feel lucky I kept my head down. The noise was deafening, drowning out the screams I knew we all shouted. But unlike those movies, neither of the women tripped, but instead kept up with me—Summer even passed me.

Finally, the rumbling and crashing died away, and we were left in an eerie silence. And total darkness.

There were two good things about our situation. One, we were all alive and well. Two, the tingling sensation stopped completely. Of course, we were now trapped in a pitch dark train tunnel populated by creepies, which even I couldn't see in this darkness. I supposed it was good no train would be coming down the tracks after us, but it was of little consolation at the moment.

A light erupted beside me, and I saw Summer

standing there with a flashlight in her hand. She saw me looking and hefted her handbag.

"I keep a lot in here."

I dug my own flashlight out and flicked it on. After this case, I would buy one of those lights for hikers that strap to your head. In the glow of my own light, I could see tears streaming down her dirty face.

"Are you all right?"

She nodded, then looked back the way we had come. Our lights filtered through the dust that hung heavy in the air and illuminated a mighty wall of rock and concrete that sealed the tunnel. "There were twelve people there."

"Do you think any got out?" Liz knelt on the ground and had also been crying. Her phone was on and working as a flashlight.

I shook my head but said nothing.

Summer wiped tears from her cheek. It only served to smudge the dirt on her face. "They thought we were crazy. They wouldn't listen."

"There was nothing we could have done," I said.

Her brow creased, and I knew she didn't believe me. "We should try to go back. Try to help them."

"We can't. It's completely blocked. And I doubt the ceiling is stable over there." Escape was my primary concern right now. The deadly magic may have been gone, but there were creepies down here somewhere, and I wanted to get out before we met up with them.

Liz pushed herself to her feet and joined us. "Now what?"

"Find a way out of here. Let's keep moving down

the tunnel. There's bound to be a service door along the wall before too long. And that could lead to an exit."

When the others failed to move, I turned and walked away from the rubble, down the tunnel. Liz rose and followed. Summer still stood, staring at the collapsed roof.

Liz and I exchanged a look, and then she motioned for me to hang back while she went over to Summer. She spoke softly to her, and I couldn't hear what was said, but it roused the young doctor, and she turned and came over to me, Liz close behind.

"I'm okay." Her nose was red and her cheeks wet, but her eyes were determined.

Finally, we started walking in silence down the tunnel.

We flashed our lights on the walls occasionally as we walked. The train tunnel had a high ceiling made of stone blocks with arched supports every now and then. It was wide enough only for one track, which ran down the center. A narrow elevated walk ran along both walls. Ahead, I saw creepies milling about in the pit where the track was. For some reason, they left the aisle alone. One of them saw us and started taking tentative steps in our direction. It was humanoid and completely black. The emaciated body sported long, bony arms with fingers so long and thin they looked like claws. Hairless and bald, it was cursed with big, bulging, inhuman eyes that reflected our light in an eerie glow.

I had seen creatures like this in many of the dark and desolate places of the world—cemeteries and subway tunnels being the most common. Of course, they were also found in hospitals, hanging around the most desperately ill. These bizarre and terrifying supies couldn't physically affect a person. That is, they couldn't scratch, or bite, or injure someone. But I think their touch had an effect on the mind or the soul.

Whatever the case, I had no interest in letting these things touch my friends or me. Grabbing Summer's hand, I gave her a tug toward the right-hand walk.

"Come on."

"I think it would be easier just walking here . . ." she trailed off. She stopped dead in her tracks and stared in undisguised terror at the creepies that now crept slowly toward us.

"You can see them?" I said, incredulous.

Summer nodded, her jaw hanging slack.

"Let's go!" Without releasing her hand, we ran to the side where the wall rose to the walkway. There was no ladder near us when we reached the wall. I tried to let go of Summer's hand to form a cup for her to step in, but she squeezed my hand tighter.

"Liz! Run!"

I whipped around to see that Liz still stood in the middle of the tunnel. She cast her cell phone around like a flashlight to look around the shaft. One creepie stood in front of her, but she couldn't see it. Others crept toward her, their featureless faces devoid of expression.

"Son of a bitch." Dropping Summer's hand, I charged the monster.

The creepie reached out and grabbed Liz's arm with its bony hand. Her reaction was immediate. She moaned and lowered her arm, then stood still, her head lolling tiredly to one side. I slammed into the thing, and it reeled from the impact, releasing its hold on Liz and stumbling away.

Every creepie in the tunnel stopped at that moment and stared at me. If they had mouths, they would be slack-jawed.

"Oh, no," I mumbled. Taking Liz by the wrist, I ran, half pulling, half dragging her toward the wall. The creepies, as one, recovered from their shock and surged forward in a charge toward us.

We reached the wall before them, and I was glad to see Summer hadn't been idle. She managed to find a way up and now leaned over the edge of the walkway, lowering her hand to us.

"Get up!" I shouted at Liz, who looked at me dazedly, but I could see her mind mastering itself as she did so. I stuffed her wrist into Summer's hand. Then, I knelt and hoisted her unceremoniously above my head. Liz came to herself as I did this and scrambled up onto the walk.

I whirled around to face the oncoming hoard. The creepies had all stopped, forming a semi-circle that hemmed me in by the wall. But they didn't attack. They all just stood there and examined me with a mixture of curiosity and something else. *Fear?* Maybe. They now knew I could see them, and they were confused. They weren't sure what would happen if they touched me. They didn't know what I was and were afraid I might pose a threat.

"Simon! Grab my hand!" Summer's voice was urgent behind me.

If I took my eyes off them, they would attack, I was sure of it. As soon as they saw weakness, they would come. Carefully I raised my hand as I glared at them all, trying to intimidate them. Summer's warm hand gripped mine and started to pull. Air hissed between my teeth as I took one big breath. The creepies tensed as one.

I spun around and pulled on Summer's hand, launching myself up as best I could. My feet scrabbled at the concrete wall as Summer heaved. My free hand made it to the lip, and I pulled as hard as I could.

A sensation as cold as ice gripped my ankle and began to spread quickly up my leg. I thrashed wildly and kicked out with my free leg, and the creepie detached. Then I scrambled the rest of the way up to land, panting, on the walkway.

"What the hell was that about?" Liz said.

"Where are they?" Summer looked all around the pit, her ponytail bobbing as her head moved here and there.

"Right down there." I nodded at the pit as I gazed over the edge. They crowded around the wall right below us but made no attempt to climb.

She shook her head. "I can't see them."

"What are you two talking about?" Liz insisted, annoyed.

Normal humans couldn't see creepies. Never had I seen anyone notice them, and their response to my acknowledgment of them showed it wasn't supposed to happen. Yet Summer saw them. For a brief time, she could see them. A suspicion forming in my mind, I took her hand once again.

"Look now," I said.

Summer leaned over and stared down into the pit, then recoiled. "Why couldn't I see them before?"

"I think you have to be touching me."

"See *what?*" Liz said, exasperated.

"This!" I grabbed her with my free hand.

She followed our gaze down and gasped.

"What the hell are they?"

"I'm not sure. But they don't mean us any good. I call them 'creepies.'"

"Have you always been able to see them?" Summer asked.

"That's why I approached you that day at the subway. You were leaning over the edge, and one was reaching for you. I had to get you away from it."

Summer gave me a curious look. "You were more gallant than I had given you credit."

Liz let go of my hand, as though to test the theory, and then grabbed it again.

"This is bizarre," she muttered.

"Welcome to my world."

"This was what you couldn't tell me," Summer said. "All those vague answers. You figured I wouldn't believe you."

"Yep."

Slight pause. "You were right."

"Let's get moving now," Liz urged, as she stepped closer to the wall.

The three of us went more carefully down the walk, Liz using my light because they both refused to let go of my hands.

"Liz," Summer said as we walked. "Did you feel anything back there in the tunnel—right before Simon ran up to you?"

Liz frowned, then shrugged. "I kind of just felt tired, you know after that happened. Why?"

Summer looked at me for a moment. "One of those things touched you."

Liz stopped walking. The girl kept her face as blank as always, but the fear in her eyes was unmistakable. "What did it do to me?"

"Not sure. It may have drained some energy from you, but not much. You'll be fine. Let's just be glad I stopped it and that we're away from them."

After several minutes along the path, we came to a junction, where another tunnel met ours. That tunnel was like the one we were on, with no service door in sight.

"Normally, I'd say we should stay in this tunnel. There's bound to be a door there nearby. That might not be true in the other one."

"But that means we'll have to climb down with those *things*," Liz said.

"I don't want to go down there," said Summer.

"Okay," I relented. "We'll stay on the walk, but it might take us longer to get out."

Around the corner we went, keeping away from the edge and taking each step with care. This tunnel was much like the other, with dingy rock and concrete walls, and the dirty floor below. The walkway here was filthy from disuse. Maintenance men didn't come down this tunnel often, which didn't bode well for finding an exit.

"Mr. Kane," Liz said as we walked, still holding my hand. Some of the creepies followed along in the pit, as though hoping one of us might fall in. "How did you know that car was going to crash into the store? Or, the cave-in? Or any of it?"

"I got a feeling."

"A premonition?" Summer asked.

"No. I felt the magical energy used to make it happen. If it were a normal accident, I would have been just as surprised as you."

"Using magic?" said Summer. The skepticism wasn't absent in her tone, but after seeing the creepies, it was weak.

"Yes. Magic exists, just like those creatures do. Your world has just become a much bigger and scarier place than it was.

"Someone did those things on purpose?" said Liz, sticking with her train of thought. "Causing all those horrible accidents just to kill me? Why?"

"Your stepfather and his friends are doing ritual magic. Powerful magic that has made them overnight successes. I suspect their methods somehow angered a group of nasty supernatural beings."

"What kind of beings?" Summer asked.

"Fairies."

Liz stopped in her tracks, the chain of hands forcing us to stop as well. "*Fairies?* Are you saying they're real?"

"Yup," I replied.

"But fairies aren't nasty," said Summer.

"You're thinking of Tinkerbell. Everyone always

thinks of Tinkerbell. But they're not like that. They're creatures of the moment. They're fickle, and they don't give a shit about humans. If a person crosses them, they get even. And they can be vicious."

"But why go after me, if it's Sebastian they want?" Liz said.

"Because they like to hurt their victims before they kill them. And they do that by hurting their loved ones."

Liz laughed. It was a dry, derisive laugh, flecked with irony. "Sebastian Gray doesn't love me. He doesn't love anyone. If I died, he'd just have one less pain in the ass."

"I doubt the fairies know that," I said.

"Hear that, fairies!" Liz called out loudly. "Sebastian Gray doesn't love me. So, don't waste your time." Her high teenage voice echoed off the walls of the tunnel, her words repeated over and over. And I wasn't stupid enough to believe the fairies didn't hear her.

Sometimes I acted before I thought. Call it a weakness, but sometimes I liked to put on a little show to enforce my will—or to teach a lesson. My hands grabbed Liz's shoulders, and I shook her roughly.

"Don't do that again," I hissed.

The girl opened her mouth to speak, some goth-inspired rebuke ready on her lips, but I raised a finger to silence her. The angry glare on my face morphed into a frown of concentration as I listened intently to the sounds of the tunnel. Another train, racing on a different line than ours, rumbled in the distance. Rats and other small vermin scurried in the pit. Water dripped slowly onto stone from somewhere nearby.

But for a second, I thought I heard more. Something different—something . . .

It was gone, whatever it was.

"Look," I said, my voice almost a whisper. "We're not out of the woods yet. Although I don't feel the tingle of magic anymore, we're still in danger. Someone, or something, wants us dead, and until we get to the safety of my apartment, we need to exercise extreme caution. Got it?"

Liz nodded, but her demeanor was hard. Her hatred of Gray overshadowed any sense of fear she had. That was dangerous. My hands opened, releasing her, and I took both their hands again and continued down the tunnel.

With all of her disaffected posturing, I kept forgetting Liz was just a kid. Though smart and mature for her age, she couldn't suppress her childish behavior forever. I just hoped no harm would come of her outburst.

The wet scrape of our shoes on the concrete path echoed eerily throughout the tunnel, which ran straight without any more junctions. About a hundred feet ahead, our path curved to the right, hiding the walkway in the bend.

Something was wrong. The mood in the tunnel had changed, and I wasn't convinced it was just the tension of our argument. My gut told me something was up, and I doubted it was my imagination. This wasn't a supernatural feeling, but the ordinary tug of intuition that comes naturally to an investigator.

"Simon," Summer leaned forward and whispered in

my ear. "The creatures are gone."

I looked down into the tunnel, my gaze scanning one way along the course of the pit, and then the other.

The tunnel was empty. The creepies were indeed gone.

They were a staple in these dark, dingy places. An ever-present evil. The only other time I saw an empty subway pit was right before the roof at the platform fell in. They had felt the magic, too. Now I felt nothing, and yet they fled.

Something terrible was coming, and I had no idea what it was.

Chapter 23

Have you ever been so unsure of what to do in an emergency that you just stood like a statue, unable to move? Well, that was me. My feet rooted themselves to the concrete walkway, and each of my hands gripped the girls' hands like vices. Dread crept into my heart, and I knew all hell was about to come loose.

"What's wrong?" Liz's tone remained bland, but the fear behind her words came through loud and clear.

My eyes felt glued to the upcoming corner. The new threat would come around it any second now. "Something's coming—something bad."

The two women followed my gaze. Then Summer gritted her teeth. "We have to go that way. Going back is just . . ."

The platform. Death. She grieved for those poor people who died because we were there.

My mind barked the order to shake my head vigorously, but it only quivered. This new dread froze my body and spirit, and a moment passed before my mouth started working again. "Whatever it is, it scared off the creepies. That's no small feat."

"You don't think you can protect us," Liz said. It was not a question.

"I don't know."

"Then let's hurry. Maybe we can find a door and get out of here before that *something* comes."

My head finally shook like it should. "There's no time."

"The junction," Liz said. Two simple words broke through our dispute and forced our heads to turn to the girl.

"We turned a corner at a junction. There is a way back."

"I don't want to go down there," the young doctor said, motioning toward the tunnel floor.

"They're gone, Summer. It's our only option." The three of us turned around and hurried along the walkway, back the way we had come, all the while looking for the first ladder that presented itself. The girls went first, with me taking up the rear. Now, that wasn't from some misplaced chivalry or anything. Women these days were as equal as men. But I had the gun and needed to be between them and the baddie.

A noise echoed from behind, but I didn't stop to listen. Someone—or something—was coming behind us, but a glance back revealed nothing.

The ladder wasn't far away, and we climbed down. Once again, I led the way across toward the other side of the tunnel. Once on the walkway, we should have an easier time finding a doorway out.

We were only halfway across when Liz screamed.

Summer and I whirled around. The girl stood still

as she stared in horror back up the tunnel from where we had come, her limbs frozen in terror. I followed her gaze and at first, saw nothing, but then a form materialized out of the shadows. No more than four feet tall, a humanoid being with skin the color of dried mud advanced toward us. The creature wore a thick, leather jerkin in a shade of brown that almost matched its hide. A single-edged knife was tucked scabbard-less in its belt. The sneering face resembled an old man with scraggly, gray hair, a long nose ending in a point, and bulging eyes. The fingers of its hands were more claw than finger and wrapped around the shaft of the pikestaff it carried. This was a dwarf or goblin of some kind—humanoid, but not human. However, there were three features of this creature that made identification easy: the pike, the steel boots on its feet, and the sack of a hat on its head—a hat dyed with human blood.

Of course, I knew it was blood because I recognized the monster. The Redcap, in Scottish folklore, must keep the dye in its cap fresh or it would die, so the goblin hunted the countryside along the English border and murdered anyone it encountered. We were far from Scotland, but the Redcap was no immigrant. The fairies sent it like they had the changeling and the ogre. Yet this was the first time they targeted me.

The fairies' new killer flashed us a malicious grin, the sharp, yellow fangs protruding from its lower jaw, glistening with saliva, and it advanced, hefting its pikestaff, the huge axe-head at its tip large enough to lop a head off someone's shoulders.

"Run!" I shouted. Liz stood there, transfixed with

terror. Summer roused and, grabbing the girl by the arm, pulled her away from the goblin. That brought the teen back to her senses, and the two ran down the tunnel, the ladder and walkway forgotten as they raced toward the junction.

The Redcap burst into sudden and swift motion. With far more agility than I would have given it, the thing sped past me and closed on Liz.

"Shit!" Gray's *stepdaughter*. The murderous bastard was after her.

The goblin may have loved its Medieval weaponry, but I fully embraced the modern. The gun whispered as it slid from its holster, and I took aim and squeezedThe blast echoed throughout the tunnels and was repeated as I fired again. Anyone with shooting experience knew better than to trust the first shot. The first round clipped its left shoulder. The second hit square in the back.

The Redcap stumbled but did not fall. Still, my ploy worked. The little killer turned toward me, its old man's face twisted with rage. With another burst of speed, the goblin charged me, the steel blade of the pike rising into position like a batter preparing to swing. The gun roared, and the single shot grazed its head behind a pointed ear. The pike, which looked almost twice the Redcap's height, swung in a wide arc toward my neck.

I could argue my choice of action was the best one, but I didn't choose—I reacted. My feet flew straight out from under me, and I fell with a thud on my ass. The mighty axe flew over me as I went down, with a whoosh and a breeze that blew my hair. As the blade passed over, I raised my gun and fired twice more, both rounds burying in its chest.

The Redcap shrieked and stumbled backward into the shadows, its pike dropping and clattering to the ground.

My breath, escaping me in great gasps, was the only sound over the fading footfalls of my fleeing friends. Could that be it? Could the Redcap be dead? A sense of dread in the pit of my stomach told me otherwise.

Falling on your ass isn't the smartest thing to do, and I realized that as I rose painfully, an ache running up my spine and a soreness on my butt that promised to make sitting miserable. With my gun aimed at the body lying motionless on the ground ten feet away, I approached using slow, deliberate steps. The gun's magazine could hold eight rounds, but I had one in the chamber, which made nine. That left four to protect me from the goblin. My mind told me it would be enough to finish off an already wounded creature, especially one so small. Yet my hand shook as I held the gun toward the body. My right arm throbbed with renewed pain—the gun's recoil did a number on the break. If the bones had been healing up, I just reversed the process.

Feet crunched on gravel with each of the three careful steps I took toward the monster when it suddenly shot with inhuman agility forward into the shadows. The damned fucking thing abandoned me for Summer and Liz.

The tunnel reverberated with three more shots, all of which hit the creature in the back. But in true horror movie style, the bad guy kept running without slowing at all. The same thing that caused the goblin to fall and lay motionless for several seconds didn't even phase it. The Redcap seemed to have learned to soak the damage from my gun.

"Dammit!" I muttered and took off in hot pursuit. The creature was focused on Liz and wouldn't let anything get in the way of killing her. I had to get in the way, and I had to kill the thing. The goblin was worse than the ogre, who was only a violent brute. You could run away from an ogre. This thing would hunt you down until you were dead. The monster reveled in the kill and was not likely to leave either woman alive. Because I was sure, Summer would try to fight it.

The junction appeared out of the darkness, and I skidded around the corner, then came to a stop. The Redcap was gone. Terror wrenching at my gut at the thought of the pretty doctor being beheaded by the monster, I jogged forward, scanning both sides for any sign of the others. A ladder rose to the walkway I had wanted us to take, and beyond it was a door. The hinges creaked as the opening shifted slightly. At least I knew where to go. The ladder proved awkward with my aching arm, but I refused to let it slow me down, and once up, I raced through the door.

A maintenance room, about fifteen feet square, stretched before me in all its utilitarian glory. Tools and equipment leaned against each wall, leaving the center of the room for the horror that awaited me.

Liz was crumpled on the ground at the back of the room, while in the middle lay Summer. The Redcap knelt on her legs and stabbed her over and over with its long, single-bladed knife.

Chapter 24

Without hesitation, I fired the last round into the bastard's head, creating a three-inch hole and splattering blood everywhere. Then my gun clicked empty, the slider remaining locked open.

The shots knocked the Redcap from its position atop Summer, and it fell forward, throwing its hands out to prevent a face-plant on the concrete. Slowly, the murderous thing rose to its feet, shaking its head and causing blood to splatter around. The Redcap stretched and turned to face me. The hole in the goblin's face, bigger on this side, was already healing. The ugly, old-man face twisted in a grotesque mockery of joy as the bloody knife raised above its head.

All nine rounds had been emptied into the four-foot monster, and the goddamned thing was not only still alive, but seemingly unharmed. The tattered clothes that hung on its body were riddled with bullet holes, but the body they covered remained unscathed.

With a sudden shriek, the monster charged, the knife swinging in an arc that would have pierced my heart had I not jumped backward. The blade only managed to cut a minor gash in my chest and slice up my shirt, which quickly soaked red. The Redcap didn't hesitate but made a horizontal swing with the weapon meant to open my belly and spill my guts on the floor.

Instead of jumping back again, I lunged forward. His arm struck my side, the blade missing me. My right hand clutched his neck, and I squeezed with all my might as I clasped his knife-wrist with my left, trying to force the steel edge away from me. He grabbed a handful of hair with his free hand and pulled backward, and we began a macabre dance about the room as each of us struggled for dominance.

I didn't stand a chance. The monster's neck rippled with muscle, and I couldn't get my thumb into position to crush its Adam's apple. My broken right arm lacked the strength it needed, while the Redcap fought with inhuman fortitude. Soon, the pain on my scalp became too much to bear. Releasing its throat, I shoved the creature away, threw his knife-arm from me, and stepped back.

The creature released its grip on my hair, giving me at least a few seconds to think as I staggered back to the door. My gun made no impression on the goblin whatsoever, and he overpowered me right away.

The Redcap shook its head and cleared its throat.

How do I kill this bastard? What do I know about goblins? They're Fae creatures—I think.

Fae!

The goblin charged. The grotesque smile had gone, and the thing was all business as it lunged forward to slice me to ribbons with that long-bladed knife.

I ran, not out the door, nor toward it, but to the side. As fast as my feet would take me, I raced in a circle around the edges of the room, scanning the piles and boxes of tools as I went. The Redcap followed relentlessly, but I didn't dare look back. With my longer legs and larger frame, I had the advantage with speed, but the room was small, and Summer's plight took away the luxury of time. There was something I needed, and I had to find it fast.

Aha!

In true hero fashion, I launched myself through the air into a box of ceramic tiles, spinning my body around as I hurtled toward it. My body crashed in un-heroic fashion into a stack of boxes that proceeded to unload itself all over the floor. Pain shot through me from every corner of my body, but it was necessary given the situation. The pile of maintenance debris scattered loudly around me, and I fished for the one I wanted. The goblin swerved to follow, only seconds from dropping on top of me with its deadly blade raised above its head.

The fingers of my right hand wrapped around a railroad spike, and as the Redcap descended on me, I caught its knife-arm with my left hand and smashed the sharp end of the spike into its face with my right.

By "sharp end," I meant the sharpest end. The tool was filed down to a point but was still dull. My makeshift weapon broke skin and bone and embedded itself into the bastard's face.

The Redcap's reaction was sudden and violent. Dropping the knife, the goblin reeled backward, shrieking, tearing its own face apart in a vain attempt to extricate the spike from its hideous face. Smoke poured from the wound, and the sizzling sound of searing flesh filled the room. The stench was horrible.

Another crampon in hand, I launched myself on the monster, driving the metal stake in and out of its neck and chest. The monster's skin burned with each touch of iron, making the Redcap convulse in agony.

In a matter of seconds, the creature stopped its convulsing and went limp, its arms falling to the floor, and a final breath issuing from its dried, chapped lips.

The iron spike clanged on the floor as I rushed to Summer. Blood seeped from several wounds, but none seemed to have hit anything vital. Putting pressure on the worst injury, which was in her stomach, I fumbled for my phone with my free hand.

A call to 911 made, I had them patch me through to Ross. He listened as I explained where I was and what I needed.

"I'll be right there," was all he said, then hung up.

In the time I waited for help, I focused on stopping the bleeding as best I could. My hands pressed hard on the wound, and I concentrated so much that my hands felt hot as I worked to staunch the flow of blood that covered everything. Time dragged on like an eternity in Hell, though it was probably no more than fifteen minutes. Paramedics arrived first and took over for me. More medical personnel came soon after, followed by cops. They ignored me, and I ignored them. The blood from her wounds filled my mind. Summer's blood on my hands. On my pants. On everything.

How could I have been so stupid—so *arrogant*—to think I was indestructible enough to keep them safe. I brought Summer on a stakeout—I turned it into a fucking date! And now she was dying because of my arrogance and my flippant attitude toward my work and my enemies.

Well, that wouldn't happen again. Ross was a cop. It was his job to risk his life for others. But I wouldn't endanger anyone else. Never again.

Finally, Ross came and brought me out of my daze. He had medics work on my injuries, which I barely noticed, and then took me aside for my story. The words came out in a stream of monotone syllables as I told him everything, about Gray and his order of magicians, and Liz, and Summer. And, of course, I told him about the Redcap.

Ross and I looked at the corpse of the goblin. The creature wore a pendant around its neck. It bore strange symbols, and I had a sudden feeling it might be important.

"Mind if I take the pendant?" I asked with a nod toward the body's chest.

Ross shrugged. "I guess. Just remember to bring it to me when you're done with it. Technically, it's evidence, but I think you'll learn more from it. And fill me in on what you learn. All of it."

With a curt nod, I knelt and pulled the chain from around the Redcap's neck.

Ross stared down at the goblin and shook his head.

"With all the bullet holes, were the spikes necessary?"

"The bullets didn't hurt it. Fae creatures are immune

to normal weapons."

He shot me a look, and I shrugged.

"The spikes are iron. The Fae are sort of allergic to the stuff. It burns them."

Ross considered that for a moment. "That was some quick thinking on your part. If that's true, why aren't you armed with an iron weapon?"

"A mistake I plan to fix."

"So, this Sebastian Gray is involved with Mann and Cook?" Ross said, changing subjects.

"He's the ringleader, I think. He and Mann were surprised to hear about Cook's death, and Mann always followed Gray's lead."

"I'll bring him in for questioning."

"Don't mention Liz's involvement."

"You think he'll do something to her?"

"I'm sure of it. He doesn't give a shit about anyone but himself. She's just baggage, as far as he's concerned."

"Okay," Ross said. "I'll keep her out of it. You want to be there?"

"No. I don't want him to connect you with me. He's gunning for me."

"I'm not afraid of him."

"You should be."

"Lieutenant . . ." Kravitz said, coming over from Liz. "We're taking them to the hospital."

"Will Summer be okay?" I asked.

Kravitz shook his head. "She's lost a lot of blood, but her wounds have stabilized. She's lucky—anyone else would have died by now. I don't know how she survived, but I'm not going to complain. She's in serious condition, but we have her ready to move, and she's got a chance."

"My question is," Ross said as Detective Kravitz went off to take the women away, "why did the Redcap go after Summer if it was after Liz?"

"Knowing Summer, she got in the way. Once the thing took her down, it couldn't stop stabbing."

Chapter 25

Ever since I was a kid, I hated hospitals. Not because of the antiseptic smell or the pain from their shots or the taste of their medicines. Creepies skulked everywhere in the place, and no one else saw them. My parents told me I was being stupid and let my imagination run away with me. But I knew better. When I discovered my enhanced healing, I vowed to avoid hospitals whenever possible. Now I found myself at Mass General for the second time that week. This time, I didn't hesitate at the entrance. Summer and Liz were in the ER when Ross and I arrived. With a flash of his badge, Ross got us to the rooms where they had been taken. The two women had adjoining operating rooms, and through the doors' windows, I saw doctors and nurses clustered around them.

I wasn't one of those emotional hotheads you see on TV that try to force their way into the O.R. despite the risks. Instead, I did the only reasonable thing I could think of: I took a seat on a nearby bench, leaned my head against the wall, and considered the events that brought us here.

Unfortunately, I wasn't the only one there. Detective Ross cleared his throat meaningfully. The cop wanted to talk, and he usually got his way—he was relentless like that.

Even the minute or two of inactivity on the chair let the joints in my neck stiffen, and they creaked in protest when I gave him a tired look before my head dropped back where it had been. The dull thud against the wall emphasized my lack of interest in talking.

"I'll get us some coffee," Ross said. "Then we'll talk about what happened. We have to, you know."

The deep breath I released as I stared blankly up at the ceiling formed the best affirmative I could manage. Ross understood my need for time, and he offered it to me, even though it was too short. We had work to do, and I wouldn't be any use if I were too upset about Summer.

The events of the past few hours ran through my head, and I tried to piece things together. Sebastian Gray had stopped at an old anthropologist's home. Then, he shot off like mad when he left. Had he seen us? Did he know we were parked there? If he did, he might have had time enough to get his group together to cast those spells—especially if they already planned to meet, which I suspected.

I shouldn't have let Summer come. That was stupid of me.

The fairy was a clue to all this. Though clearly unhappy with me, it didn't show the hatred it had for Gray. Nope. The fairies had nothing to do with the "accidents." Yet they had *everything* to do with Gray.

It had to be Gray and company—The Order, I decided to call them, since they were an ordered group
of magicians. And by "magicians," I didn't mean
illusionists, like on stage. Wizards would be a better
term, but then you'd think of Gandalf and Harry
Potter. These men were nothing like them. They used
Ceremonial Magic with elaborate rituals and rites to
cast their spells. They didn't wield wands or carry staffs
or anything like that, and their magic wasn't quick and
obvious. It was slow and subtle and far more potent
than it should have been.

The Redcap. Now that reeked of fairies. Goblins
were believed to be related to them—like another
species of them. The fairies sent the Redcap.

And they sent it after Liz.

I hoped Gray wouldn't come to visit Liz in the
hospital. If he made it clear he didn't care about her, the
fairies might leave her alone. How could I protect Liz
from fairies if they were determined to kill her? They
were too much to take on, and I didn't have the ability.
So far, I'd been lucky. But my luck would run out if I
kept going like this.

And that brought me to a line of thinking that had
been going through my mind since I stopped pushing
on Summer's chest. The time to worry about Liz and
Summer was gone. The best thing I could do to help
them was to get off my ass and do what I do best: catch
supernatural bad guys. In this case, The Order. The
fairies targeted them for something they were doing. If
I put an end to The Order, the fairies should stop their
attacks. I had to quit wallowing in guilt, stop messing

around with Summer, and get back on the case.

My mindset, I was ready for action again. Ross found me pacing in the hallway, muttering to myself when he showed up with the coffee. My face was set when I took the cup he offered.

"Let's talk," I said.

Ross got us access to a conference room in the hospital. He told them to tell us if anything changed with Summer or Liz. The room was a standard small box of a place with white walls, no windows, and a small conference table. The chairs didn't roll but had padding and felt comfortable enough. A little black device resembling a big three-legged spider sat on the table. The audio conferencing unit sat dark and silent, but I unplugged it anyway. This was for Ross' ears only.

There, with the door shut, I told Detective Ross everything that had happened, including how Gray and Liz fit into the case. It was time to forget about client confidentiality and work on solving the case as quickly as possible. Which meant full disclosure. Some of this I had told him back in the subway, but that was the Reader's Digest version. This was unabridged.

Detective Joseph Ross listened intently to the whole story, taking notes as he did so. He sat there for a while in silence when I finished. The call to action pulled at my mind, and I sat fitfully, my knee bouncing with nervous energy as I waited for Ross to speak.

"We need to find out what Gray and his pals are doing. I could bring them in for questioning—ask them about their relationship to Cook."

"That would put them on the defensive," I said.

"We've got to catch them in the act, which means figuring out where they meet."

Ross shrugged. "Not hard. I can have them tailed."

"No. Too risky. You're not on the Order's radar now, and I'd like it to stay that way."

Full disclosure, Simon. "There's a safer way. I planted a device in Gray's car. It lets me track him."

"A radio tracker? Kind of high-tech for you, isn't it?"

That forced a smile on my face—the first one since everything went to shit. "It's actually a stone talisman. A spell's been placed on it to let me find it."

"Of course it is," Ross said with a wry grin.

"We just wait until he goes there. Then, we show up and catch them in the act."

He nodded and took a sip of his coffee.

"I've got a question for you, Simon." He leaned back in his chair and took another sip. "Why don't you just zap them with your own magic? Fight fire with fire, and all that?"

I laughed, but not from mirth. The detective had no idea how wrong he was with his question. Yet, it was still a good one. The nature and extent of my abilities was a secret I held close to my heart. But it was time to open up to him. If anyone was ready to hear this, it was him. And he'd make a more valuable partner if he knew my limitations.

"I'm not a superhero, Ross. Yet I do have special abilities. I can see supies—supernatural beings—for what they are, instead of how they want us to see them. When a spell goes off around me, I can sense it—I can feel the magic, so to speak. My body heals itself with incredible speed, although my arm is taking too damn long. I can channel my energy to activate and use magical artifacts and talismans. That's it."

"Hmm," he said, "All passive stuff. What can you *do?* What can you actively make happen?"

That earned him a frown. With only a moment's thought, he cut straight to the heart of the matter. Under his simple, gruff exterior, the detective was a smart man.

"Nothing. I've never been able to intentionally use supernatural abilities, aside from activating a talisman, and it's not an *active* ability—it's just meditation."

"You've never made anything happen on your own? Do you think you can't, or have you never tried?"

Again with the astute observations. "I've never tried."

"Why not? I mean, if I found I had powers like that, I'd try to learn what I could do."

"That can be dangerous."

"How?"

My gaze wandered past my partner as I searched my mind for the right words to explain it. "Let's take Gray and his Order, for example. They didn't plan to make the tunnel cave in—at least I don't think so. They just cast a spell to make me die. The fact that others would be killed in the process didn't occur to them. They might not even realize they were responsible for those specific accidents."

"What are you getting at?"

"Magic is wild. It's dangerous and unpredictable.

It's why I don't study magic. And it's also why I haven't tried to use my abilities in any active way."

"Hmm. Well, I agree with you about magic. You always made it sound like science. It's all trial and error and trusting in what others have done before you. Your powers aren't like that. This is a natural ability we're talking about, not something you learned from someone. You should try to figure out what you can do."

"But what if I can't control it?" I said. "What if my powers are strong and I lose control? Whether it's natural or not, I could still kill people."

"What if you could have used your powers to help Summer and Liz? You can't let 'what-ifs' lead your life."

My chair almost tipped over when I rose and started pacing. The room was too small for it, but I made do. Those last words pierced me deeper than the Redcap's pike. The urge to hit him when he spoke forced me to back off. Ordinarily, I wasn't an emotional man, but that nearly pushed me to my limit. The women's fate affected me more deeply than I cared to admit, and as a result, I would not be at my best.

With a deep breath to calm my nerves, I stopped and turned to face Ross once more.

"It's too dangerous," I said, but my voice was weak—unconvincing.

"And you think bottling it all up isn't? If it's in you, it's gonna come out. And you'll want it to come out on *your* terms rather than on it's."

So much wisdom from such a simple man. He surprised the hell out of me. Still, he had a point.

"Okay. I'm convinced. I'll try to learn to use my abilities actively. But not now. I can't risk any surprises. We need to stop Gray, and we need to do it soon before more innocent people are hurt."

"Good," he said with finality. "Now we're on the same page. Tell me how this doo-hickey of your's works, and we'll come up with a plan."

Chapter 26

The next hour was spent working out our plan. You'd think it would be one hell of a good one after a solid hour's work, but no. After a lot of talking and arguing, we settled on merely waiting until Gray took his car somewhere suspicious, then I'd pick up Ross, and we'd head over there.

The plan was far from perfect—hell, it was hardly a plan at all—and there were many flaws. For instance, Gray and company were likely to take another shot at me once they realized I wasn't dead. And that meant more bad luck. So, I needed to find a way to change my fortune for the better. Or, ideally, to prevent them from changing it at all.

A doctor came to us as we left the conference room. The man looked tired and solemn—not a good combination.

"What's the verdict?" Ross said, cutting through all the niceties and sugar-coating the doctor was prepared to feed us.

Doctor Wheeler, as his name tag read, cleared his throat. "Well, Miss Borden is out of the woods. Her wound was deep, but the blade missed all the vital organs. It was touch and go for a while, but we repaired the damage and patched her up. She's on her way to recovery now." The doctor followed up with a hopeful smile.

"And what about Summer?" I asked.

That was when his smile took a nosedive.

"I'm afraid her injuries are more severe. We're still working on her. But we're hopeful."

"What are her chances?"

"If we can repair the damage to her . . ."

"*What* are her chances?" I had no interest in hearing the details of how badly I screwed up.

The doctor's face went grim. "Fifty-fifty."

Ross put his hand on my shoulder, but I shrugged it off.

"Right." I turned to the detective. "Kindly drop me off at my car, so I can get to work."

"Simon," he said softly. "You need to rest."

"There's no time," I snapped and strode away toward the exit. "Come on. I've got a lot to do."

"That's bullshit, and you know it," Ross said as he drove me to my car, which was still parked outside Bullfrog Records. "We're in a waiting game, and you could as easily wait in the hospital, or in your apartment."

"There's something I have to take care of first."

"Regarding the case?"

The simple answer I was tempted to give would do nothing but waste time. "When Gray discovers I'm still alive—a fact we haven't tried to hide—he will most certainly try again to kill me. I must prevent that."

"How can you, if you won't do magic?"

"Connections. There's someone who might be able to create a charm, or ward, or something that can keep me safe from the Order's spells."

"And the identity of such a person is bound by client confidentiality?"

"No," I said. "It's personal."

Oakwood Manor was a large country home in the Blue Hills area south of Boston. Jessica Bride owned the house that sat on ten acres of forest, abutting the Blue Hill Reservation state park. A successful psychologist in Boston, she made plenty of money and bought the manor as soon as she could. A tall cast iron fence encircled the property with a massive gate blocking the main drive, but Jessica usually kept it open when she was home. If she had any flaw, it was her trust in the decency of others.

Jessica was what I would call an old friend. I met her several years ago while I tried to come to grips with the supernatural phenomena that tormented me. Her help was invaluable.

The gate stood open when I arrived at ten o'clock that evening. The Camry's engine rumbled like a caged tiger as I navigated down the long, paved driveway lined with immaculately landscaped hedges, and came to a stop at the steps to the front door. The expensive brick house had an English Manor feel to it with its arched doorway, three gables, and two chimneys. The driveway continued on and circled around to make it easy to leave.

After I rang the doorbell three times with no answer, I tried the door. Unlocked, it opened onto a foyer. A chandelier hung from the vaulted ceiling to shine on the white walls with oak trim. Many coats hung on pegs adorning the walls. But the place was eerily silent. My professional paranoia got the better of me, so I brushed the shirt back from my hip and placed my hand on the gun's grip.

Not being a cop, I resisted drawing my weapon as I went from room to room on the first floor, looking for clues to their whereabouts, or for signs of trouble. The sliding glass door to the back deck stood open. Beyond the deck and the spacious backyard, woods rose up tall and dark. And filtering from gaps in the trees was the light of a fire.

All the tension that had built up upon entering drained out of me at that moment. They were out back having a bonfire. When I stepped out onto the deck, I understood. Magic tingled in the air, causing the hairs on my arms to rise and filling me with a sense of exhilaration. Somewhere nearby, a group of people worked on a ritual, and already the place was thick with its power.

Of course, this made sense, considering Jessica was a witch.

Dr. Bride was the High Priestess of a coven of witches. They called their religion Wicca, which they claimed came from the old Celtic nature religions that existed in the UK before the Romans arrived. I doubted that and didn't agree with the religion, but I couldn't argue against their magical tradition. Though many covens didn't exhibit much magical weight, Jessica's was the height of Wiccan power.

She was having her circle tonight. Good for me! More experts on the topic to help me.

The well-tended grass soaked my shoes from the earlier rain as I crossed the backyard toward the line of trees. They said Wiccans danced naked in the moonlight. Now, that would be a welcome sight!

I drew my flashlight and scanned the tree line. A clear trail led into the woods at the far end of the yard, and I crossed the green expanse, the wet grass soaking my feet. The prints of many bare feet decorated the well-traveled path, and I followed along, certain it was the right way. Voices drifted to me from the trees ahead—the sound of a dozen or so women lifted in song. Witches weren't the old, ugly crones of Hollywood camp, and they didn't cast bones, cackle, or chant evil things. Oh, no. They danced and sung and made merry, and somehow managed to weave magical spells in the process. There was some chanting, of course, but by and large, their rituals tended to be upbeat. At least that was the case with Oakwood Coven. They were never solemn in the practice of their religion. And there was a lot to be said for that.

The bonfire light shone brightly ahead, and I pocketed my flashlight. Presently, I found myself on the edge of a large clearing, in the center of which burned the fire. Thirteen women danced around the blaze.

And they were all naked.

The witches rollicked to no music save for the sound of their voices, which rose high and melodic into the night air. Light and carefree, they made their way around the fire, which burned in a pit in the center of the clearing.

From the safety of the woods, I stood and watched the spectacle. There was something about watching a bunch of naked women dancing that kept a man's attention. My gaze locked on them but not only because of the festival of flesh. The coven danced with purpose, and my professional curiosity was piqued, as well as my voyeuristic interest. At first, it looked like they were merely dancing, enjoying the chill of the evening and the warmth of the fire. But as I looked on, I noticed a subtle pattern taking form before my eyes. They moved in two circles, one going clockwise, while the other went counter-clockwise. They weaved in and out as they did so, giving the impression of two loops of rope that were somehow entwined. And the singing. The verses of a magical spell filled the air with their clear, light voices, and its power, which I had felt back on the deck, tingled strongly around me. That power was similar at its core to what I felt during the "accidents," but infinitely more wholesome. The crackle of energy warmed my heart even as the heat of the flames warmed my face. If anyone could help with my current dilemma, it was Oakwood Coven.

The dance grew faster as they weaved in and out, and I felt the spell coming to a crescendo. Then, the power released—sent off in whatever direction the witches wanted it to go, and the tingling ceased. The women all collapsed to the ground at that moment, spent and panting. To anyone else, it would have looked like they just had sex. For me, well, it still looked like sex, but I knew better. The coven pooled up a lot of magical energy and directed it outward. Much of that energy came from them, which left them exhausted.

I stepped out from my hiding place and approached the fire, clapping and smiling wanly.

"That was wonderful," I said. "Truly amazing!"

None of the women ran for their robes, but lounged about on the ground, laughing and talking. A few shook their heads at me, but with looks of humor, not scorn. One woman, however, rose to her feet. A beauty of twenty-seven stood in the remains of their circle, facing me, her hands on her hips. She showed no sign of modesty as she flashed a stern look. Her body was stunning with her athletic build and lack of tan lines. Brown hair cascaded over her shoulders. Her expression was hard, but her brown eyes were warm with humor as she addressed me.

"Why are *you* here, aside from the cheap thrills?" Jessica asked.

"There is nothing cheap about you, Miss Bride," I said and bowed low.

She snorted but smiled. The High Priestess of Oakwood Coven walked over to a large rock and picked up a dress. She pulled it over her head and let the cloth fall into place. It was a simple thing, resembling something a common girl from the Middle Ages might have worn with its dark, earthen colors and the cord she now tied around her waist. She padded over to me but stopped a few feet away. Half a head shorter than me, she seemed even tinier in her bare feet.

Brown eyes steeped in intelligence and wisdom scanned my body and then an eyebrow raised. "You're dressing down. Either you're on a case, or your dad cut you off."

"A case," I said. She knew me well.

"Then let's talk."

Jessica tossed her head back toward the other witches. "I'll be back shortly." With the confidence that came from years of experience in these woods, she plunged into the darkness of the trees and led me back down the path to the house.

We walked in silence for a couple of minutes. It's funny; I'd never had trouble talking to anyone. I spoke my mind, and everything was okay. But not with Jessica. Somehow she made it hard to find the words. Finally, I forced myself to speak.

"How have you been? You're looking good."

There was a pause, and she continued walking without even a glance.

"I'm doing fine."

"It's been a while."

"It has been."

"I think the last time I saw you was . . ." I trailed off, thinking.

"When you dumped me."

"Really? I was sure I had seen you once or twice since then."

We reached the house, and she led me into her office. A forest scene surrounded the room, painted on the walls with stunning realism. Books about Witchcraft and other obscure religions lined a shelf against one wall. A couch sat beside the door. Her desk looked like it had been sliced from the trunk of some enormous tree with its rough edges sanded into smooth grooves. On it rested statuettes of her God and Goddess, an incense burner, and other witchy things. A laptop computer sat to one side, its screen closed. She didn't like computers but understood the need for them.

Jessica took a seat behind her desk and motioned for me to sit at one of the two in front of it. She wanted to keep things professional. Well, I guess I couldn't blame her.

"What is it?" Her tone and expression were both flat.

That was it for socializing. To be honest, I didn't expect more than that.

"I've run afoul of an order of magicians, and they're casting spells to kill me."

She frowned. "How?"

"Well, have you heard about the subway tunnel collapse?"

Her eyes widened for a moment, but she remained composed.

"That's a pretty specific target for a spell. How do you know it was magic?"

"I felt it." She knew about my ability to sense spells. She didn't know all my powers, but she knew that one. "And they didn't target the subway. I was almost hit twice by cars within minutes before the cave-in."

She nodded grimly. "Probability, then. That makes sense. But to produce something that grand in scale with such a generalized spell would take an awful lot of power. My coven is strong, and yet we couldn't hope to pull off something of that magnitude. Magic is far too subtle."

"They've apparently found a way."

"Yes," she said. "And there's your key to defeating them. Find out how they build so much power, and take it away."

She said it as though it were an easy thing to do.

"But to do that, I need to stay alive. Me and my partner."

Jessica raised an eyebrow. "You have a partner? Why, Simon, you *have* grown."

"Cool your jets, Jess. He's just a cop that hires me now and then to consult."

"Still, an improvement."

"Can you help us, or not?"

She paused and considered me for a moment. There was more going through her mind than my request, and I was glad my Wiccan ex-girlfriend wasn't the vengeful type.

"A pair of charms. And they must be strong enough to protect you against an incredibly powerful force." She let out a breath. "I guess my coven isn't done tonight."

"I could pay you," I offered.

She shook her head. "That would cheapen it—and its effect. The reason for making the charm has power. Greed is a poor conduit of magical energy."

"Yet that seems to be the Order's main objective."

"Again, their power source is the key to their undoing."

"And it's a separate thing? It doesn't just come from

the ground?"

"Oh, they would be practicing in a powerful location. That is certain. But it wouldn't be enough. They're likely using some object of great power for their rituals. Remove it, and they will be bereft of their magical might."

"Okay," I said, rising. Jessica walked me to the front door.

"How long before they're ready?"

"It could take a couple of days, but I hope to have them ready by tomorrow night. Until then, I recommend you stay someplace safe. Someplace with strong powers of good. A church, perhaps."

"You blessed my apartment."

She shook her head. "That won't be enough."

"I've added some artifacts to the mix to act as a magical barrier. But they only work on a place, not on a person."

"Then stay home. I'll call you when they're ready."

The raw wind hit me as I stepped through the doorway onto the stoop. It would rain again soon. Turning suddenly, I smiled at Jessica.

"It's good to see you. It really is."

She hesitated, and for a moment I thought she might embrace me. Then the wall went back up, and she shook her head, frowning. "We're not friends, Simon. Not anymore. Stay safe. I'll call when they're ready."

She closed the door.

"That could have gone better," I said to myself as I drove home. It had been three years since I last saw Jessica, and she was as beautiful as she had ever been.

Chapter 27

I liked my apartment. It was big. It was spacious. It was comfortable. As prisons go, I could do worse. Until Jessica delivered the charms, it was best I stay put in the safety of my home. I find it amazing how a place I loved so much could be claustrophobic when I was forced to be there. And I had no company. So far, Ross had been under Gray's radar, and I assumed he would remain so as long as he didn't mess with the magician or his cronies. I stood in my apartment, staring out the picture window at Boston Harbor. Clouds approached from offshore, bringing rain with them.

The coming storm reflected my mood. Two women I cared for were in the hospital because of me. Jessica's coldness shocked me—she was always a kind and forgiving soul. The old wounds I gave her ran deeper than I expected. What did that say about me?

With a shake of the head, I turned my back on the impending storm and went to my laptop. Jessica had given me a useful bit of information. Casting spells as powerful as the Order had been throwing around required a location with a high amount of natural

She was a bit colder, but that was because of me. I didn't handle her well. Of course, I'd never handled any woman well.

power. There shouldn't be many sites rich in magical energy in the city. All I had to do was list them.

The list proved harder to build than expected. After all, I couldn't just Google "places of strong magic in Boston." Certain types of structures were commonly built in areas like that. Cemeteries, graveyards, and burial grounds were full of the stuff. Not because of the bodies themselves, but because people chose where to bury their dead carefully, and they tended to prefer locations with high magic content. The same was true for holy ground. Churches were often—but not always—built on magic-rich soil. The people who picked these spots didn't necessarily know why they chose them. They just *felt* right.

Boston sported several cemeteries and graveyards, of course. Yet they were all public places that people visited. The old ones were now tourist traps and sat right out in the middle of everywhere. The Order couldn't use them without being seen.

Churches posed a different problem. Priests had a thing about people doing ritual magic in their churches, so those currently active were out. My searching uncovered no abandoned ones, though many had been torn down to make room for apartment complexes and businesses. Unlikely candidates though they were, they still made the list because there was nothing else to put there.

My eyes ached when I finally glanced at the clock on the wall. The black and white circular device read 12:05 with its long, elegant arms. I closed the screen of my laptop, leaving the *Haunted Places of Boston* website half read.

I took a shower before bed. The grime from the subway tunnel and the blood of the Redcap—and of Summer—rinsed gratefully down the drain. But no amount of soap could wash away the guilt. Bringing her along was foolish, and completely my fault, and may still be the death of her. She was innocent with nothing to do with any of this. Now she fought for her life in the same hospital in which she worked. They would blame me, of course, if she died. They would be right. The place would be off limits on those rare occasions when I needed medical help. That somehow seemed fitting.

My thoughts followed me to bed, and so sleep eluded me. A half hour of tossing and turning and I finally rolled out of bed in desperation at the futility of it. Usually, I'd go for a long drive if I couldn't rest. The Ferrari made good therapy. Yet I had no such therapy available to me in the apartment. At least, not unless I wanted to drink myself into oblivion. The bar in the living room tempted me, but I shook my head at it. I didn't deserve that kind of escape. No. When the hospital called about Summer, I would be sober.

With steaming mug in hand, I returned to the computer and flipped it open. The website I had been reading appeared and there, in a blog menu on the right side of the screen read a title that woke me more thoroughly than the coffee ever could.

"Mystery Church of the Great Boston Fire"

This sounds good. The mouse cursor slid quickly to click the link, and I read the article that appeared moments later.

The Great Boston Fire destroyed sixty-five acres of Boston's downtown back in 1872. The page focused on a church that had been a victim of the fire. There seemed to be no record of the church's name, denomination, or of anything regarding its history. The article *did* go on to build it up as a mystery with a haunted past involving Satan worshipers. Of course, it did. This was, after all, a web page on the Internet, so naturally, there were ghosts and Satanists.

Knowing better than to trust the word of one blog post, I did some research and verified that a church had indeed existed on that spot before the fire. A warehouse stood there now, old and forsaken. My gut told me to check the place out. My supernatural gut told me to listen to my normal gut. An abandoned warehouse on holy ground in the middle of the city. No place could be more perfect—and its address put it along Gray's path on the day I tailed him.

The urge to take action welled up inside me. If I could stop the Order tonight, then Summer might have a chance. Of course, I didn't have Jessica's charm yet, and I didn't want to bring Ross into harm's way without one. It didn't make sense to go off investigating their lair tonight.

But making sense was for suckers. Lack of sleep and my rage toward Gray and company for hurting Summer and Liz made acting rash a natural course of action.

I concentrated and sent my feelers out for the talisman in Gray's car. Rocky came to life and reached out to me far from the old warehouse. They stopped for the night. The multiple attacks they made against me probably bled them dry of power. This offered a window of opportunity I couldn't pass up.

Back in my bedroom, I reloaded my gun. Into a backpack I stowed a first-aid kit in the main compartment, along with my detective kit—I planned to dust for fingerprints. From a big box of batteries, I grabbed some AA's and replaced the ones in my flashlight before stuffing it in my jacket pocket. The cells weren't old, but as it sucked to have your flashlight die in the middle of a dark room, it became standard procedure to always replace them. Once again dressing down, I threw on old blue jeans and my Army jacket, with a Metallica t-shirt underneath.

This time, I took a taxi in case the warehouse was being watched. The rain, which had finally come during my abortive attempt at sleep, arrived as a light mist that dotted on the car's window. Another reason why I should have waited, but I grimaced and pushed the thought aside.

The warehouse rose into sight along a dark street lined with other similar-looking buildings. It was old, built during the first years after the fire. Two stories high, the immense brick building nearly filled up a city block. Wooden boards covered most of the windows, and the place looked dingy with disuse. No one walked along the deserted street as the taxi drove by. That made sense, considering the late hour.

The cab stopped around the corner, and I got out and strolled casually to the place. The front door refused to open, but fresh footprints led to and from it, and the knob was cleaner than it should have been.

Someone used it recently and had a key. A dark, narrow alley separated the building from its neighbor, and I went down there, looking for an easy way in. A broken window on the second floor was the only entrance I could find. A fire escape led up to a boarded window near it. It looked like I could shimmy my way on a narrow ledge from the blocked one to the broken one.

The ladder on the bottom of the fire escape stopped above my head, and jumping up to it with my arm in its current state was out of the question. I muttered some unkind things about my limb in frustration. *How the hell do people live with shit like this?*

A wooden crate promised to give me a boost to the fire escape. The box scraped loudly on the ground, forcing me to stop now and then to listen for trouble, but I got it into place without issue. Once on the crate, I worked on freeing the ladder. This proved difficult, but eventually, it swung down with a deafening *clang* that reverberated throughout the alley. Once again I listened, yet no sound of pursuit came.

Negotiating the ladder was no piece of cake, but before long, I found myself at the top of the fire escape, looking at the ledge.

That "ledge" I had seen from the street turned out to be only a few inches wide and ran the length of the wall to the corner.

Yeah. This was the *easy* way in.

My undercover work boots scraped on the small wet surface, and I took my time, relying on my left arm to keep me from falling. Inch by inch the broken window came nearer until it stood before me, revealing a dark and silent room beyond. With my arms protected by the Army jacket's sleeve, I cleared away the remaining glass from the edges and climbed through.

The glow of my flashlight revealed the contents of an old office. Devoid of furniture, the room was littered with old newspapers, porno magazines, and beer bottles. Bird shit carpeted the floor. A single open door to the hallway creaked slightly on its hinges.

Seeing no sign of recent use in the room—the Playboys were two years old—I cautiously entered the corridor. My sixth sense tingled, but I couldn't identify its cause. Though not as dependable as Spider-Man's spidey-sense, my mystical intuition usually gave me more warning. Most of the time, it alerted me to magic, but every now and then it prefaced some kind of weird supernatural event. This didn't feel like a spell. Whatever the case: magic or otherwise, it couldn't be a coincidence. This place *had* to be the Order's sanctum.

The hallway stretched out before me as I stepped through the door, passing several offices before ending at a door leading to the warehouse's massive open area. The floor of the passage sported less debris and, thankfully, less bird shit. Each room resembled a copy of the first one—signs of use by partiers and the homeless, but nothing recent, and nothing occult.

Only four office doors decorated the hallway walls, two on either side, all standing open. The light clicked off, and I stepped to the opening and stood, listening. Silence settled around me.

In fact, it was *too* quiet. In a place like this, especially at night, I should hear the sound of rodents and birds.

With all the bird signs on the floor, I should have heard the flutter of wings. Where were they tonight?

Something moved behind me, and I whirled, my flashlight causing shadows to dance as it aimed back down the hallway. The corridor ran empty to the boarded window at its end. It wasn't really a sound that I heard—more of a feeling—but my gut told me something had crossed from one room to the other.

Back along the passage, I went, placing one foot, then another, with plenty of time to listen in between. The nearest pair of doors approached slowly. Whatever it was, it had gone into one of those rooms. No sound came from either opening. No breathing, no movement. Nothing. Then, I flashed the light around the room to my left. The shadows retreated from the beam, but nothing else moved. Boards covered the window across the room, neatly cutting off the imagined intruder's only escape route. I shone the light in the other room, but with the same result.

Get a hold of yourself, Simon. You're too nerved up.

I went back to the opening at the end of the hall and stepped out onto the landing.

Moonlight filtered through second story windows to illuminate the expansive warehouse ground below, its shortage of boxes and crates managing only to make the place seem bigger. In addition to its immense size, the room was different from the offices I had visited by its total lack of debris. No bottles, no magazines, no trash. The well-maintained floor pushed my lips into a triumphant grin. With increasing excitement, I turned the light down. What I saw took the breath momentarily from my lungs.

   In the exact center of the floor, painted in red, was an enormous pentagram.

Chapter 28

The circle was big—probably nine feet in diameter, as that number had magical significance. And it looked like they used blood.

After snapping an aerial picture of the scene, I descended the metal staircase that led from the landing to the warehouse floor and carefully approached the ritual place. The site was old, at least a week—maybe more. The blood, dark and dry, crumbled when I scratched the circle's edge with a pocket knife. The remains of old wax from candles was still in the cardinal points along the ring's perimeter, but dust had already begun to cover them.

Though I had no doubt the Order used this warehouse and this circle for their rituals, they stopped using it before their attacks on me. They either abandoned this location for another or made a new one somewhere else in the building.

I stepped closer to the edge and extended my psychic feelers outward. The strange vibe that hit me when I entered the warehouse still prickled the skin of my arms and neck, but it didn't come from there. The ring had almost no magical residue left. No, the vibe came from elsewhere in the place, which meant I should search for a newer site around here.

A sudden noise echoed in the expansive chamber, like the scrape of a shoe on concrete.

My light flashed toward one end of the warehouse. The creator of the sound stepped out from a doorway into the room. The humanoid figure stood about five-eight, or five-nine. Black robes covered its form, its face hidden behind a hood.

My gun raised to aim at the intruder with my left hand, while I held the flashlight with my right.

"Identify yourself!" I challenged.

"Why, Simon," the mysterious man said. "Is that how you greet a friend?"

A frustrated growl escaped my lips, but I didn't lower my weapon. "Aleister Crowley? What the hell are you doing here?"

The man pulled his hood back to reveal the plain face with those un-plain yellow eyes.

"Undoubtedly the same thing you are doing—investigating the supernatural."

My eyes narrowed. "What do you mean?"

"There is something here."

"You feel it, too?" I asked.

The strange man chuckled. "My dear Simon, of course, I do. We are alike, you and I."

"Let's agree to disagree on that point," I said.

"Please put your weapon away. You have nothing to fear from me."

I lowered my gun. Though I didn't trust him, I didn't

think he meant to hurt me. The man was mysterious, all right, but he wanted me on his side.

I turned my attention back to the warehouse and walked around, scanning the littered floor for another ring. Crowley joined me.

"What are you doing?" he asked as we strolled aimlessly around the open area.

"Looking for a magical circle."

"Other than the one in the center of the room, I take it?"

"Yes. Other than that."

"What makes you think the feeling we share is caused by magic? Many things can cause that sensation."

"And the circle is just a coincidence?" Sarcasm came naturally to me when talking to people who annoyed me. Aleister Crowley annoyed the piss out of me.

"Learn to see beyond the obvious. Your senses are telling you something. Listen to them."

The scraping of my own shoes stopped, and I turned to face him. "Look, Obi-wan, I didn't invite you here, and I didn't come because of some random feeling. This is a case, and frankly, you're in the way . . ."

A sudden sensation shot through me, like the one I encountered upon entering the building, but stronger and more urgent. An entity of some kind lurked in the shadows across the room. Something magical, maybe, but a *thing*, not a spell.

"We're not alone," I whispered.

"What do you think is here?"

"Whatever it is, I'll bet it's not here to talk."

"Then reach out with your *inner* senses. Visualize

our guest in your mind."

My eyes rolled, which, of course, he couldn't see.

The darkness was near complete, and only vague shadows remained as I strained to look across the room. A shadow moved. The shape had no discernible form in the poor lighting, and it blended with the rest of them to the left. The thing vanished before I could figure out what it might be.

"It's on the move," I hissed.

The recruiter made no response but backed away with cautious steps, farther from the gloom across the room.

Either with great courage or stupid curiosity, I didn't retreat but flicked my flashlight on instead.

"Turn it off, you fool!" Crowley called from somewhere far behind me, as a scream pealed all around the room—a cry driven by anger and guided by malevolence. This was no human vocalization but the call of something supernatural.

Almost immediately, I felt a presence behind me. "Good. Cover my back." Switching the flashlight to my other hand, I reached slowly for the holster on my right hip.

At that moment, two things happened. First, something smacked my hand, sending the light flying. The small metal cylinder whirled through the air, causing shadows to dance all around me, before striking the ground and going out. Then clawed fingers raked along my back.

A scream tore from my lungs as I lurched forward and spun around, gun in hand, aiming at . . .

There was nothing there.

A frown creased my face. Something had been right behind me. The pain of those claws still throbbed, and I felt the presence directly before me. Yet I was alone, save for the shadows that penetrated every inch of the place.

"What the hell?" I said, confused.

"Feel it, Simon." Crowley's voice echoed around the room. "Reach out to the being. Touch it with your mind."

"You know what it is?"

The mysterious man ignored my question. "Go on. As you can perceive its presence, so you can perceive its *nature*. Reach out. Understand it. That's the key to its undoing."

A sudden pain shot through me, as sharp talons raked my left arm. Tension exploded in immediate action, and I spun around and fired in the direction the monster must have been. The bullet ricocheted off a distant wall.

"Your gun is useless here," Crowley said. "Use your gifts."

Shadows swirled in the fringes of my sight as I backed my way to the nearest wall. If I couldn't see this thing, I should at least present as little a target as possible. The creature stalked me out there, but the room was darkness and shadow. Moonlight filtering in through a skylight above created just enough light for them to play in. Crowley was right. The beast was invisible, or something like that. Besides, I doubted bullets would hurt it. My gun, useless against this thing, went back into its holster.

A supernatural monster in this room—something unclean, demonic. The taste of inhuman rage burned in its essence as I stood with my back pressed firmly against the wall. The fairies didn't summon this thing. They dealt with Fae creatures.

Could the Order have summoned something like this, and then left it here? That might explain why they abandoned the warehouse.

But what was it?

A shadow moved from the corner of my eye as another attack came, this time along one cheek. My hand went instinctively to my face where welts already began forming.

"You must *try*, Simon."

"I don't know how!"

"Let go. Don't force it. Feel the presence, then expand on that feeling. Stretch out to understand its form, and then its nature."

Fine! After all, what choice did I have? I was a sitting duck to this thing I couldn't see and couldn't shoot. The essence of malevolence surrounded me, and I focused on it, touching it with my mind. Strength. Power. Evil. The entity had all those in spades. My thoughts spread out along it. The demon was big, but how big? The sensation of its presence stretched across the room, in all directions. The fucking thing filled the room. Yet the monster had no solid body. Part of it existed in this world but only part. A dimensional being. *What does it look like?* At first, nothing came to me, but then a shape began to form, then twist and shift and it turned into something else. The blasted thing had no shape at all. An amorphous monster that filled the room, taking advantage of the items in it, mimicking them, like shadows.

Shadows!

This was a shadow creature. A being that existed in this world only as dark tricks of light. Every place where the dim illumination pushed at the darkness became part of the demon. How do you fight a shadow?

A smile stretched across my face, and my chuckle echoed in the room.

With a sudden burst of motion, I sprinted across the room toward the huge sliding warehouse doors. The shadows around me surged in pursuit. The attack would strike me any second. My legs, my arms, my neck. All were exposed to it.

My body struck the wall between two of the large bay doors, causing a flash of light in my head and stars to dance around me. Running in pitch darkness. Great idea. My hands fumbling desperately with the shapes on the wall, I found what I was looking for and flicked its switch.

With the loud clicking of a relay, the many overhead lights flickered and came on.

The shadow creature screamed from all around me, its agony ringing clearly as it was forced back and away. The flashlight was not nearly strong enough to hurt the entity, but I was on the right track. A silent "thank you" went out to whoever had paid the electric bill. My brilliant plan could just as easily have been a dud.

The creature wasn't gone, by any means, but it was pushed off, relegated to the corners where the light failed to reach. At some point, I'd have to come back to get rid of the thing, but for the moment, I was content to leave it trapped there.

Crowley walked over to me, clapping his hands like a proud father after his son caught his first softball.

"You see, Simon. There is far more to your gift than you know."

"Okay, I'll bite. Tell me what kind of things I can do."

"Join us, and we'll teach you."

"Ah, yes. Your cabala of magicians. No, thank you."

"There's so much you could learn. You could be powerful."

"I don't want power. It corrupts."

"But you want to know what you are, and we can show you."

"Which can be done without me joining your group. That you won't tells me you've got some selfish reasons for recruiting me."

The recruiter laughed. "Of course I do! The addition of one as talented as you would benefit my companions and me."

"Again, I don't have to be in your club to be an ally."

"Simon," Crowley looked me in the eye, his face set. "Allowing someone with as much magical potential as you to remain wild and uncontrolled is dangerous. We have no intention of controlling your actions but to ensure you learn to manage your gift. Right now, your powers are chaotic—destructive. Surely you understand that?"

Score one point for Crowley—he made sense. Yet

I had a strong aversion to following rules, and I didn't want to belong to a cult, or cabala, or any other group that did magic as a single unit. After all, I was trying to stop one at the moment.

But I wanted to get rid of him for now. "I'll think about it."

"Good." Footsteps echoed around the room as he strolled off toward the hallway from which he had come. "Call me when you're ready."

"Hey, Crowley," I called as he walked away. "Is that *really* your name? You don't look like the real Aleister Crowley, and I'm pretty sure he's dead."

The strange man chuckled. "There is power in a name, Simon Kane. Remember that."

Chapter 29

No cars drove on the wet street when I exited through the front door. The rain, now no more than a light mist, invigorated me and I chose to walk the three blocks to a road bearing cabs to hail. The thought of waiting on this dark, deserted neighborhood for an Uber sounded like a bad idea. Once seated and on my way, I stared out the window and thought about my little adventure.

In my hurry to leave the warehouse, I had forgotten to ask Crowley a couple of questions. One: did he know anything about the Order and the circle there? And two: what the hell was that shadow thing? That last question dominated my mind as I rode in the cab back to the apartment. The two possible culprits, as I saw it, were the magicians and the fairies they angered. The monster was a demonic creature, so no Fae would never summon such a thing.

That left the Order. Could they have summoned the entity to hunt me down and kill me? No. That wasn't their MO. So far, I'd only seen them manipulate probability, increasing the chances of things happening.

Summonings went down a whole different path of magic. Demons . . . well, magicians didn't summon demons if they could help it. They were hard to control, and the consequences were always too high. Their current magical focus was too successful to risk a summoning. Besides, the thing seemed to be stuck in that building.

Maybe Gray and company summoned the entity some time ago but couldn't get rid of it. That would explain why they abandoned their lair. Or, perhaps it was a ghost enhanced somehow by the residual energy from the Order's experiments. Both of those theories were a stretch. Again, not their type of magic, and wouldn't their increased luck make mistakes like that less likely to happen?

Anyway, I doubted the creature had anything to do with my case. The Order had clearly used the place for their spellwork but abandoned it some time ago. *Back to waiting for Gray's car to move,* I thought as I watched the tall Bostonian buildings whiz by. A quick check with Rocky told me it sat unmoving in the direction of Liz's home. A great weariness came over me, and I longed for sleep as the urban landscape whizzed by.

My cell phone yanked me out of my stupor.

"Yeah?" I breathed through a yawn.

"It's gone, Kane." The grumble of Ross' voice betrayed his frustration. He had that I-want-to-hit-somebody-but-there's-no-one-around tone I'd heard too many times. Most of them were because of me.

"What's gone?"

"The damned body! The corpse you made of that Redcap monster. It's been stolen."

My face in the window frowned at me. "How?"

"The truck never got back to the hospital. The medical examiner's office called me to find out why the body didn't arrive. A cruiser found the ambulance parked on the side of the road on its route to Mass General. The driver and crew were asleep, and the cadaver was gone. No sign of intrusion and the men had no idea what happened. None of them even remembered pulling over."

"Sounds like fairies to me. They cleaned up their mess like they did with the ogre."

"Shit! I was afraid you'd say that. This is gonna cause me a lot of trouble, you know. Luckily, I didn't tell anybody that what we had wasn't human."

"Too bad it's gone. I hoped to find out more about the creature."

"You don't sound surprised, Kane. Did you know this would happen?"

"I had a suspicion."

"You could have warned me."

"Would it have made a difference?"

The muttered response was barely audible. "Well, I've got shit to clean up, now." The call clicked dead.

Even after what I had been through, I was glad not to be in his shoes. It was nice not having to answer to anyone. Frankly, I didn't know how he put up with it.

The bag dropped off my shoulder to land on the floor as soon as I entered my apartment. My jacket fell shortly after, followed by my abandoned boots, all forming a breadcrumb trail to my bar. Two shots of whiskey went down, and I poured a third before my mind went to work again.

Every inch of my body screamed for bed, but I couldn't give in yet. One last revelation of the evening still hounded me. I read the creature's "nature" and understood it. That had never happened to me before, so why now?

The answer came to me right away: because I never tried before. In all cases, my gift just did its thing without any conscious thought of my own. This time I reached out and touched the creature with my mind and learned a lot about it. Crowley was right. Ross was right, too. I possessed the power to make change in the world. There was no downside to what I did. With a spell, one wrong move, one wrong word, and bad things happened. This ability belonged to me, and I was, therefore, meant to use it.

My arm still hurt. Bones took a while to heal, even for me, and I kept tweaking it. Maybe my gift could speed up my existing supernatural healing.

The whiskey burned as I drained the glass and set it on the bar, then I went to my bedroom and changed into comfortable clothing. Back in the living room, I took a seat cross-legged on the floor by the picture window. I rested my right arm on my lap and concentrated on it. Like at the warehouse, I reached out to the injured limb and tried to imagine the bone under the skin and sinew—the long, white of the radius, broken about midway down. Healing had begun, but the halves had not bonded. The image in my mind sped up as I pictured the break mending more rapidly. It looked like one of those time-lapse pieces in a PBS documentary. A warmth spread from my chest down my arm. Something told me I shouldn't focus on the sensation, so I didn't. Instead, I continued to think about the appendage healing itself. At last, the spell ended. The magic gave me a little nudge to stop, and I did.

All remained still in the apartment. The dull thumping of a bass beat filtered in from some floor below. The dim lights cast a warm glow about the room. Boston Harbor continued to twinkle at me through the picture window, the rain now a mist that beaded on the glass. I raised my arm and twisted the wrist gently, testing it.

Searing pain shot up from it and I grunted.

The spell hadn't worked. But I swore I felt the power, felt the magic do its thing.

A yawn forced its way up from my chest and out my mouth, drawing my attention to it. Exhaustion overwhelmed me, more so than before I started my little experiment. *Maybe I'm too tired.* Carefully, I stood and stretched. *I could always try again in the morning.*

Morning came, and still, I slept. The night haunted me with dreams of shadows, all moving and swirling and reaching for me. Finally, my eyes opened and refused to close, but my body resisted the day and remained still for a while. My eyes and my body fought between getting up and going to sleep, and I just waited to see who won.

My eyes emerged victorious, and my body, resisting to the last, dragged itself out of bed and into the shower. At some point, the hot water and steam did their magic, and my mind began to work. Then I took a seat at the computer with a cup of coffee and a bagel, ready to research the shadow creature. It was during my fifth sip of joe that I realized I had been using my right hand. Curious, I set the mug down and flexed my arm experimentally. The bone still ached, but not bad. Though not fully healed, the break itself appeared to be gone. The attempt last night hadn't been fruitless. The magic worked!

This was big. The mending spell proved beyond doubt I could use my gift to create a change in the physical world. Excitement welled inside me, threatening to burst out. I had power—*real* power. Not the ritual crap the Order did. Hey, I might even be able to go head-to-head with the bastard and win.

My head shook violently, as though to eject the idea physically from my brain. No. These were dangerous thoughts. If I thought of my gift as a weapon, I'd be no better than Sebastian Gray himself. Last night's spellwork was a fantastic breakthrough, but I couldn't let it go to my head. Like Ross suggested, I would ex-periment to test my bounds. To try it out and to use it in the field only in dire need. To do any less would send me down that slippery slope to corruption and turn me into the same type of creature I hunted.

With a deep breath, I pushed the thought from my mind. Back to work, Simon. That monster was demonic and clearly evil, but I didn't know why it was there. For some reason, I needed to find out.

Nothing matched, although I came across

something similar. People all over the Internet described entities called "Shadow People" that resembled the shadows of people cast on the wall. Yet they didn't quite fit with my monster. First, in nearly all accounts of Shadow People, the creatures could never touch anyone. Second, they appeared only in your peripheral vision and would disappear once you turned to look at them. The horror I fought had gotten physical with me, and I looked straight at it the whole time. My attacker didn't look like the shadow of a person—it was all the shadows in the room at once.

Perhaps these beings were related to the one in the warehouse. After all, they did have their similarities. But how did the thing become solid enough to scratch while remaining immune to physical harm? And why did it attack me? The creature left Aleister alone and made a beeline for me. The odd sorcerer knew the thing—he understood it. Why didn't he clue me in? Why didn't he help? Well, he did. He gave me advice, teaching me how to fight it, like a—

That bastard!

Crowley summoned the thing. The tingle I felt there was the creature, but there was something else. The prickle of magic. That asshole brought the shadow monster there and sent it after me to—what? See if I could defeat it? Was the whole scene some kind of proving ground?

Of course. The wizard wanted to test me, and he wanted to show me that I needed him and all his "advice." This was just an elaborate ploy to recruit me!

The chair flew back as I leaped from my seat and

paced around my living room. "He doesn't want me trifling with him," I growled as I stalked angrily past the morning view of Boston Harbor. "What I'm going to do to him will be no trifle."

Of course, I had no idea where to find him. "Aleister Crowley" wasn't in the phone book. Without a real name to go by, I had to wait until he came to me. Then, things would get interesting.

The sorcerer and his monster were distractions and had nothing to do with the case. Clicking the little X's on each of my web browser's tabs felt invigorating. After closing all my work on the shadow creature, I was left staring at a single page about the warehouse—the remains of my research on the Order.

Was that all I had? An address to a warehouse they abandoned at least a week ago? Yup. Well, no, there was something else. Phone in hand, I flipped through my gallery and examined each of the pictures from the old building in turn. The magical circle was huge. The Order must be bigger than I thought. The spellcasting area was big enough for at least ten magicians. Nine— magic loves threes. Their use of blood meant their spells weren't wholesome, like Jessica's coven was.

Jessica. She would know. This was her specialty. I texted the pictures to her with the message, "What can you make of these?"

My thumb hesitated over the power button—I had a voicemail.

"Mr. Kane, this is Liz. They're discharging me from the hospital in about an hour, and I want to see where things stand regarding the case. Please call as soon as you can."

I hit redial and waited for four rings before she picked up.

"Yes?"

"It's Simon. Can you talk?"

A pause. "Yes."

"Unfortunately, I haven't much to add after the incident in the subway," I said.

"So, you're still on the case?" She sounded surprised.

"Of course I am. Why wouldn't I be?"

"I figured . . . You know, after everything that's happened. To you, to your girlfriend . . ."

The long breath I took was unintentional, but I didn't regret its help in conveying my annoyance. "I'm a professional. When I take a job, I see it through."

"Then nail that bastard to the wall." Anger. Hatred. Those words failed to describe the message conveyed across the line. From a controlled lack of emotion to this . . . The girl wanted Gray dead.

"Your stepfather did not send the Redcap after you," I reminded her.

"No, he just tried to *bury us!* He's a murderer, and he'll keep on murdering until someone stops him. Stop him, Simon. You *have* to." Liz's voice quavered a little on those last words.

"Oh, I will. Count on it."

"Good. I'll let you know everything he does when he's at home."

"That's not wise, Liz," I countered. "Gray's dangerous—he could hurt you."

The girl snorted. "Do I care? I'm not sitting quietly

while he's still at large. I'll do my part."

The frown I now wore was also unintended, but I let it slide. If Gray found out I was working for her, he wouldn't hold back because she was a kid. I didn't want to have to decide between her life and stopping the Order. The choice would be hard.

"Then be careful. The man's dangerous and clever. He'll use you against me if you're caught."

"Don't let him win. If he gets me . . ." She took a breath. "Don't let *me* get in the way of doing your job. Do you think I'd be any safer if you backed off?"

"Point taken. Just don't let it come to that. Be careful, and don't take unnecessary risks."

"Right." The phone went silent.

Steam wafted from my mug as I tipped the coffee pot over it. "What have we got?" The hot drink focused my mind as I wandered around the room. "We have an order of magicians with at least ten members that are casting spells to give them luck." I took a sip as I mentally ticked off the items. "Somehow, they've managed to piss off fairies, who declared war on the Order's families." The view out my window beckoned, and I stopped to watch as life bustled outside. A boat loaded with tourists made its way slowly out to sea.

"Now my client is about to do something stupid that might not only get her killed but screw up my investigation."

My feet paused in mid-stride, a frown creasing my face.

And I was stuck at home until Jessica showed up with the charms. If she didn't show up soon, I might have to go out and do something rash—like pay a visit to my old pal, Sebastian Gray.

Chapter 30

Over the next two hours, I pored over the Internet in search of more holy sites in the Boston area. Aside from active churches, there were a couple of Native American burial grounds and one cemetery that had promise. Nothing reached out to me.

At one o'clock in the afternoon when my doorbell rang, I closed the screen of my laptop and went to the door, bringing my right hand to the gun at my hip. One deep breath to steel myself, and then I put my eye to the peephole.

My father stood there, dressed as immaculate as ever, his suit expensive and perfect. The mostly-gray hair was flawless as though he had just come from the stylist. The fidgeting and nervous glances he cast around him raised some flags in my mind.

Frowning, I opened the door but did not step aside to let him in. He noticed, and his expression hardened for a moment.

"Simon," he said. "I'm not here to yell at you. I think I've done enough of that in the past few months."

"So, why are you here?" My voice remained hard.

Dad never came by without wanting something.

"There's a dinner party tomorrow night, and I'd like you to come with me."

A second passed where my mind went blank. The blink of my eyes brought me back. "Why?"

"Because I'm to bring a 'plus one,' and your mother—well, let's just say she's got other things to do."

By "other things," he meant to drink and maybe cheat on him. Yeah. Winners of the "World's Best Parents" award, twenty-seven years straight.

"And I'm sure it would be great to keep me out of trouble for a night."

"I'm making an effort here, Simon," he gritted. "The least you could do is try."

"Sorry if I don't trust you, Dad. I haven't had much reason to."

The mental struggle showed in the slight tightening of my father's jaw, and the extra creases in his brow. The man was fighting to be civil. Again, not like him.

"I'm a good businessman," he began. "But I'm a mess as a father. I'm trying to make amends."

"Isn't it a bit late for a midlife crisis?"

"If you don't want to go, say so," he growled at me.

I looked away. Huh. Did I actually feel bad for him? "Sorry, Dad. You caught me off guard. This isn't like you."

"Well, that's what happens when you try to change, isn't it?"

"Makes sense. Still, I'm busy on a case, so I don't think I can go."

A cloud passed over his face. Subtle. Most people

would never notice, but I did. Could he be *disappointed?*

"I see." William Kane's voice was steady, carefully mastered. "Well, the invitation's open in case you find the time."

A hand raised, a card offered between two fingers.

"This has all the details. Please, try to come." With that, he turned and walked off. No goodbye, no nod, nothing. Expensive shoes clacked tersely on the hallway without a single scuff to show he'd been rattled. The man was trying his damnedest to remain calm.

My eyes descended to the card. A big formal party at Donald Kress' mansion. One of my father's business relations. Possibly the only man in Boston richer than him.

Of course, I had no interest in going—right up until he acted like a father.

Only an hour later, I lost my patience. Any typical day, I could spend hours at home listening to music, watching TV, or hanging out online. Tell me I couldn't leave, and the place became unbearable. Over and over, the events of the past few days ran through my mind, and I stared at my notes, looking for something—anything—I could do while I waited.

Then it hit me!

"The professor!" my voice rang out. "Of course! Professor . . ." Pages flipped as I searched for the info. "*Doctor*. Doctor Owen Donnell. I'll go visit him and find out what Gray was up to."

Keys jingling in my hand, I stopped at the door. Oh, yeah. The prison. My safety and all that shit. My gaze strayed to the spacious and comfortable living room, and I frowned. Every instinct I had told me to stay put, but I knew, even as I told myself that, I couldn't. The caged animal always wanted to escape, even when it meant being hunted to death. With a battle of wills that took far less time than it should have, I threw open the door and passed beyond the protection of my wards into the wide world.

The Camry purred as it pulled up to the curb outside Doctor Donnell's house. The same yellow Beetle sat in the driveway as I strode up the walkway. That woman from the other night was there.

Less than a minute went by before the door opened. The twenty-something blond from last night stood before me. The shoulder-length hair still hung behind her head in a ponytail. Up close, I realized that although she was not unattractive, she wasn't the type to tempt a man to adultery. A plain, unassuming face held eyes that radiated honesty and morals. The wan smile that greeted me as the door opened faded when recognition—or lack thereof—struck her. A second or two of confused frowning crossed her face until it finally settled on cold professionalism. Brown eyes scanned up and down my body in suspicion.

"May I help you?"

"My name is Simon Kane. I'd like to speak with Doctor Donnell."

The woman's expression became instantly guarded. "The doctor is not taking visitors. Sorry."

The door swung to slam in my face, but I stopped it with my foot.

"My apologies, but I desperately need to talk to him. This is police business, and I'm helping them."

"I don't believe you. Now go, or I'll call the cops!"

"Please do." A confident smile tugged at a corner of my mouth. "And ask them if Detective Ross is working with a private investigator named Simon Kane. I'll wait right here." I withdrew my foot, and the door slammed in my face.

Five minutes later, the woman returned and gestured me inside, her expression apologetic. "I'm sorry, but you have to be careful these days."

I stepped past her across the threshold. "Of course, you did the right thing. Except I wouldn't have opened the door until I knew who it was."

"Yes, well . . ." she said, her face turning red.

"Were you expecting someone?"

"That's personal."

"Actually, I need to know if our interview will be interrupted. Remember, I'm one of the good guys."

The woman's face seemed to deflate, as though she were giving up a personal dream. "No. Nobody's coming. I just hoped it was—a friend."

"Ah," I said.

The reason for the lady's sudden mistrust became quickly apparent. This was the house of an elderly man. The doctor wasn't just a retired professor. The man was old, and she was almost assuredly his nurse. I couldn't have been an acquaintance with the introduction I gave. The house was neat and clean, the living room decorated in a style one or two generations old, with many photos on the mantle and end tables. Most of the pictures were taken on location at archaeological dig sites and in primitive villages, many in black and white.

I turned to face the nurse as she followed me into the room and I offered my hand. "And you are . . . ?"

The woman shook my hand. Her grip lacked confidence. "Lacy Stoddard."

"Nice to meet you, Miss Stoddard."

"Mr. Kane."

"How is the doctor doing?" I took a seat on the couch and smiled pleasantly at my host.

The nurse sat in an easy chair that faced me. "Same as always. He doesn't remember much, and he's pretty weak. He spends most of his time in bed these days."

I nodded.

"Someone else has been here to see him. A man, driving a BMW."

The woman blushed. "Sebastian."

"Right. Do you know why he came—what he was after?"

"Well, to visit me."

"Ah, of course. And he comes here often?"

The woman shrugged. "About five times, now."

"How did you two meet?"

"Well, he came at first to see Dr. Donnell, but when he discovered his condition, we ended up talking. We hit it off, and he's been coming to see me ever since."

The nurse's eyes suddenly narrowed. "Is he in trouble?"

"He's a person of interest. In fact, you should call the police if he shows up again. And don't let him in. The man is dangerous."

Lacy sat still for a moment, staring ahead of her, not meeting my gaze. "Yesterday, he invited me to Cape Cod for a vacation."

"He's married." I eyed her as I said it. Reactions speak volumes.

"Of course he is!" she spat. Sincerity. Good. Miss Stoddard trusted him until I started talking about him. That trust crumbled at once. The woman should be helpful from that point on.

"When he came to visit, did he just spend time with you? Did he ask questions about the doctor, or see any of his papers?"

Lacy wiped her eyes. "I let him rummage through his notes. He said he worked at the university. He doesn't, does he?" When I shook my head, she grimaced. The voice that came from her next was soft, deflated. "He was so sweet and sincere."

"Can you show me what he looked through?"

The nurse led me into a room that was clearly the anthropologist's office. Bookshelves lined two of the walls, and a couch took up the third. The fourth was behind an enormous oak desk with a window behind it. A large box sat on one corner of the table, and a pile of notebooks and papers lay in the center.

She smiled weakly and stood by the door while I went to work.

The papers strewn about on the desktop were all about fairy lore, and the beliefs of Irish locals, both old and new. Dr. Donnell seemed to have quite an interest in the Fae, in a healthy, scholarly way. But I didn't see anything that could be useful to Gray.

At last, I uncovered a notebook that had been set aside. The corners were dog-eared and showed signs of recent use. The book flipped open to a page that had most likely been read recently. It contained the following passage:

Witches danced in their circles and communed with fairies, who gave of their power to aid in their magic.

This was a clue—it had to be. Finally, I found a link between the Order and the fairies. Not much of one, admittedly, but it was a link nonetheless.

An email arrived while I drove home, but I chose to wait until I was safely back in my apartment before reading it.

Back under cover of my protective wards, I dropped the bag of papers on the bar and grabbed a beer. Then, I pulled out my phone and checked the email.

It was from Jessica.

Simon,

The circle troubles me. It has definite roots in The Golden Dawn, but it goes beyond that. I see elements of Satanic ritual, and other traditions as well. One sigil I recognized from somewhere, but I don't know its origin or meaning. It's the complex symbol with the crisscrossing lines bounded by circles. I have a bad feeling about the whole thing, but I can't tell what this circle was used for. All I can say is these magicians are quite knowledgeable in esoteric lore and are pulling from multiple sources in a way I've never seen before.

Be careful.

PS: The charms will be ready later today. I will call then.

Jessica.

Later today. Good. I wanted to take the offensive against Gray and company, but I knew I couldn't until I had protection from their spells. Without her charm, I'd be dead from a car accident, or a coyote attack, or by a safe falling on my head long before I could get to them.

Weapons—my mind turned to them since I planned to go on the warpath. I had my gun, of course. But the circle at the warehouse was big enough for a large coven, and I didn't relish a gunfight with nine or more evil zealots. No, I wanted something more. Something to give me an edge.

My gift. Okay, so Crowley proved his point. I had abilities beyond those I had seen before. So far, I healed faster than normal—my already fast normal, that is. My psychic sense could be used actively to probe the nature of things. None of them were helpful in a fight. There had to be more things I could do—I only needed to find them. Which meant experimentation. *What other abilities should I try?*

There was precognition or telling the future. Nah. Too confusing. If I saw the future, could I change it? If so, then what would stop someone else from changing that future? And if I couldn't do it, what use would the power be? The whole subject made my head hurt just thinking about it.

Object reading sounded interesting. That was where you held an item dear to someone and got visions about that person. I didn't know if the dream showed what was currently happening, what had happened in the past, or what was going to happen to the person. There was only one way find out.

Then there was telekinesis—or psychokinesis. Yes. That was the one. Moving objects with your mind. It would even the odds if I could fling random stuff at the Order's members, in true Jedi style. Hell, I'd stay hidden and take a bunch of them out before they realized what was going on.

My gaze drifted down to the beer bottle in my hand, and a slow grin spread across my face. Tipping my head back, I finished off the drink and set the empty container on the coffee table. Like with the healing exercise, I sat down cross-legged on the floor and focused my energy on the bottle. My thoughts went out to it, picturing the object sliding across the table and falling to the carpet. I wanted it to move. I *needed* it to move!

Nothing happened, except a small headache.

Again and again, I tried, with no luck. I filled a shot glass with whiskey and downed it, then attempted the trick again with the smaller item. Still nothing. Finally, I shoved the glass angrily off the table with my hand. There.

Maybe I wasn't ready for psychokinesis yet. Too bad. Object reading, then. I needed an item to hold. Something relating to the case, like Gray's keys, or one of the candles from the circle. But I didn't have anything like that.

The pendant. That weird amulet I had taken from the Redcap. Now, that might give me something useful.

With shoes discarded in the living room, I padded to my bedroom and retrieved it from my nightstand.

Once more sitting on the floor, though this time away from all the furniture, I held the talisman in my hand before me. About two inches in diameter, it was made of a metal heavy for its size. Gold, or brass—it was too dirty to tell. The symbols depicted on its surface were unknown to me, but it didn't look Celtic. Pictish, perhaps?

No!

No *thinking*! My eyes slammed shut, and I relaxed, performing the breathing ritual I did when meditating. Then I looked at the amulet again. Instead of examining its details, I only took in its shape, its size, and the feel of the thing in my hand. It felt cold and hard against my fingers. This was a pendant and wasn't meant to be held. It needed to be worn—it *wanted* to be worn. Without thinking, I slid the chain around my neck and let the metal disk fall against the skin of my chest.

A hallway stretched out before me—the neat and tidy upstairs hall of some suburban home. A single light in the ceiling cast a soft glow as I walked swiftly, intent on my quarry, a woman running ahead of me. Tall and attractive, with long brown hair that cascaded over her shoulders and bounced from side to side as she ran. The white nightgown fluttered behind her, giving an impression of the ghost she was soon to become. I strode after her, confident. There was no place to hide. She burst through a door to her right and disappeared within. Her screams of terror brought a smile to my lips.

Striding purposefully into the child's bedroom, my eyes rested on the woman standing at the crib, stricken by the carnage that lay before her. She screamed and screamed, keeping her back to me as I approached. The woman would have to turn around. Though I could kill her from behind, I saw no point in it without seeing the terror in her eyes. I had to play with my toy first.

The halberd raised above my head for the blow that would sever her arm . . .

Chapter 31

"Spoonman" by Soundgarden suddenly blared in the child's bedroom. The space around me changed and the woman—the woman I was about to kill—vanished. My head whipped around in surprise. The living room of my home spread out before me. No crib and no woman met my gaze, only a couch, coffee table, the bar, and piano. The scent of freshly spilled blood had gone.

I was disappointed.

My cell phone rang again, the ringtone blasting all its grungy goodness into the air. My mind came back to me then. The whole scene was only a vision, and in it, I had been the Redcap. And I had enjoyed it. Now I wanted to vomit.

This out-of-character emotion had to be a property of the object reading. I'm no killer, yet the goblin was. The dream not only conveyed images but *emotions* as well.

The phone rang for the third time and I grabbed it. "Hello?"

"Hello, Simon."

"Summer? How are you doing?" My heart leaped,

and I woke up immediately. *She's going to be fine*, I told myself.

A slight pause crackled over the airwaves.

"It's Jessica."

"Oh." My heart crumbled. It wasn't her. "Hi."

Another pause.

"I can bring the charms over at ten o'clock. Your partner will need to be at your place as well. They must be bound to each of you."

"Okay," I said. "I'll let him know."

"Good. See you then."

"And, Jess. Thanks."

A moment's hesitation passed before she hung up. *Could she be jealous? Nah.* We established long ago how incompatible we were.

But Summer. I wanted so badly for it to be her. To hear her voice and know that she was okay. It would have made the rest of what had to be done bearable. But there was still no word.

Retrieving the shot glass from the floor, I poured in more whiskey and drained it again. Then I speed-dialed Detective Ross.

The call went straight to voicemail, but I didn't leave a message. The man never turned off his phone or let the battery die, and although he could have been on a call or out of range, I doubted it. A sneaking suspicion told me that something was wrong. Nothing supernatural, this time—just a hunch I couldn't shake. Since I needed to talk to him anyway, I decided to pay him a visit—and quickly.

The Camry rumbled appreciatively when I started

her up. The Ferrari wasn't right for the case, and with its NASCAR engine, this sleeper could hold its own against the Italian sports car. At mid-afternoon on a weekday, there was hardly any traffic. With the added benefit of my muscle car, I made excellent time navigating the streets to Ross' house.

Ordinarily, I wouldn't check the detective's home during the day, but my hunch pointed me there. Whether it was a normal instinct or some supernatural premonition, I didn't dare forsake it. Still, I called the department and asked for him. They told me he went home to rest. Something about working late last night. As usual, my gut was right.

Detective Joe Ross lived in a small ranch in a lower-middle-class neighborhood. The houses here were small, typically ranches and split-entries. All had postage-stamp yards, most of them well groomed. Only a few homes had garages, but Ross' neighbor was having one installed. Construction men swarmed the place as a backhoe dug into the ground.

Ross' house sat dark and quiet with no lights in any of its windows. The tires of my car crunched on the gravel beside the curb as I pulled to a stop. Professional courtesy taught me to park on the side of the road so as not to get in the way of the owners or the police. Dew soaked my shoes as I crossed the grass lawn to the small concrete stoop that was the closest thing to a porch the house had.

The doorbell rang dully beyond the door. There was no answer. I tried it again. Nothing. I knocked. My apprehension grew with each attempt to reach him. My fists pounded on the door as I called his name.

Apprehension turned to fear, and it tingled along my spine with a shudder. My raised hand paused in mid-swing for another pounding on the door.

That tingle . . . Not fear. *Magic*!

I tried the doorknob, which wouldn't give. In the movies, detectives would shoot the lock off the door and burst in. I doubted it was that easy.

The window beside the door revealed an empty living room. Removing my coat, I held it to the glass and smashed it with the grip of my handgun. The jacket dropped to the ground, and I reached in and unlocked the window.

Once inside, I looked around my gun at the ready. An eerie silence filled the place, the rumble of the backhoe dull from outside. There was nothing "homey" about the living room. A couch taking up the far wall looked like it doubled as a bed. A rectangular, particle-board coffee table sat in front, police files spread over its surface. No pictures adorned the walls, only a flat-screen TV and entertainment console.

The hallway that led throughout most of the house also lacked all personal charm. *Jeez, Ross*, I thought as a stalked down the corridor. *Learn to live a little.* Two doors greeted me halfway down the hall, one an office, the other a bathroom. Both Spartan.

A noise called my attention to the door at the end of the hallway. Someone was in that room, trying to be quiet. The gun in my hand pointed at the door, and I took slow, cautious steps forward.

The door flung wide open, and the dark form of a

man entered the passage, a revolver aimed at me.

"Freeze!" we both shouted at once.

Relief sighed past my lips and my weapon lowered. Ross did the same. The cop stood there in his suit, the jacket missing and his shirt untucked. The tie was gone. He rubbed his eyes and walked to me.

"Simon? What the hell are you doing here? Did you break in?"

Right. Broke in. "We've gotta get out of here. Right now."

"Why? What's going on?"

"Outside first. Come on!" I turned and headed down the hall, checking to make sure my partner followed. He did, so I bolted to the front door, unlocked it, and threw it open. The sounds of construction flooded the house. Ross met me at the door.

"Run!" I shoved him out onto the stoop.

He got the hint, and we both ran full-tilt toward the Camry.

The house blew up in a rush of flames and heat and wood.

Chapter 32

A sudden wave of heat struck me from behind, and I was thrown to the ground, getting a mouthful of grass in the process. Luckily, we were far enough away to avoid the worst of the blast. The wind left my lungs, my back felt like it got an instant sunburn, and I ached all over from the fall, but I'd live. The ringing in my ears annoyed the piss out of me, though.

"What the hell?" Ross shouted from the ground beside me, and I had to read his lips to get what he said. He pushed himself to his feet and turned to face the burning remains of his house. The poor man's jaw drooped like he just got the biggest shock of his life. I was afraid I expected something like that. That tingle foretold a catastrophe of this magnitude. On a good note, the prickle vanished. The Order was apparently satisfied.

The place descended into chaos. My friend's house was in ruins and engulfed in flames. The construction workers ran around like ants whose anthill just got squashed. At least one talked anxiously on a cell phone. 911 was taken care of.

"No, no, no . . ." Ross fumed, running his fingers through his hair. "What the hell did you morons do?" With surprising suddenness, he turned to storm toward the workers.

I grabbed him by the shoulder and pulled him around to face me.

"It wasn't them," I said.

"What do you mean? Of course, it was!"

My head shook with slow purpose, and I met his gaze, my eyebrows raised.

Dawn broke over Marblehead.

"You were in the house," he said, working the details out in his head. "You got one of your little vibes, right? This," he motioned toward the house, "was Gray's work."

"Exactly," I said.

Hatred seethed through him toward our common enemy, but he swallowed it with effort as he stared at his burning house.

"That's why you came here. To warn me. You saved my life."

"Well, I saved your life, at least. I came here for something else. The tingle hit me at your door."

"A tingle?" If he was going to ask why I had come, he lost the chance. The foreman of the construction workers joined us by the curb, stepping over shingles and clapboards that had been thrown everywhere in the explosion.

"You the owner?" he addressed Ross.

The detective nodded.

"Anyone else inside?"

Ross shook his head. "What happened?"

The man wiped sweat from his brow. He glanced at the burning wreck that was my friend's home and then grimaced. He didn't want to answer the question.

"A gas line explosion. But I swear we couldn't have hit any line. We had the plans. We dug in the right place."

"Could the plans have been wrong?"

The foreman shrugged. "I guess, but I've never seen anything like this in all my twenty years in the business."

The two men walked off toward the other workers. Ross had work to do, and so my news had to wait. Sirens blared in the distance, growing steadily louder as I pulled the Camry to a safe place a few doors down. From there, I watched the spectacle unfold.

The fire trucks came soon, and they had the blaze under control in less than an hour. Kudos to them, and good luck that the house had a single floor.

The Emergency Medical Techs checked us both out before attending to the workers. One said I was the luckiest guy he'd ever seen when he found no injuries to show for the ordeal.

Ross and I talked to the police, which went quickly since he was one of them.

Finally, the two of us lounged by my car, watching the men work.

"So, why did you come?" the detective asked.

"I took you up on your suggestion and used my gift intentionally."

He raised an eyebrow, but his gaze remained on his ruined house.

"What happened?"

"I had a vision where I saw through the Redcap's eyes."

Ross frowned. "The thing you killed? How is that?" He looked at me suddenly. "You think it's alive? That the fucking shit walked out of the ME's van?"

"No. It showed what the monster did before it died."

"How'd you do that? Seems like a pretty random thing."

"Not so random." I handed him the pendant.

Ross looked the metal disk over, examining the sigil. "What did you see in your vision?"

"The Redcap killed a family."

He gaped at me. "And you didn't think to *lead* with that? Who? What family?"

"No idea. I only saw what it saw, and the carnage had mostly finished. The goblin chased a woman into a child's bedroom. There were already bodies there. Lots of blood. I—the Redcap—raised the halberd to attack her. Then the vision ended."

Ross considered my story for a moment. "Can you describe the woman?"

"Tall, brunette. Good looking. But I only saw her from behind, though I could describe the hallway and bedroom."

"That might help." He pulled out his cell and dialed a number.

"Mrs. Mann? Hello, this is Detective Ross. Do you have a minute to talk? Is your husband home? No? Good. I'm going to put you on speaker phone. I have

Mr. Kane here."

He pressed a button and held the device near our faces.

With a nod to me, I leaned closer and spoke clearly.

"Mrs. Mann, I'm going to describe a person and a place, and I want you to tell me if it sounds familiar. Ready?"

"Ready," came the woman's voice over the speaker.

"The upstairs hallway of a house. Tan walls, forest green carpet. A painting of a farmhouse. A woman, about five foot ten, with long, brown hair. Attractive. A child's bedroom is off the hallway about midway down. It's a baby's room, with a decorative wooden crib, white carpet, and sky blue walls—"

"Elise. Elise Powell. The Powells are friends of ours. That's little David's room." There was a pause. "Did something happen to them?" Her voice was apprehensive.

My mouth opened to answer, but Ross cut me off. "We don't know, ma'am. Please, give us the address, and we'll check it out."

"22 Opal Lane, Brookline. It's just down the road from me. I . . ."

"Don't go there," Ross warned. "It's important you stay clear of the Powells for the time being. I'll call you when I know more. Don't go to that house, Mrs. Mann. Am I clear?"

"Yes." Her voice was small. It wavered enough to reveal the terror welling inside her.

"Good. I'll talk to you later," said Ross, then pocketed his phone.

"Let's go." He gave me a meaningful look as he said it. He expected to give the woman some bad news.

Chapter 33

Brookline. The case began in this comfortable suburb, and now we returned. Quietly upscale, the big houses and immaculate lawns appeared safe and sane. But Ross and I knew differently as we pulled up to the curb. The Powells owned a beautiful, large white house, full of gables and trim. A white picket fence separated their yard from their neighbors but left the lawn open to the sidewalk. A walkway curved from the decorative front door to the driveway which ran two cars wide to the garage. The glow of lamps illuminated the windows, appearing out of place in broad daylight.

We walked without speaking up the drive, then on to the door. Would anyone come when we rang the bell? I didn't expect it. Ross pressed the doorbell, and we waited. There was no answer.

Nothing but the brisk spring breeze could be heard. All else was silent. *Deathly* silent.

"Any tingles?" he whispered.

I shook my head.

The detective opened the screen door and gave me a quick nod toward the front door that stood slightly ajar.

Ross drew his service revolver, and I followed suit with my .45. Carefully, he pushed the door open. The stench of death assailed my nostrils. A staircase rose to a hallway on the second floor. The living room spread out to the left, while the kitchen opened up to the right. My partner motioned toward the stairs and then worked his own way into the room.

"Police!" he called, following the Boston PD playbook.

The muzzle of my gun pointed up at the landing above as I mounted the steps in a slow, careful manner. Though the Redcap was no longer here and Mrs. Powell was likely deceased, this was the home of a member of the Order, and he was unaccounted for.

The hallway ran perpendicular to the stairs, which gave me a choice. First, my gun aimed down the left-hand path. Nothing but walls, floor, and closed doors. Then I turned around.

A gasp escaped my mouth, and I stood, jaw agape, my weapon forgotten in my hand.

The setting of my vision stretched out before me in all its creepy glory. The same light in the ceiling cast the same glow on the same carpet. Even the pictures on the wall were identical. Everything. There, before me, the door to the child's room hung open.

Images of what I would find in that room forced themselves into my mind. A brutally butchered woman and child. Blood everywhere. Probably decapitation. The calling card of the Redcap.

Somehow, I was strangely excited. A side-effect of the object reading. Even that spell had its dangers!

First one foot and then another stepped slowly down the hall, not out of caution—because no one was there—but out of a reluctance to see my expectations laid out before me. Mr. Powell might have been guilty as sin, but his wife and child—they were innocent.

At the door, I paused, my feet refusing to move. No deep calming breaths—not in this stench. There was nothing for it but to step in and witness again what I saw in the vision. In one fluid motion, I stepped in front of the doorway and leveled the gun into the room.

The room was trashed. The crib lay on its side in a corner. A wooden nightstand was in pieces on the floor, the light on the baby monitor still lit. Blood everywhere, on the walls, on the sheets, on the furniture. A great pool of the stuff had soaked into the carpet.

Yet there were no bodies.

What the hell? The mother and child were clearly murdered in that room. So where did they go? Without stepping into the crime scene, I leaned my head in and glanced around. Nothing. No drag marks led into the hallway. The windows were all closed, and I could see no sign of blood on the frames. No one could have removed them without leaving a trail.

Except, of course, supernatural creatures orchestrated this hit. Fairies could have done it. They might have levitated them or something, though I couldn't see why. The standard Fae revenge plan would be to kill the family and let Powell find them. The man would tear himself apart from anguish, yadda, yadda, yadda. And where was the Order member?

"Clear!" came Ross' shout from below.

"Right!" The rest of the upstairs rooms were all as they should be. Apparently, the child's bedroom was the only place where violence occurred on this floor.

"Clear!"

Heading downstairs, I found Ross in the door to the dining room, his face deathly pale. Once at his side, I glanced into the room and saw why he hesitated.

Elise Powell, whom I recognized from my vision, had been nailed to the opposite wall, crucifix-style, beside a window that bathed the room in daylight. She was naked and covered in blood, occult symbols drawn on her chest. "Drawn" wasn't the right term. The sigils were *etched* into her flesh with some kind of thin knife or scalpel. The child hung on another wall, in a similar fashion, his body marred in the same manner.

On the table lay the naked body of what must have been Mr. Powell.

Bile rose in my throat as I stood there, aghast. Ross looked like he had just thrown up, but I couldn't tell from the smell since the stench of rotting flesh overwhelmed everything else.

When I looked back at the figures on the wall, I lost it too, vomiting all over the carpet. It wasn't the blood that did it—I'm not squeamish. It wasn't the ritualistic way in which they had been placed—I had seen that kind of thing before. They were a mother and child. I couldn't reconcile that. One look at that baby and I lost my breakfast, last night's dinner, and anything else that was in my stomach.

Get a grip, Simon! my voice shouted in my head. *Compartmentalize. Don't think of the people. Think of the evidence. The clues.* Out of habit, I took a deep breath, then regretted it because of the reek of death in the air, and threw up again. When I looked up, I had mastered myself.

"What do you think? This is your expertise." No mention of my embarrassing moment. Just got down to business. He was a pro.

The nightmare on the wall had to wait, or I might lose it again, so I instead approached the table. Besides, I knew what happened to them. The Redcap killed them upstairs and placed the bodies here. The husband was what surprised me the most. The fairies had been using a strategy of suffering, trying only to hurt the Order members. The changeling tried to drive Mann and his wife crazy. Tom Cook was murdered savagely, but that was probably a message to the others—or perhaps he had no loved ones to target. The obvious plan was to send the goblin to kill Powell's family as a warning, or a threat, to him. That they killed him, too, meant they had other designs.

Jeff Powell was also naked with his limbs splayed out. Cords tied his wrists and ankles to the table's legs. The eyelids had been cut away, and they propped his head on a book, forcing him to watch as they dealt with his family.

Cause of death was from two neat, deep cuts across each wrist.

Okay, I understood the torture. Yet something about the whole thing didn't sit right with me. I was missing something, but I had no idea what.

"What d'you think?" Ross said as I stepped back,

frowning. "Why would they do this?"

"It doesn't make sense." My voice sounded distant, as my mind struggled to understand the riddle spread out around me.

"Damn straight," Ross scratched his head as his gaze scanned the scene. "Why would they do this to one of their own?"

My head whipped around to face him. "What?"

"Well, they were all friends, right? Powell was a friend of Mann's. I figure he was part of their cult. So, why would they—"

"Of *course!*" In three long strides, I crossed the room to the mother and took a close look at the symbols carved into her skin. With a handkerchief from my coat pocket, I wiped the blood from one.

I knew that symbol. I had seen it before.

Pulling out my phone, my thumb tapped like mad on the tiny rectangle and up came the picture of the magic circle from the warehouse. The sigil Jessica had pointed out—the one she didn't know—zoomed in to fill the screen and I held it up next to the mark on Mrs. Powell's chest.

The two were identical.

"Kane, tell me what the hell you're thinking!"

A smug grin lit my face as I turned to face him. "This wasn't the Order. It was the *fairies*."

Ross frowned and looked up at the corpses on the wall. "Those are ritual symbols. Do they do ritual magic?"

"No, they don't, but Gray's group does. The Fae took their revenge out on Powell and his family and posed the bodies to cast the blame on the magicians. They want us to take the Order down."

"They're sending a message?"

I nodded. "The Redcap killed them, we know that, so it was the fairies. Why else would they set them up to resemble a magical ritual?"

Ross rubbed his chin absently with his hand as he considered my theory. "Hmm. On the surface, it makes sense. But I don't think that's it. It doesn't sound right."

"Why not? It fits their *modus operandi*."

"Well, I just figured fairies are pretty smart. I mean, they'd know by now we *are* trying to take down the Order."

My gaze strayed across the carnage and I shrugged. "Maybe it was a message to him—and to the rest of his group."

I pointed to the mother. "See that mark on her chest. It matches this." The detective stared at the image from the warehouse that glowed on the phone I held before his face. He flashed me a curious look.

"Tell you later," was all I could say. We needed to stay focused on the task at hand.

Ross examined the picture, and then inspected the sigil on the body. "They're the same. Kane, the fairies aren't just trying to frame them. They're showing us what the Order is *doing*."

My head cocked to one side as his thoughts started to gel in my mind.

"These Fae thingies wouldn't have been able to duplicate this symbol so closely if they hadn't seen it before," Ross continued. "And it can't be a coincidence they randomly chose a sigil the Order uses. How common is that mark?"

"Exceedingly rare. In fact, it's new to me."

"Then either they've watched the magicians do their rituals, or they found the bodies after they were discarded."

"You're right," I said, and understanding dawned on me for the first time since this case began. "And I think I know how the Order upset the fairies."

The front door suddenly burst open, and multiple sets of footsteps came running through the house toward us. We both drew our guns and aimed them at the door as two figures charged into the room.

Before us stood the towering figure of Richard Mann beside the eerily cool Sebastian Gray.

Chapter 34

Mann stood still, gaping at Mrs. Powell, his face wracked with terror and anguish. Huge hands clenched and unclenched at his side, and his face turned red.

Gray, on the other hand, stared at the woman's body with grim detachment. The magician seemed more interested in the position and condition of her body than of her death. He was a psychopath. That's what made him far more dangerous than his hulking comrade.

The big man stepped around the table and moved toward Mrs. Powell.

"Don't move," Ross commanded.

The brute stopped and glared at the detective, as though seeing him for the first time. Mann was beside himself with rage and grief and wasn't likely to follow orders, especially by the cops. Tripwire tension filled the room, and we all remained frozen in place.

"Richard," Gray spoke calmly to his friend. "Ease down. This is no time for rash actions. He is a police detective. We need to work *with* him."

The words seeped into Mann's brain almost visibly,

then he finally cast a glance from Ross to his associate, and then up to Mrs. Powell. A growl of dissatisfaction forced its way past his frown, but he stepped back to join his companion like a well-trained guard dog.

"Detective," Gray addressed my partner. "Jeff was a friend of ours. Can you tell us what you've learned so we can have closure?"

Ross approached the two, his gun lowered but still in his hand. "First, you need to leave this room. This is a crime scene."

The two turned and let the detective guide them to the living room.

When we were all seated, Ross called the station. The police were on their way, in force.

"I could bring you both in for questioning on this case, but I'd rather discuss things here if that's okay with you."

Gray nodded. "Of course, detective. We're here to help in any way we can." The man sneaked a glance at my face as he said it.

Ross scanned each of the men's faces in turn. "Tell me what you thought when you came in and saw— what you saw." A nod of his head motioned toward the dining room.

"I thought, who the fuck did that?" growled Mann. That was Richy Rich trying to be nice. How he could have won over a woman like Rebecca made no sense. Oh, yeah. I forgot he was "lucky."

"Of course, I was horror-struck," Gray said matter-of-factly. "To see something as gruesome as that done to a friend . . ." The man shivered on cue.

"Funny, you didn't come across as one wracked with grief," Ross said, his eyes scanning the tall, cool man for a tell. "In fact, you hardly seemed surprised."

The sociopath shrugged. "I'm afraid I've learned to internalize my grief, always having to put up a strong front for my siblings whenever tragedy struck. Trust me, I'm grieving inside. Jeff was a good friend."

"Do you know why someone would want to kill Mr. Powell or his family?" Ross asked.

Gray shook his head, and Mann shot him a glance.

"No one would want to hurt him." The handsome monster kept his expression calm, in control. The man showed no sign of emotion whatsoever, aside from arrogance, of course. No one could grieve from what he just witnessed and not show it in some way.

"Did anything you see there look . . . *familiar*?"

Gray narrowed his eyes, but Mann looked about to burst from his seat.

"What are you trying to say?" the baby ogre snapped.

"I'm not accusing you of their murder," Ross said, the slight twitch of the corner of his mouth revealing his pleasure at Mann's outburst. "But I think Mr. Powell was familiar with some of the occult images in there. I thought you, as his close friends, might also recognize them."

"Of course not!" Mann shouted, but his friend calmed him down with a stern look.

"I'm sorry, detective," Gray said, taking control of the conversation away from the man with the anger issues. "Neither of us is familiar with the occult. We're businessmen. But Jeff was a bit, shall we say, *odd*. He had some interests he kept to himself. I once asked him what they were, but he told me I didn't want to know. I left it at that."

Big Richard calmed himself as Gray spoke. He realized his smarter friend had the situation well in hand, and he didn't have much to fear. He fixed me with a cold stare that read "I don't know how you're still alive, but I hate you for it." I smiled back at him. His face heated up again, like a red version of The Hulk on the verge of becoming the monster.

"I realize you must consider us suspects in this case," Gray was saying, apparently in response to something Ross asked as I was distracted. "But I assure you that could not be farther from the truth, despite what your Mr. Kane might argue." The cool bastard tipped his head toward me.

"On the contrary, Mr. Gray," I cut in. "I believe that, in this particular crime, you are innocent. In fact, I think our investigation would be best served down other avenues." I motioned to my friend. "Detective?"

He frowned at me, surprised and angry. To him, the interview was not over, and he thought I would think so, too. Still, it wouldn't look good if we argued in front of the others, so he turned to the two men.

"That will be all for now," Ross said, rising. "Until this investigation is cleared, I want you both to stay in town."

The rest of us stood, and the detective led them to the door.

"Of course. Please don't hesitate to call if there's

anything we can do to help." Gray played his hand as smooth as ever, and I could tell Ross wanted to put his fist in the man's face.

When the two were climbing into their car, Ross shut the door and whirled on me.

"What the hell was that? We *had* them. This was our chance to interrogate the bastard. It took me this long to get that chance, and you *dismissed* them. I thought you wanted to bring their group down."

"I do, but any more questions would have been useless, except to tip our hand to what we know."

"What do you mean?" he fumed.

"The suspect can often learn as much from an interrogation as the cop asking the questions—"

"Don't patronize me, Kane . . ." he began, but I held up my hand to stop him.

"He wasn't going to give us any information, Ross, though he was likely to get some things from us, either about our suspicions or about the crime scene."

"And we had the killers . . ."

"*Think*, Ross! They didn't kill their own friend, and they wouldn't have left any evidence if they had. The fairies did this, and they were sending a clear message."

"To who?"

"To us, to the cops. The Fae wanted to show somebody what Gray's Order is doing. Those two are using people in their rituals, and they're laying them out the same way the fairies did to the Powells."

A slight pause followed as Ross' mind switched to the new information. "You're talking human sacrifice. How would that upset fairies? The little buggers don't care about us, you said so yourself."

"There are some people they *might* care about. This city sports a group who worships the Fae. They do rituals to call to them, talk to them, and to pay homage to them. These guys are freaks, and I doubt they ever saw a living pixie, but the fairies would like any humans who actively try to make them happy."

"Nature lovers," Ross said. "Okay. And I take it the Order is abducting them to use in their rituals."

"That's my theory."

"Why? Why abduct those people in particular?"

"I don't know. But there's one way to find out."

Chapter 35

The first stop was my office for the brochure on the fairy-lover group, *People of the Wing, Followers of the Fae Path*. Funny how serious fairy worshipers didn't realize fairies had no wings. The pamphlet had no address; only a phone number. A single call to the department and a few curses got Ross a location. Now, I had assumed they would be based out in the woods somewhere, so they could hug their trees, or do whatever it was they did to worship the little shits. So, naturally, I was surprised when we pulled up to a big complex in the heart of Boston. The fairy-lovers' unit was on the twelfth floor— the top floor of the building.

In the hall outside the door to apartment 1220, I couldn't feel any farther from fairydom. *Knock, knock, knock*, Ross' fists banged heavily on the door. At first, there was no answer, then the door opened slightly, stopping at the length of its chain lock, revealing the sliver of a man's face.

"Is this the *People of the Wing*," Ross growled.

The eyes widened, and with a squeal of terror, the man ran off back into the unit. We exchanged surprised looks. "Now *that's* suspicious," he said.

"Police!" he cried, but when a door slammed farther in the apartment, he kicked the door that was still ajar. The thin chain broke, and the door burst open. In an instant, the detective had crossed the threshold in pursuit of the fleeing man.

The two of us raced through the small yet immaculately decorated living room and through the bedroom door. Fairy art hung all over the walls of a place that had an odd mixture of masculine and feminine decor. The open window in one wall drew our attention, though. Ross stuck his head out and then cursed.

"He's going up!"

Without a word, I ran back into the hallway and mounted the steps to the roof, taking them two at a time. The door at the top of the stairs was not locked, so I burst out into the chilly Boston air.

The roof looked almost identical to those you saw on TV with its flat rooftop and the occasional satellite dish or antenna, and the small structure for the staircase. The garden, however, made all the difference. Standing in the middle of the expanse, in a large fenced-in area, was Boston's own little Fairytopia.

A massive wooden box filled with soil covered a fifty-foot square section of the roof, inside which grew saplings, decorative bushes, and many species of flowers. Narrow paths led into the garden to end at a fountain in the center. Posts rose here and there with candles on them to provide light.

This nursery sat between me and the wall where

Ross was likely still climbing the fire escape. The fleeing suspect wouldn't bypass the artificial woods, considering it formed a formidable little maze.

An opening in wire fencing stood before me, so I stepped through and followed a narrow path that wound between a bed of roses and marigolds. The trail led back and forth through the garden, winding its way inexorably toward the center. Once there, I found myself in a small clearing, the middle of which was taken up by a fountain. Decorative benches lined the circular area, and four paths entered it at even intervals. If it weren't for the incessant honks from the cars below, I could have forgotten I was in the heart of the city.

Light, barefooted steps headed my way down the opposite path. In one fluid motion, I went to the side of the trail and ducked down to conceal myself behind a collection of small saplings. The approaching footfalls were quick and erratic, betraying his panic.

A man in a flowing white gossamer robe burst into the clearing, and as he did, I gave him a hearty shove to one side. The momentum of his mad dash sent him careening toward one of the benches, where he struck it and flipped forward to sprawl in the daisies beyond. His bare feet stuck up comically above the back of the chair.

I laughed. I laughed long and hard, in part because it was hilarious, but also to signal Ross—no, it was only because it was funny.

The poor man struggled to stand up, ruining more of his flowers in the process. This only made me laugh more as he pulled himself unceremoniously from the garden into the clearing.

"Don't bother running," I chuckled. "I'll just knock you down again."

The suspect stood about five foot five, and with his flowing gown, immaculate blond hair—now disheveled—and delicate features, he was the poster boy for effeminacy. Blue eyes stared at me, a mixture of terror and anger in the fragile orbs, which were wet with tears. The man's vulnerability made me pity him, but only a little. *The People of the Wing* people hassled me constantly at every psychic fair and every other paranormal-related event in New England.

My chuckling subsided, and my tone softened. "Take a seat. We only want to ask you some questions."

"N-not until you identify yourself." The guy tried to sound tough, but in his current state and with his light, wispy voice, he was pathetic.

"You should have asked that before you ran. My partner is Detective Ross—that's right, a cop. And my name is Simon Kane, and you sent me a brochure." From a jacket pocket, I produced the pamphlet, but his face changed visibly at hearing my name.

"*You're* Simon Kane?" Awe clung to every word as he spoke. "The rich private eye who always takes jobs about magic?"

"The occult in general, but yeah. That's me. So will you sit and hear us out?"

The man lowered himself daintily onto the bench over which he had flipped. The man made a poor attempt at primping his hair and brushing the dirt off his face and robe.

Ross emerged into the clearing from a third path, his

face set in that I-want-to-punch-someone expression.

"Everything's fine," I said. "This young man is ready to talk now."

The detective glared at the little guy and growled, "Why did you run?"

"I-I'm sorry, officer." The man trembled, but not from the chill air. "I didn't know you were a policeman. We usually get, well, bullies looking for us."

The detective's voice softened a little. "What kind of bullies?"

The man in the flimsy robe shrugged. "You know, testosterone junkies. Guys who want to hurt people they don't understand."

"And I look like a testosterone junkie?"

The man gasped, putting his hand to his mouth. "Oh my! I didn't mean that. Not you . . ."

"Hey! Just answer the questions," Ross cut him off.

The man nodded vigorously, looking plenty relieved. "Go ahead."

"What's your name?"

"Oh!" the little fairy-man laughed nervously. "Terry. Terry Goodchild."

A unisex name. Of course.

"Terry," I said, trying to fill the "good cop" role of the interview. "Are you and your group targeted a lot?"

"Occasionally. We get more of them than we get recruits."

"What do these bullies do?"

"They egg my place now and then. Spray paint. Stuff like that. Some guys have chased us and called us names."

"You should open a PO Box," Ross said. "Damn sight safer than giving out your real address."

Dirt flew from Terry's head as he shook it with vigor. "No way! That's what we used to do. But after two of us disappeared while checking the box, we decided not to use an address at all."

The two of us exchanged glances.

"Two of your people went missing?" The incredulity on Ross' face was comical. "Why haven't I heard?"

"I don't know."

"They were never found?"

Terry shook his head.

The detective frowned. "If your group was involved in two missing persons cases, I would have been told about it."

"*We* didn't report them. Their families did."

"They didn't know about your club," I said. It wasn't a question.

"They'd never understand. We like to keep a low profile. Even with the fliers. Like, we'll only give them to people that might be interested. People like you."

"You never told the police these two people were connected?" Ross asked.

The man gave Ross a look that said: "Cops can be bullies, too."

The detective grunted. "I see. Are you aware that by your silence, you might have condemned those people to their deaths?"

Terry's face paled.

"When did they go missing?" My voice remained calm. Every time Ross opened his mouth, the poor guy practically became a gibbering mess.

Tears welled in the man's eyes as he thought for a moment. "Paul disappeared three weeks ago. River, a week before that."

"Two of your people vanish within a week of each other, and you never thought there could be a connection?" Ross' voice rose threateningly.

Terry's nerves started to fray, and he began to stutter.

"We—we didn't think they were connected. River was talking about quitting. Everyone thought she just left."

"But you pieced it together eventually," Ross interrogated.

The guy dropped his head and stared miserably at his feet, the soft loam squishing up between his toes.

"Ahem," I cleared my throat as Ross opened his mouth to scare the guy again. "How are you certain they both went missing at the post office?"

"It—it was their t-turn to check the . . . the . . ."

"Breathe, man!" At once, I dropped to one knee before him and grabbed his head with my hands. "Take a breath. Hold it. Now let it out." The man did as he was told.

"If you want to help them, answer my next question *truthfully*."

Terry took a moment to calm himself, then gave a curt nod.

"Okay. Ask."

"Does your group practice magic? Of any kind?"

Panic threatened to return as he stared at me in surprise.

"Trust me, Terry. I won't scoff. Magic is real and you know I believe that."

"Yes." The man tried to get his breathing under control. "Yes, we do."

"What type? Wiccan? Golden Dawn? Satanic?"

"No!" His features twisted with distaste. "We do *fairy* magic."

My eyes narrowed suspiciously. I couldn't help it, despite my promise not to scoff. "And how is that done?"

"The power to do it is inside us, so we don't need rituals." He looked away from us, and his face turned red. "Though we usually go here and dance and sing. It works. They give us power—the Fae. Through them, we make the magic happen."

I stood up and stepped back. "Okay. Have there been more disappearances since Paul?"

He shook his head.

"Well, Detective, I think we're done with him."

Ross addressed Terry. "I'm going to have to take you in for further questioning . . ."

Chapter 36

Backup was called, and I talked some more to our prisoner as we waited.

"Before the first disappearance, was your group approached by any interested people?"

Terry thought for a moment. "Well, there was that writer. He said he was writing a novel with fairies in it and wanted to give an accurate portrayal."

Ross joined me and hung up his phone. "Which writer would that be?"

"Are you ready for this: *Tom Cook*," he said, and his voice practically squealed with glee. "His stuff is so good. Have you read any of his work? Never mind. Everyone has! Personally, I prefer *Darkness Strikes*, but *Darkness Strikes Back* was as good a sequel as he could have done. Anyway, if he wants to paint an accurate picture of fairies in a novel, then I'm all for it."

"And you told him you can do magic?" The answer was obvious.

"Of course."

"Did you explain to him that the Fae gave you the power to do the spells?" Again, I knew what was going on, but I had to cross my t's.

Yes. Well, not right away. On his second visit, a few weeks ago, Tom said he wanted more details about the magic, and so I told him. This kind of made him mad—he told me I should have mentioned it before."

"I'm sure he did. Let me get this straight. The famous Tom Cook comes out of the blue and asks lots of questions about fairies and the magic you do. Then two of your people go missing. Shortly after, Cook returns and finds out the *fairies* produced the magical energy for your spells. Is that it?"

Terry gasped, and his hand went back to his mouth. "Do you think *Tom* . . ."

"That's police business, Goodchild," Ross growled.

The man once again looked miserably at each of us, then put his head in his hands and wept.

"It's all my fault," he sobbed. Moving away from the scene, we let him wallow in his guilt and discussed the new development in a corner of the living room.

"The Order took his friends," Ross said as we stood by the broken door to Terry's apartment, leaving the poor man sobbing on the couch.

I nodded. "That was weeks ago. When they discovered that they couldn't extract the magical power from them, they stopped grabbing the fairy-men."

"You mean, they used these people as *batteries?*"

"They *tried* to use them as batteries. But yes."

"How do you figure?"

"The Powells were arranged to be the center of the spell. Sacrifices. Magicians only have one use for a sacrifice: *power.*"

"But Gray and company didn't do that to the Powells."

Sometimes Ross frustrated me with his moments of ignorance. The man was usually pretty smart. "The fairies laid them out the way the Order did to Paul and River."

"Okay," Ross said at last. "That gives us something to charge them with if we can tie the disappearances to them. For that, we'll need bodies, and according to the files, they were never found."

"I think I know where you can look."

The detective cast a suspicious glance my way.

"Their last hideout," I said. "An old warehouse with the remains of a magical circle." I gave him the address.

"Good, we'll head out once my men get here."

"No!" There was no way I'd go back to that place, even though I suspected Crowley removed the creature. "You and your men should handle it. Remember, I'm not a cop. And the Order is after me. I should be getting back home."

He shrugged, clearly aware that I held back. "Whatever. Go home, then, before Gray and Mann cast another bad luck spell at you."

"Agreed. Call me when you find something."

Chapter 37

The warehouse was off limits for me now. Though I was sure Crowley summoned the shadow creature and must have removed the beast when I left, I wasn't about to take that chance. And the strange little sorcerer wasn't likely to sic a monster after the cops, so they'd be safe enough.

There was other business for me tonight—something I highly doubted Ross would have gone along with.

The Camry purred as it handled Storrow Drive, the occasional *thump* of the tires on cracks barely noticeable in the cabin. The shy orb of the April sun peeked tentatively from the clouds as it lowered toward the horizon. Night was falling, but I knew The Mother Load would be open. Nick got most of his business after dark.

Three people were browsing in the aisles when the little bell above the door announced my arrival. Nick looked up from his place at the register and smiled.

"Simon!" the big man boomed. All faces turned to examine me before returning to their shopping. "What brings you here? I hope the stone worked for you?"

"Of course," I said in a hushed tone. "I need another item."

"Oh!" he said with enthusiasm, although he carefully matched my volume. "What item do you want?"

"Something that can trap a supernatural entity."

Nick frowned.

"Hmm . . . highly difficult—and dangerous. I'd recommend against it."

I allowed one small shake of my head. "No choice."

"What kind of being?"

"A fairy."

A single eyebrow raised on the man's dark face, but his frown remained. "What type?"

"A pixie, I think. About six inches tall, no wings, but can fly. Invisible to normal people."

Nick nodded. "Building a cage is easy. Iron is their Kryptonite. They can't pass through it, and its touch will hurt them. A fairy will never willingly enter anything made of iron."

"Which is why I'm here. If anyone has something that will do the trick, it's you."

"Hmm . . ." he said, his great brow furrowed.

"There is something," Nick said at last. "Wait here." The tall man came out from behind the counter and went to the door in the back. I waited patiently by the register. Outside, the traffic increased as rush hour came into full swing. A horn honked, and I jumped instinctively. So many of the recent attempts on my life involved cars that I must admit I was a little paranoid.

Nick appeared through the door only a few minutes later and joined me at the counter. An old, dusty book was in his hands, which he laid gingerly before me. Oversized, with a hard cover and old, tattered pages, the tome resembled a spellbook.

My head shook its dissatisfaction. "I don't do spells. You know that."

A deep, throaty laugh burst from Nick's chest as he flipped the cover open. "Relax, Simon. This is not a spell I'm showing you." He turned the leaves of the book with gentle reverence until he landed on one about midway through.

"Here." A big, dark index finger tapped on the page. "It is not a spell, but if you follow the instructions exactly, the trap will respond to the fairy's own magic, creating an invisible cage through which the being cannot escape."

I skimmed over the section. "Looks like a ritual."

"No . . ." The shopkeep stretched that word as though to sound like I was being ridiculous. "Simply craft a symbol."

"There has to be iron in the thing you draw with."

"Hence this," Nick said and placed a small wooden box on the table beside the book. The big fingers of the shop owner were surprisingly gentle as he lifted the lid and grinned at me. "Ta-da!"

Inside the tiny, velvet-lined chest was a three-inch long piece of gray chalk.

"Made with iron, I suppose?" I asked.

"A strong mixture. It'll do the job quite nicely."

"Okay, I'll take them."

"Of course you will," Nick said jovially. "You always do."

"Well, you're the best."

"This is only part of the trap," he said as he slid the book into a bag. "You will need a lure, and that can be more difficult."

"No worries—I've got that covered." The man took my credit card and rang up the order. The price was undoubtedly tremendous, but as I never asked, he hadn't told me. The two of us had a nice arrangement: he would always find the right item for me, and I would always buy it regardless of the cost. No haggling "Of that, I have no doubt."

"Hey, Nick," I asked as I pocketed my wallet and grabbed the bag. "Are you aware of any magical orders at work in the area?"

The store owner raised an eyebrow. "There are more here than you would think."

"How about one led by a Sebastian Gray?"

The shopkeeper frowned and shook his head. "You know I don't discuss my clients. Some of my best customers prefer a certain anonymity."

"I thought *I* was your best customer?"

Nick grinned. "You certainly are a generous one, but you understand."

"You can't tell me what Gray or his people have been buying from you?"

"I'm sorry, Simon."

"They're dangerous. I'm trying to take them down, and the more I know about them, the better."

"All the more reason why I can't tell you. A colleague

of mine lost his shop because he talked too much. A curse destroyed his place and nearly killed him."

"Humph." *That was disappointing.* "Well, I get it. No more questions. What would I do if The Mother Load blew up?"

"Find another specialty shop, I suppose."

"None are as good as yours, Nick. Keep your secrets, and live long and prosper." I gave my friend the Vulcan salute.

The man's smile curled wide around his face, and he laughed a booming laugh that drew everyone's attention to him. "Take care, Simon. Do not underestimate that which you plan to trap."

The smart thing to do would be to go home and wait for Jessica to show up at ten. Time, however, was a commodity I couldn't waste. Setting the trap at home wouldn't work because of all its protective spells and charms, so I found myself driving out of Boston proper to a small secluded park. The sun had gone, and the streets were illuminated by myriad lights. The wind, still chill, had driven back the clouds, revealing a black sky speckled with twinkling stars. The moon was already rising in the distance, and it made me smile—a person can come to miss the sky if it's hidden long enough. Leaving my car parked at a metered spot on the edge of the park, I grabbed the bag from The Mother Load and set out across the expanse of freshly mowed grass toward the woods at the far side.

The Order started their nasty work by kidnapping fairy worshipers and sacrificing them in their rituals.

They stopped using them after only killing two. I needed to learn what they were doing now, and I knew of only one source of information. But to talk to the pixie, I first had to catch it, and that wasn't easy. Hence the trap.

The trail I followed through the woods was paved and lit with decorative streetlights. Trees rose up on both sides, giving the illusion of a tunnel of wood and leaves. A trash can was set every couple hundred feet, each beside a park bench. The biting ocean breeze managed to find its way down the path every once in a while, making me shiver. A woman dressed in sweats ran past in the other direction. She smiled at me as she went by.

After a few minutes' walk, a small clearing opened up to the right of the trail, revealing a well-groomed garden. A white gazebo stood in the center. Nobody moved in the area, and the streetlights were the only technology in sight. If I were to lure a fairy to me, this would be the place to do it.

The gazebo's floor was dirty and wet from muddy sneakers. That wouldn't make a good place for a chalk circle, unless I cleaned it off, which I didn't want to do. Besides, the pixie might see the symbol there before stepping into the trap. My gaze pivoted upward and broke a triumphant grin. Although the roof of the gazebo was pointed, a flat ceiling had been installed underneath the conical top.

I fetched a metal garden chair from the grounds and placed it on the gazebo floor. With the book propped to the right page, I studied the sigil for some time, then opened the box and removed the chalk. Standing on my improvised perch and using a flashlight to see by, I drew the symbol on the gazebo's ceiling. This took some time because the design was complicated, the light was unsteady in my mouth, and the chair kept wobbling.

Finally, I finished my drawing. After a quick inspection, I cleaned up and put the book and chalk away in my backpack. I set the pack aside and stood in the center of the gazebo, underneath the symbol, concentrating all my thought on the fairy I had seen following Gray out of that house. I pictured the little bastard, its size, its delicate features, the little pink tongue when it gave me the raspberry. My mind called out to it, not with words, but with *intention*—willing the little creature to me.

Though I understood the fundamentals of magic, I avoided using it. Only three times had I cast a spell. Two went horribly wrong. Luckily, this was the one that worked. A couple of years ago, I had cast this spell to ask a fairy what I was. The little guy had been less than communicative, but I was able to discern that the fairy had no idea what I was, though he knew that I wasn't entirely human. The spell was a bitch to pull off because it resisted the summons.

My mind cast about first for the Fae in general, and then for one I wanted. After what seemed a lifetime of searching, I found the tiny bugger and then the real work began. The pixie wouldn't come for no reason—I needed to give it one. The image of Terry formed itself in my head, and I sent it out to the creature. As expected, the little guy reacted, coming closer. Simon's ego drifted to the background as Terry took center stage in my psyche. The facsimile of the fairy-lover beckoned to it, and the Fae critter came to me.

At last, I opened my eyes, the spell complete. Hovering in the air about twenty feet away, illuminated in the glow of a nearby streetlight, was the fairy. It cocked its head and regarded me with a mixture of curiosity and suspicion.

"Come here, little guy," I said gently, giving a curt nod. "I just want to talk to you."

The miniature man shook its head but continued to regard me with interest.

I stepped backward toward the far end of the gazebo. *Come on, you little monster.*

The pixie smiled then, a grin that didn't instill me with any comfort. The smile dripped with mischief—the kind of violent mischief a psychopath got right before it slit its victim's throat. Then, all the streetlights went out at once, bathing the garden in the silvery glow of the rising moon.

Chapter 38

My eyes squinted as I strained to see the fairy in the near dark. The flashlight clicked when I flicked it on, but nothing happened. No light came out. The fairy used magic to disable all electrical devices.

Great. And I hadn't felt it coming. So, Fae spells didn't trip my Magic Sense. This was the first sign that I might have made a mistake.

The fairy continued to hover in place, and I could still make out its nasty smile. Luckily for me, the nearly full moon cast a fair amount of light. But the little guy wasn't alone anymore. Another fairy stood next to it.

No. Not a fairy. The newcomer stood less than two feet tall and didn't hover. It had a short, skinny body dressed in black. Its oversized head was round, with red glowing eyes that tilted inward in an evil glare. The wide slit of a mouth peeled into a smile full of long, interlacing, needle-like teeth. The effect reminded me of an angler fish. This was the second sign that I shouldn't have done this. I dropped my useless flashlight and drew my not-useless gun.

The little monster, which must have been some

kind of fairy-kin, started walking toward me. Its stride was short, due to its size, but it moved faster than I expected. Within a few seconds, it reached the gazebo stairs, but instead of mounting them, it went around the structure. *Oh, boy,* I thought miserably.

If it was related to fairies, it might still be susceptible to the trap. But I doubted I would be that lucky. I backed my way down the stairs as it approached, my gun raised.

"I just want to talk," I said.

It made a grotesque croaking noise that I took as laughter, but I didn't shoot. The last thing I wanted was a fight with a fairy. I really, really, *really* didn't want a fight.

The monster continued around the gazebo, and so I backed myself toward the main trail.

"Come on, I just wanted help against a mutual enemy!"

The thing didn't laugh this time. It stopped and tensed, as if for a spring. The ugly maw opened, and it hissed at me.

The air came alive with thunder as I fired three rounds at the thing. The first shot missed. It opened its mouth wide and took the remaining two shots right into its vast maw. It didn't chew them up, like in a cartoon. They simply vanished.

That was the third sign . . . or the fourth. Aw, hell. This was a *bad idea*.

The monster formed a wry grin with that slit of a mouth and then charged.

I dove to one side, rolling in the grass. Then, I rose

and ran past it in a mad dash for the path. Civilization presented my only chance, I thought as I ran. The ogre attacked me in the middle of a swamp. The Redcap, in an abandoned subway tunnel. Fairies liked to keep themselves a secret to normal humans. It wouldn't want to be seen by a street full of people.

The fairy-kin was fast for its small body, but I had long legs and healthy lungs. I sprinted out of the garden and onto the path, heading back the way I had come. The creature raced in pursuit as I made the turn, slowly gaining on me.

I thought desperately as I ran. Its immunity to bullets made my gun useless. But it was Fae, which gave it their weaknesses. That meant iron. A nice, strong iron walking stick would be a handy addition to my standard gear. I'd consider that if I survived the night.

Though I was in good shape, I couldn't run forever, and I already started slowing down. But my pursuer seemed to have an endless supply of stamina. Any time now, I would feel the sting of those stiletto teeth entering my leg.

I stopped suddenly, spun around, and pistol-whipped the fairy-kin in the vicinity of its temple. In mid-stride, the wee beastie was in a precarious position, and it flew tumbling into the brush beside the path. Without hesitation, I sprinted to it, put the barrel of my gun an inch from its temple, and fired.

The bullet made a hole in its head about an inch in diameter. There was supposed to be a much bigger and messier exit wound, but nothing happened. It was as though the creature absorbed the bullet.

The fairy-kin sat up and smiled, sending a shiver through my entire body. Then I did the only thing that made sense.

I ran.

Running away from danger seemed to be a recurring event in this case. And I was getting pretty tired of it. As I burst from the woods and charged headlong across the grass toward my car that sat waiting for me on the curb, I struggled to work out a plan of action.

There were no other cars, and I couldn't see any people. So much for having a crowd scare it off.

It was still behind me, I knew, but I thought I had a head-start this time. The shot it took to its head had slowed it down some. I holstered my gun as I ran and drew my keys from my pocket. The Camry's lights flashed as I approached, and with another button press, the trunk popped open.

With a final burst of energy, I sprinted ahead and reached the back of the car with about ten feet between us. My eyes scanned the interior of the trunk but saw nothing.

The fairy-kin leaped into the air and struck me in the shoulder. We both went over, and I landed on my back on the road with the monster on top of me. It must have looked comical, with me underneath a doll-sized monster that struggled to bite me while I held it at arm's length from my face. One of its razor-sharp teeth scratched my nose.

The tiny cut bled, and it sent the cannibalistic Fae into a frenzy. The thing shoved itself with more strength than I would have given it at my arms, and I almost lost my grip. There was little I could do. With such a small body, most of my fighting skills were useless. Try wrestling an American Girl doll and tell me you could wrap your arm under its tiny neck, or place your feet under its little chest to kick it away from you. I tell you, it's impossible!

A desperate thought came to me, and I rolled to one side and slammed its head as hard as I could against my car's bumper. It shook its head, disoriented, for just a second before trying again to force its way to my face.

My arms shook as I banged it against the bumper again and again. Each hit caused it to pause, and it eased up a little.

When the monster shook its head from the last hit, I pulled it to me and then shoved it with all my might under the car. The oversized head rolled and bounced in the cramped space almost the full length of the vehicle.

Rising quickly, I scanned the interior of the trunk, feeling around with my hands. The seconds ticked away in my mind, and I knew I would be running again if my hands didn't find anything useful.

A scrambling sound came to me as the persistent little bugger crawled with amazing swiftness toward my ankles, just as my hand wrapped around something cold and hard.

Leg muscles burned in protest as I leaped back from the car. The fairy-kin emerged from under the bumper, its teeth clicking as it tried to bite my moving ankles.

"Fore!" I shouted and swung the crowbar with all my might. It was an old-style iron tool, not one of those new-fangled aluminum jobbies—my car guy insisted on it. It connected with the monster's head with a dull crunch, sending it several yards to one side, where it landed in a heap in the grass.

The noise it made now was more like a whimper. Iron. Fairy Kryptonite. *Nice*. Confidence exuded from me as I strode toward it, hefting the crowbar as I went. Now it was *my* turn to smile.

The fairy-kin was trying to stand up, a deep gash in the side of its head leaking blood. Fairies bled. Interesting.

It looked up at me with what could only have been fear, as I raised the crowbar and brought it down on its skull. Over and over I swung, each time transforming its head into a ball of mush, bit by gory bit.

Finally, I stopped, the doll-sized corpse very much dead. Satisfied, I strode over to my car and used my elbow to close the trunk—my hands were covered in blood. Then I returned to the scene of the carnage. What I saw made me frown.

The fairy-kin was gone.

The grass was still matted down from where the creature had lain. Its blood disappeared, too, being absorbed into the ground. Before long, there would be no trace of the fight left. Thankfully, the red stuff faded from my hands and clothes as well. Lucky me.

It wasn't dead, of course. Killing a fairy was not an easy task, and took more than beating it with an iron club to do it. All I could do was kill the body it used in our world and send it back home. My plan, of course, was a bust. I summoned the fairy, only to lose it when it sicked Fido on me.

Exhaustion hit me as I walked back down the trail toward the garden to retrieve my backpack. My legs wobbled and ached, and I wanted nothing more than to lie down and rest. The lights were still off in the clearing as I plodded up the steps to the gazebo in the moonlight. Then I stopped short, my mouth hanging open.

There, in the middle of the gazebo, trapped in an invisible cage, hovered the fairy.

Chapter 39

"Well, well," I said, smiling. "It seems I get to have my talk with you after all."

"Shrivel up and die," it said in its tiny voice.

"Look," I said, trying diplomacy for the first time ever. "I think we got off on the wrong foot. I admit that shooting your changeling might have been a bit rash. But after all, it was pretty rude. The truth is, we're on the same side. You're after Sebastian Gray and his cohorts. So am I."

The fairy stopped flying around, trying to break from the trap and looked at me. He seemed skeptical.

"You killed our ogre," he said.

"It tried to kill me."

"You killed the Redcap."

"Again, it tried to kill me, and my client."

"You keep getting in our way," he retorted.

"Let's stop throwing the blame around. I want to stop Gray's Order as badly as you do. They're doing ritual magic and sacrificed some of your human followers. I understand why you're mad at them. Tell me where they are and what they're doing, and I'll take care of it."

"Screw you!" he said.

Really? "Did you, or did you not send us a message with the placement of the Powells' bodies?"

"We sent the human's *friends* a message, not you, you stupid prick!"

"You know, I always thought fairies were, well, polite."

"Fuck that," it said and began pacing in mid-air. "Let me go!"

"Not until we've reached an agreement," I said calmly. "First, I need you to promise not to attack the families of the magicians."

"No!"

"Your tactic won't work on them. They're psychopaths. They don't care about anything but themselves."

"You lie!"

"I'm not lying." It was getting harder to stay calm.

"Then you're wrong."

"I don't think so. But we'll be a lot more successful if we work together."

The fairy laughed then. Tiny, high-pitched, mocking laughter. It pissed me off.

"Then just tell me where the magicians meet, and I'll let you go."

The pixie snorted. "You can't beat them. If we can't, you can't."

"Don't bet on that. I've got a few tricks up my sleeves. Just tell me where they meet."

"I'd tell you if I could," he said. "I'd love to see you go in there and get yourself killed. But I don't know where they meet. They moved. Now, let me go."

"What are they trying to do?" I asked, ignoring his request.

"Get filthy rich. Let me *go!*"

"They did something to get you mad. Something worse than sacrificing a couple of human fans of yours. What is it?"

"Fuck off!"

"Tell me, or you stay here forever!"

"They hurt us, okay? Now, let. Me. Go."

I frowned. "They hurt you? Seriously?"

It nodded its tiny head and said nothing. It was telling the truth.

"I see. But I need to know what they're trying to do?"

"We don't know what they're doing. They just hurt us, and so we hurt them."

"This is going nowhere. I'll let you go now. But don't try to attack me again."

I grabbed my backpack and pulled a cloth and a water bottle from it. I poured some water on the fabric, and then walked into the "cage" and, standing on tiptoes, I wiped off the chalk sigil. The fairy flew out and then vanished.

Well, that was shit, I thought, then thought again. Actually, it wasn't shit. The Order had hurt the fairies. How? Physically? Was that even possible? I shot one, and it didn't get hurt at all. It just vanished and went back home. I ran a hand through my hair. *Great. More thinking and more research. Just what I always wanted.* But that meant it was time to go back home to my apartment and its safety wards.

The charms! I glanced at my watch. "9:36 pm" glowed on the tiny screen, and I swore. Jessica and Ross were showing up at my place at ten, and I had less than a half hour to get there! I raced back to my Camry, gunned the engine, and peeled out towards home.

Chapter 40

Although rush hour had ended, Boston's streets were still alive with traffic. I found myself stuck in a wall of cars no more than three blocks from my home. As I sat in my car that hadn't moved in at least five minutes, my phone rang.

"It's me. Jessica. The charms are ready. Shall I come over now and deliver them?"

"Yeah," I said. "Traffic's bad, but I'll be home soon."

"You went out? I told you not to." Her tone talked down to me, as to a child. That was a detail I had forgotten about her. Funny how I only remembered the good times.

"I ran out of toilet paper."

"This is no joke. Those men are dangerous, and you're pushing your luck."

"Pun intended, I'm sure. But I had things to do. I'll be home in a few minutes."

Frustration hissed over the line.

"Okay. And make sure your friend is there, too. We need to bind the charms in person."

"Understood." I hung up on her before she could

hang up on me. Juvenile, I know, but still satisfying.

The Camry jumped ahead two car-lengths as I dialed Ross.

"Yeah," came his voice over the line.

"The charms are ready. Meet me at my place right away."

"Okay. I'll be there in fifteen."

"Good."

"We've been interviewing the whole fairy group, and made some progress . . ."

The detective's voice shifted to the back of my mind as a strange feeling prickled through my body. Magic seethed all around me, building up to something big. Subway-explosion big. All of a sudden, my motionless car didn't feel safe anymore.

I pocketed my phone, turned off the engine, grabbed my backpack, and vacated the car. Horns honked at me as I weaved between stopped cars on my way to the sidewalk.

A deafening crash made me spin around, despite all the warnings in my head.

Something that I could only describe as space junk had landed on my car. A massive pile of metal, antennas, and solar panels stuck out at odd angles from the spot where the front seat of my Camry used to be. Several smaller chunks of debris fell among the parked cars, causing some panic, but the worst was done.

The tingling returned almost immediately, and I knew that I had to get out of there before more people died. Pandemonium reigned around me as I passed the cars that now tried in vain to escape the metal hail. A windshield smashed to my right, a steel rod protruding from it. Curses flew from my mouth as I leaped onto the sidewalk and ran down an alley . . .

. . . right into a group of gangbangers. Yeah, like all big cities, Boston had its gangs. Like most people, I knew nothing about them. I left them alone, and they left me alone. But there was no mistaking the gang-like posturing of the four men that I nearly plowed into.

"Where are you going, asshole?" said one Hispanic twenty-something, whom I took to be the leader. The others closed ranks around me. Well, I guess bad luck came in all shapes and sizes.

"I don't have time for this." My fist shot out before he could wipe that smug look from his face and jabbed him hard in the throat.

The tough guy grabbed his neck, his eyes bulging, and staggered backward, choking horribly.

The others descended on me in an instant. Fists and clubs came from all directions and pummeled me to the ground. I went down right away, covering my head with my hands. This caused the fists to disappear, only to be replaced with feet. Sneakers and work boots kicked me repeatedly in the head, the stomach, the back, and half a dozen other places.

When a person received a beating like this, everything shut down. You pulled yourself into the fetal position you took in the womb and wished you were back there. Logical thought ebbed away as you lay still and let it happen. This was where my mind went, and it damn near ended me. Luckily, there was another part of my head that was stubborn enough to refuse being killed by a bunch of losers. If I were going to die, it would be at the hands of something really bad-ass.

Risking the loss of one arm from my head, I reached to my hip holster. With all the flying feet and clubs, nobody noticed. They *did* notice when I fired a round into the crowd of them.

That changed the dynamics of the fight a bit. At the sound of the shot, they all bolted, running down the alley as fast as they could. All but one. One banger fell to the ground, his hands covering a bleeding stomach.

I stood slowly, and the world began to spin. My body dropped to the pavement, and I threw up. The seconds ticked away like the life of the guy I shot. Guilt finally overcame my nausea, and I crawled over to the poor young man who lay like a slug, holding his wound.

"Give it pressure. I'll call for help."

Although the tingling had stopped, I didn't dare stick around. Gang members were easily startled, but they'd soon return—and in greater numbers.

With as much speed as I could manage, I hobbled back to the street and worked my way carefully to my home, calling 911 as I went.

Both Ross and Jessica were waiting when I stumbled into the reception area of my apartment building. They ran to me.

"I'm okay," I croaked as they held me up.

"Like hell you are." Ross' bedside manner was like a steel pillow—awkward and out-of-place.

"You need a hospital." Jessica frowned as she examined the bruises on my face.

I shook my head and instantly regretted it. "I'll be safer upstairs."

"It was Gray again." The rage Ross suppressed emerged in a guttural growl, like the tiger you heard right before it pounced on you.

A slight tilt of the head was all I could manage of a nod. "Satellite fell on my car."

"That was *magic?*" Jessica breathed the words in awe.

Ross grunted. "Yeah. It's their MO."

The witch said nothing, but the horror screamed in her silence.

Once inside my apartment, I felt better. I was still a wreck, but I knew I was safe. They laid me on the couch, and Jessica went for a wet cloth and Ibuprofen.

I told Ross about the attack, and the guy bleeding out. He called it in.

"Do you think those men would have attacked you without the spell in effect?" Jessica asked.

"Oh, yeah. But I would have known better than to go down that alley."

An hour's rest made all the difference. My heightened healing took care of my head and most of the bruises. My back and a couple ribs still ached, but I was ready to get back to work.

"The charms must be bound to you," Jessica said to us and held up one of them. It was a small piece of rawhide shaped in a ball and sewn shut, holding the bulk of the charm within. A string was attached, turning it into a pendant. The witch stood on her toes to loop the thing over my head, and let the tiny bundle fall down, touching the skin of my chest.

A sweet odor filled the room as Jessica lit incense in a burner that hung on a chain. The brass censer swung slowly back and forth, aromatic smoke emitting through the holes in its lid. "With the blessing of the Gods and the will of Love, I bind this charm to Simon Kane. Let it drive out negative energies and keep you safe from harm." Jessica then leaned forward and kissed the leather-bound bundle.

"Now, you kiss it," she said to me.

I lifted it and put my lips to the small packet without question. This was her area of expertise, and I had full confidence in her.

The High Priestess padded to Ross and put the second loop of string over his head. Once again, she swung the censer in front of him. The detective fidgeted nervously, his eyes darting from the woman's exquisite face to me, then back again.

"With the blessing of the Gods and the will of Love, I bind this charm to Joseph Ross. Let it drive out negative energies and keep you safe from harm."

Ross' face turned beet red when she kissed his talisman. It was as though Jessica didn't realize the effect she had on men, but I knew better.

"Now you," she instructed the burly man.

The detective glanced at me. "Do I have to?" His voice was unnecessarily gruff, as though to assert his manliness.

I gave him a curt nod, holding back my laughter.

Hesitantly, he lifted the charm and gave it a quick peck, before dropping it to his chest like it burned him.

Jessica smiled but didn't comment.

"It's done. The charms are bound to you. But I'll warn you that they may not fully protect you from the Order's magic. Their spells are extremely powerful."

"I understand. These will help a lot."

"Then I should go," she said.

"Okay." My reply was curt, awkward.

The detective glanced from Jessica to me, and back again.

"I think I'm missing something," he said.

"I'm sure Simon will fill in all the details," Jessica said as she opened the door. "It was nice meeting you, detective. Both of you be careful. The Gods will be with you."

And with that, she was gone.

Ross looked at me once the door closed. "You went out with her, didn't you?"

"Yeah."

He nodded. "Now I get it."

Changing tack, he said, "That was it? We wear these things, and she says a few words, and we're safe from the Order?"

"This was just the tail end of the process. Jessica and her coven spent almost twenty-four hours making them. And they're not complete protection. We still have to be careful."

"Magical Kevlar. Got it. Now what? We don't know where Gray is, and we still don't have evidence connecting him to the two disappearances. They're guilty as hell, you and I both know it, but we need something concrete before I can bring them in."

"We know what kind of magic they're doing and that there were at least nine of them. They tried using the People of the Wing as sacrifices for power but gave up on them in lieu of a more powerful one. And then, they angered the fairies."

Ross' eyes narrowed. "Do you think they could be sacrificing fairies?"

"They're hard to catch," I said, but the trap I used tugged at my mind. "And we can't kill them. The best we could hope for is killing their physical bodies, which wouldn't produce enough power."

"Like you did with the baby," he grunted.

"The changeling, Ross. Like I did with the *changeling*."

"Yeah. It still looked like a baby to me."

"But none of this tells us what to do next," I said. "We still don't know where The Order meets. Did you find anything at the warehouse?"

"A magical circle and traces of candle wax and other ritual remains. There were blood stains, so it was likely where they killed their victims. We're doing DNA tests now to match it to the missing fairy worshipers."

"Any fingerprints?"

"Sure, but none on the system. But here's something interesting, Kane. The lights in the main room were on. It was used recently, even though the circle and remains were weeks old."

A smile tugged at the corner of my mouth. "Yeah, that was me."

"I see. I think it's time you tell me the whole story."

Sitting at the bar, I poured us both drinks, then

filled Ross in on the events, including the bit about Crowley. He seemed more forgiving of my breaking and entering than of my withholding information about the magician.

"When were you planning to tell me about this Crowley character?" he growled when I had finished my tale.

"Aleister has nothing to do with the case."

"He may or may not be tied to the Order, but he's having an indirect effect on our investigation. The guy followed you to the warehouse, and the stunt he played was dangerous. And I'm sure it tainted the evidence. Personally, I think it's too coincidental that he introduced himself to you just after you took on this case."

"I think he's watching me. He wants to find out if I'm good enough to join his little guild. I suspect he wants to see how I do against the Order to tell how useful a member I would make."

"Or how much a threat you would be. Kane, I wouldn't trust this Crowley guy. He's willing to put your life at risk to test you. That's sociopathic behavior. If he is an example of an average member of that guild, then they're worth avoiding."

"The enemy you know is better than the enemy you don't."

"You're taking a big chance, Kane. I wouldn't mess with them. That's my job."

"They might be out of your league," I said.

"Do I give a rat's ass? At least, leave him alone until after we're done with the Order, okay?"

"If he doesn't bother me, which isn't likely. Don't worry, I can handle the situation."

"Whatever. Just keep me in the loop from now on."

I was spared making any such promise by my phone.

"Hello, is this Simon Kane?" came a woman's voice over the line. It was curt and professional.

"This is," I replied.

"I'm from Massachusetts General Hospital. I'm calling about Summer Parke."

Chapter 41

My heart leaped to my throat. The last I knew, Summer was in bad shape and had lost a lot of blood. I had been expecting the worst since they took her away. The woman on the line didn't instill me with confidence.

"How is she?" I quavered only a little as I spoke.

"She's awake and doing better."

"Is she going to be okay?"

"Yes, she will. She'll need to spend some more time in the hospital, but she'll be fine."

Relief flooded through me. "That's great."

"Mr. Kane," her voice sounded more personal now, but not cheery. "She tells me you saved her life. I should thank you for that. She's a friend of mine, and I care a lot for her."

"It's okay," was all I could say. Summer told people I was a hero. But if I hadn't taken her out, she wouldn't have almost died.

"I've heard about you, Mr. Kane. You're the kind of guy who gets into trouble and sleeps around. I'll say this: if she's not the love of your life, end it now. I don't want to have to pick up the pieces again. Do you get that?"

An awkward pause followed where I opened my mouth, then shut it. At last, it opened again and, "Yeah," was all that came out.

"Good." She hung up.

"Was that Miss Parke?" Ross asked as I put my phone in my pocket. "She's okay?"

I nodded.

"You should go see her."

A groan came from somewhere in me, and I ran my fingers through my hair. Her friend was probably right, although not for the reasons she thought. I had no intention of hurting her. Summer was in danger as long as she was with me. At least during this case. It would be best for her if I stayed clear until after the Order was taken down.

My feet took me to the bar as my gloomy thoughts swirled in my head. I poured a drink without even realizing it. It wasn't until the Scotch burned in my throat that I realized Ross had said something to me.

"I have to focus on the case."

He chewed me out with his eyes but said nothing.

"I guess we just wait for Gray to use his car again," I said. I didn't like it, but there wasn't much else to do.

"Or, we could check out more of those holy places," Ross said. "It's better than staying here, and we might find more leads."

Busy work. Sometimes I forgot how adept the detective was at reading people.

Having already eliminated the only inactive church

in town, we decided to focus on cemeteries. One by one, we searched through them all. We left the historic ones alone, as they tended to be both more public and more heavily patrolled by the police.

During the day, these big graveyards could appear peaceful and harmless with their manicured lawns and orderly lines of gravestones. But at night, they were downright creepy. Each place sent a chill up my spine. Lone, gangling trees stretched long shadows under the moonlight, grabbing at us with their bony fingers. Granite mausoleums rose before us with their austere architecture threatening to spew vampires at us. Why did architects always feel that cemetery buildings had to creep the hell out of people?

The plan was to walk around them, systematically, checking tombs and any other secluded place that might work as a ritual area. Each one proved to be a waste of time. None of them showed signs of activity aside from the panties, and beer bottles left over from teenage partiers.

We decided to end our tour of Boston's creepiest places with the Mount Hope Cemetery. Though one of the City's historic graveyards, it was out of the way enough to hide a group of evil magicians.

Like at all the others, we chose to leave the car on the road and walk in. We wanted the element of surprise if we were to stumble upon them doing their spellcasting.

This was the oldest graveyard on our tour, and it felt it. Dark and forbidding, its winding roads caused us to continually look over our shoulders as we trekked along. The moon had chosen this time to disappear behind clouds, eliminating the only shred of light we had. To say the shadows were no longer a worry was no consolation, as the near total darkness made every tree, gravestone, and building equally as imposing as that demon-monster.

Eventually, we made our way into a section that appeared to be more recent, but it did nothing to help the feeling of dread that crept over me.

"I don't get it," I said. "Shouldn't the newer graves be in better shape? You know, the families of the interred would visit."

Ross knelt before a grave and shined his flashlight on the stone's face.

"It's a John Doe. He has no family."

I cast him a sidelong glance. "I thought they were always cremated."

"I've heard of a couple of churches that pay to have some homeless people buried. They believe they're saving their souls."

I walked farther down one aisle of graves and then stopped, frowning.

"Uh, Ross. Come here."

He joined me and swore.

Our flashlights shone down into a six-foot hole, where a coffin lay open and empty.

"Son of a bitch!" Ross fumed. "I have to call this in."

Something didn't feel right about the place. It wasn't just the overall creepiness of being a cemetery. There was something decidedly supernatural in the air. I turned slowly around with my flashlight aimed outward. But I didn't get all the way.

My cell phone rang. *Who could it be?* I shoved my hand in my pocket and grasped it.

Then something slammed into me, and I fell.

Chapter 42

Most people would have just fallen on the ground. But I wasn't that lucky. I dropped six feet and landed on my back in the recently vacated coffin. On top of me thudded the person who shoved me into it.

By "person," I meant the corpse of a person. Presumably, it was the body of the grave's previous tenant. It was about my height and male, and it was decomposing. Flesh peeled from its face, revealing bone in places, its eyes glazed over. It stunk horribly, and I had to force back the urge to vomit.

And it was also trying to bite me.

I didn't believe in zombies, but that didn't stop the cadaver from clawing at my face and lunging with its jaws to bite my nose off. I had to push on his chest with one hand while struggling to pull my other from my pocket. Whoever was calling could wait. Wrestling the cadaver was rough in such close quarters, and its mouth came dangerously close to my honker. Of course, I was sure zombieism—if there was such a thing—wasn't contagious, like in the movies, but I couldn't help wondering about it as its jaw snapped shut an inch from my schnoz. And considering I was wrong about their existence, I could be wrong about that, too.

I finally freed my hand and pushed hard, my arms going to full extension. My mending arm hurt like a son-of-a-bitch, but the corpse was unable to reach me. However, it knew enough to scratch. Its bony fingers raked my face and shredded my coat as it tried to tear me apart, all the while snapping its teeth together like a wind-up Halloween skull. Unlike all zombies I had ever seen in movies, it didn't moan—it just silently tried to devour me.

My elbows gave a little, and my attacker lurched an inch forward, its teeth tickling its nasal target. The stress of the past few days came down on me then, and I felt tired, more so than I had in a long time. This fight had to end, and I had to do it quickly, or I was dead meat.

I slid my left hand from the body's shoulder to its chest and squirmed with my right hand to the holster on my hip. In most movies, you killed the zombie by destroying its brain. It sounded reasonable to me, so I drew my gun, placed it against its temple, and squeezed the trigger.

The blast was deafening in the enclosed space, and sludgy blood and gray matter splattered my face. The corpse's lower jaw dislocated and hung by a single tendon, swaying back and forth an inch from my face.

But the dead man kept fighting. Its head was useless, but its body continued to convulse, and its arms still tried to tear a hole in me.

Without the head doing its thing, it was easier to handle my gun. I shoved the barrel up its left armpit and fired. Again, the deafening roar set my ears to ringing.

But the arm separated cleanly from its torso and fell lifeless—and motionless—to the ground.

I didn't want to fire another round in the confines of the grave, so I wrestled the corpse around until I was on top of it, stood up with my foot on its shoulder, and then I yanked with all my strength on its last arm. There was a sick cracking and popping sound, and then the arm tore free of its body.

Its legs continued to thrash, but there was nothing it could do to me. I picked up my gun and holstered it, then called up to Ross, who was staring dumbfounded down at me.

"A little help, here," I said and held my arms up.

He clasped my hands and pulled. Once out of the hole, I clambered to my feet, took my coat off, and wiped the rotting gore off my face. I let my jacket fall to the ground. I didn't want it anymore.

Ross stood, face twisted in disgust as he stared at me with John Doe's guts all over me. "Was that a . . ."

I shrugged as I carefully removed my jacket and wiped the blood and debris off me, using its clean inside. "It was an animated corpse, but it wasn't a zombie."

"What do you mean? I thought that was what zombies were."

"This isn't a zombie, like in the movies. Its brain wasn't functioning. The thing was a grotesque marionette where the strings were magic. I think I had been feeling the magic the whole time we were here but didn't realize it until seconds before it got me."

I picked up my flashlight and angled it along the row of graves we had been searching.

"Do you think there are more?" he asked.

I nodded. "About three more, if I'm not mistaken."

The three graves beyond the one I had fallen into had also been dug up.

Ross scanned the area with his light.

"Shit!"

I followed the beam of his light and saw another corpse shambling toward us. I scanned around and found the other two coming from both sides.

"Time to go!" I said and ran off in the only direction left. Ross followed suit.

Ahead of us, and about a hundred yards distant, was an old mausoleum. We made for it. I risked a glance back only once as I ran and verified my suspicion. The zombies could not run, but they walked faster than I would have expected.

When we reached the tomb, I tried the door. There was no chain or lock, but it refused to pull open. I looked around. The mausoleum was in the corner of the cemetery with a tall wire fence preventing our escape. There was no way out without going through the zombies.

"Ross, help!" I called. He came around, holstered his sidearm, and grabbed the door handle.

"On the count of three," I said. "One. Two. Three!" We heaved as one, and the door tried to open but seemed jammed from within.

"Again," I said. I heard the creak of strained wood from the other side as we yanked, and the door gave a little more.

Ross glanced toward where we had come from and

swore again. "So, we have to dismember them?"

I nodded as I braced for another pull. "Ready?"

He nodded, and we pulled together as hard as we could. As usual, I had been favoring my broken arm, but this time I put my faith in the magic that dulled the pain and yanked hard.

Searing pain, which had become all too familiar these days, shot through my arm, and I knew I was back to square one with the broken bone. But there was a loud snap from inside the tomb, and the door came open.

We ran inside and shoved the door just as the first of the walking dead made it to the mausoleum.

The good news was we were safe from the zombies. The bad news was we were now trapped in a tomb.

By the light of our flashlights, we looked around the place. We stood in a single chamber made wholly of granite. The walls, floor, and vaulted ceiling were composed of the stone. Against most of the walls were shelves that housed pictures and possessions of the deceased. Against the far wall was a small Christian altar. This room was a place for family members to go and pray for those entombed within. A trapdoor was open in one corner of the room. Its cast-iron lid lay beside it. A slight glow, as from candles, illuminated the hole, the magic I could feel in the air pouring out of it like the cold from an open freezer.

I put my finger to my mouth and then pointed toward the hole. "Down there," I whispered.

Ross nodded and, switching off our flashlights, we drew our guns and crept to the hole. The trapdoor opened onto a narrow stone staircase that led down into the ground. By the look of it, they went about thirty feet before opening to the right, so that the stairs appeared carved into the wall of a subterranean chamber. The scent of incense and the sound of a man's voice chanting greeted us from the room below.

I went first since the occult was my specialty. I descended the steps as quietly as possible, with Ross moving in near silence behind me. When I reached the point where the stairs emerged from the new chamber's ceiling, I stopped and peeked out into the room.

It was the actual tomb of the mausoleum. It was about twenty-foot square with alcoves cut into the wall to house the coffins. All of the coffins that I could see had been disturbed. In the center of the room was a granite altar with a circle of lit candles spaced around it. On the altar's flat surface sat an incense burner, more candles, a chalice filled with a dark red liquid, and a long, elaborate, double-edged knife.

Standing in front of the altar, facing me, was a man dressed in a black robe with red writing and symbols on it. A deep hood covered his face, which was bowed over the altar, obscuring his view of the stairs. He chanted something in Latin over and over.

And he was alone.

I quietly descended the stairs and stood outside the circle, my gun aimed at the man. Ross passed me in silence to position himself about five feet from me along the edge of the ring. He followed my lead in not crossing the line of candles.

"You can stop that, now," I said in a clear, commanding tone.

The man jumped with a gasp and raised his head in my direction, the hood falling forward to obscure his sight. He removed the hood and glared at me. The long, greasy straight hair that almost covered his face, the somewhat dark complexion, the big nose, and the many piercings gave his identity away instantly.

"Jack Deth!" I said.

"Who the hell are you?" he demanded.

"We're the police, Deth," I replied. "Now, I had expected certain people to be here, but not you. You're part of Gray's magical Order. Oh, but no. You're not. You used to be, but you must have had a falling out, right?"

Deth narrowed his eyes.

"How do you know that?" He bit his lip, telling me he didn't mean to let it slip.

"Because," I said. "Your band *Black Deth* rose out of obscurity two years ago and managed what no other goth band could do—become phenomenally successful. You hit the big time. But it was short-lived, right? I haven't heard anything about you guys for a while, now. I bet you broke up."

"So, we broke up. That doesn't mean anything."

"It means you left the Order. You were no longer receiving the extraordinary good luck your magician buddies gave you. Without them, you had to rely on your musical talent, which was pretty much non-existent."

Deth's glare deepened. "Luck magic? That's child's play. I don't do that shit, and I don't know any Gray."

"That's right. You're into death, just like your music. You're a necromancer. You raise the dead and control them like puppets."

Deth grinned. "That's true magic. That's *real* power."

"But you fucked up when you sent them after a cop!" Ross said. "Step away from the altar and keep your hands where I can see them."

I stepped forward and dashed some of the candles lining the circle with my feet. I dumped the incense on the floor and stamped it out.

Ross grabbed Deth's arms and handcuffed him.

"So, Deth," I said as I walked around the tomb. "Where does Sebastian Gray's Order meet these days?"

Deth snorted. "Why should I tell you anything?"

"Because," Ross said, stepping forward, "you just tried to kill a police officer. Giving us the information we need could make the difference between life in prison and the chance of parole."

"And just *how* did I try to commit this murder? Will your report say I sent a zombie to kill you?"

"I see lots of ritual equipment here," Ross said. "Including a pretty formidable knife. Ritual sacrifice is illegal, you know."

Deth frowned. I raised an eyebrow.

"You're gonna lie on record?" Deth cried. "What happened to justice?"

Ross shrugged. "You *are* guilty, even if your actual methods are not prosecutable. A time may come when supernatural crimes can be tried. Until then, I have to get creative."

Deth said nothing but looked Ross in the eyes,

trying to decide if the detective was bluffing. Then, he looked at the suspicious scene around him.

"Whatever. I don't give a shit about them. You can fry 'em. They deserve it. But I don't know where they meet. They move to a new location now and then, and I'm sure they moved after I quit."

"You know them," I said. "I bet you've got some ideas."

Deth snorted. "They don't meet at places they know. They meet at places of *power*."

"Like Holy Ground. Churches and the like. Sure. You'll be providing a list of all the Order's past locations."

I stepped up to him. "So now, tell us something about them. How many people are in the group? And don't lie. I can tell."

That was a lie in itself. It was outside my list of supernatural skills, but the necromancer didn't know that.

Deth frowned at me. "You have power. I can see it."

"So, no lies."

"Five," he said, studying my face as he said it.

I shook my head without breaking eye contact. "Try again." That was too small for what they were doing.

"There are nine of them. They would have replaced me. The number is important."

"What would happen to their magic if they lost a couple of members?"

"It would weaken, but they'd still have a lot of power. They'd replace anyone who leaves."

"I'm sure they're pretty powerful," Ross said, putting his face in front of Deth's. "Sacrificing those fairy worshipers would have given them quite a boost."

Deth winced and turned his head away.

"I was against it, but they had their minds set. It's why I left. It was the last straw."

"Now, I don't believe that for a second," Ross said, once again putting his face before him. "You're all about death. A few sacrifices would get you off."

"You don't get it!" Deth cried, his face twisted with disgust. "I love the dead, but I don't mess with the living. They didn't just kill them. They *tortured* them. I left after the first."

A tear welled in one eye. "I still dream about it."

"You sent your zombies to kill us," Ross said.

"To scare you away. Not to kill."

"It tried to kill me," I said.

He shot me a curious look. "It did?"

I nodded.

"Hmm . . ." he trailed off, then muttered, "Maybe my command wasn't clear enough. They should have just driven you off."

"Well, they didn't, and you're under arrest." Ross read him his rights and then glanced at me.

"Are you done with him?"

"For now."

"Then let's go," Ross said and pushed Deth toward the stairs. The necromancer went quietly, but he held a smug smile as he went.

I followed them to the stairs, but on an afterthought, I ran back and grabbed the knife. I didn't want to leave that behind.

"So, the zombies are gone, right?" Ross said to me

as we climbed.

"Should be," I said. "Are they gone, Deth?"

He snorted but said nothing.

I pushed the door open and motioned for them to go.

"After you," said Ross and gave Deth a little shove. The necromancer stumbled out into the night air.

Ross followed, and I came last. We stood on either side of Deth. I looked at him, and he smiled at me, gave me a quick wink, and muttered something in Latin.

The three corpses lurched from around the sides of the mausoleum and attacked. Ross shot the nearest one in the head. It staggered backward, and its head flew back. It struggled to keep its balance.

I shoved my gun into the jaw of the one that came for me and fired. Its head burst asunder and gore splattered behind it. I pushed it back with all my strength and then turned and ran back to the mausoleum door.

Ross fired his gun at his zombie, but the bullets did no good.

The third zombie, sent to action by the single word "Kill," attacked Jack Deth. With his hands cuffed, there was little he could do. He tried to run, but the corpse grabbed his arm and bit into it. Deth screamed and turned to face it. The zombie threw itself on him, and they fell to the ground, the puppet of death on top of its master.

I turned away and went to the door. I put the ceremonial knife to the edge of the doorway and then slammed the door closed, wedging the blade in the crack. Then I took the butt of my gun and pounded the hilt of the knife repeatedly until the blade finally snapped in two.

Instantly, the corpses fell to the ground, never to rise again.

Ross stared down at Deth's body. The necromancer's face and arms were scratched and bitten, with a big chunk taken out of his neck. Blood poured from the wound.

I knelt and lifted his wrist to check his pulse. As expected, he was dead. I shook my head at my partner.

"Well," Ross said, scratching the back of his neck, "this sucks."

"I doubt we would have gotten anything more from him."

"But I don't know what the hell to do. I have to report it. It was one thing when he was alive. I could get him for trespassing, vandalism, desecration of graves. But now he's dead. How do I explain *this*?"

All the zombies that lay scattered around the area were decomposing and had been dead long enough to be unthinkable as murder suspects. A time may come when Ross could convince his superiors that the supernatural exists as a criminal element, but that time had not come.

I shook my head slowly. "I have no idea."

"Well," he said after a moment's thought, "the evidence will clearly show that Deth dug up the bodies. We could say he set them up to scare off intruders, and in the dark, we shot them by accident."

That sounded pretty weak, but I also saw little

alternative. I walked around the area, scanning the ground.

"There are other footprints here," I said. "Looks like more zombies. We could say we were attacked by some people—*living* people—and they killed Deth.

Ross examined the tracks and nodded. "Yeah, that could work—*damn you,* Kane! Why do you have to involve me in all this supernatural bullshit? I hate lying on record. I feel like a goddamn criminal."

"Someone needs to bring these supernatural baddies to justice. Imagine how many innocent people would die if we did nothing. Besides, I believe it was *you* who involved *me.*"

"Yeah, I know," Ross muttered.

"And if you get fired from the force, I could hire you."

He flashed me a nasty look. "Don't push it, Kane."

Chapter 43

Once again, the Powells' house stretched out before me as I climbed the stairs to the second floor. At the top, I turned to see the empty hallway. Carefully, I crept down the carpeted passage toward the first door on my left. This would be the child's room. David. The exquisite tingle of anticipation rippled through me as I passed beyond the open doorway. The room was lit by the warm glow of a single night light down along the baseboard beside the crib. The child lay asleep in his bed, oblivious to what was to come. In the chair beside the bed slumped a man. Jeffrey Powell slept, a child's book still clutched in his hand.

A ringing could be heard from somewhere in the house. I frowned because I didn't want him to wake yet.

It was not yet his time to die, but I had to silence him so he wouldn't wake his wife in the master bedroom. I strode quickly across the room and struck him hard in the head with the butt of my halberd.

The ringing came again, but louder. It sounded vaguely familiar.

A grin spread across my face as I turned to the crib.

Now, it was time to play . . .

I woke suddenly, sitting up. My bedroom was dark with a sliver of moonlight cutting through the gap in the curtains.

Dammit! I hated the interruption.

I took a deep breath to calm my nerves. It was a dream, where I was the Redcap again. But now I wasn't. *I'm not that evil thing, and I don't want to kill that child.*

My cell phone rang again, and I jumped. The clock read 4:15 am.

I grabbed the phone and put it to my ear.

"What?" I said irritably.

"It's me—Liz," came a whispered voice over the line. I listened hard, instantly alert.

"Someone's here . . . in my house," came the urgent whisper.

"Your stepfather?" I asked.

"No. He left a half hour ago."

"Could it be your mom?"

"No way. It's something bad. I know it."

"How do you know?"

"I just *do*. Please, help!"

"All right. You hide. Climb out the window and run, if you can. We'll be right there."

"I'm not leaving my mom," she said flatly.

"Then the two of you need to hide. Do you have anything to defend yourselves with?"

There was a pause. "I've got something. Now, please hurry." She hung up.

Damn! I was going to tell her to stay on the line so I could hear what was going on. I couldn't call her back.

The noise might draw attention.

I threw some clothes on and ran out into the living room, strapping my holster as I went.

"Ross! Ross! Get your ass up!"

I heard a groan from the direction of the guest room. I slammed the door open. "Come on! My client's in trouble. We gotta go!"

Ross jumped out of bed and put his shoes on. He hadn't changed, so his disheveled clothes from last night were worse now. He grabbed his holster as we ran out the door.

I had run out of undercover cars. This case was starting to get expensive. But speed was necessary, so we took my Jaguar F-Type R convertible. Ross gave me a look when I motioned for him to get in.

"Can I drive?" he asked.

"Absolutely not!" I said and climbed behind the wheel.

Once we were racing toward Liz's, I filled the detective in on the call.

"You think it's Gray or fairies?" he said.

"Fairies would be my bet."

"Christ." I was sure the image of the Powells filled his mind. It was all *I* could think about.

I broke every speeding law as I shot down the streets of Boston, my engine rumbling with gusto. Luckily, there was no traffic at this hour, or things would have gotten tricky.

Ross called it in and notified them of our position and speed. A squad car raced with us by the time we were halfway there. Their sirens and lights made our going less dangerous. In better circumstances, I would have enjoyed opening the Jag up like that.

Another squad car was parked on the side of the road when we pulled up. I had to ease her down gently, so as not to tip our hat by squealing tires.

My phone rang as I got out of the car. *Damn!* I didn't have time now. Whoever it was had lousy timing. I let it go to voicemail as I focused on the current crisis.

I went to the trunk of my car and withdrew a crowbar, which I stuck inside my belt.

I sprinted across the lawn to the front door, Ross close behind. He barked hushed orders to the other cops, sending them around the house. With my gun now in hand, I reached for the doorknob.

Ross grabbed my shoulder.

"Did Liz tell you to come?"

"Yes. She said 'Help.'"

He let go of my shoulder, and I pushed the door open.

A spacious foyer greeted us, complete with hanging chandelier. Doorways opened to the left and right, but our attention was drawn to the staircase that rose from the back of the foyer. The crash of breaking glass came from upstairs, followed by a shriek of rage that I recognized as Liz.

Movies glossed over the difficulties of running with a gun. Even with the safety off, I wasn't concerned with it firing by accident. But you couldn't take stairs two at a time and still be able to aim well. I went up the stairs slower than I wanted to, but with enough care to blast anything that might come for me.

Light spilled from a room at the end of the upstairs hall, casting shadows of action against the walls.

"Let her go!" shrieked Liz, "Or so help me, I'll kill you!"

Ross and I made our way silently down the carpeted hallway, then stopped by the doorway. The door was in the corner of the room, and the ruckus came from somewhere deeper inside.

Ross nodded grimly at me, his gun also in hand.

I steeled myself and then entered the room, stepping a couple yards beyond the door to give Ross some space to cover me.

A woman stood in front of the king-size bed, dressed in a simple nightgown, her black hair hanging loosely about her shoulders. She stood still, her arms dangling at her sides. A look of awe-filled adoration covered her face.

Liz stood beside her with an expression of pure hatred—as different from her mother's as her features were similar. She wore a pair of old, black sweatpants, complete with a hole in one knee and tattered cuffs at the ankles. An oversized t-shirt sporting the band *Evanescence* hung like a nightgown over her body. She held a wooden mini baseball bat like a club before her, as she glared at her intruder.

The intruder turned to face me as I leaped into the room. This was no ogre. No goblin. No monster with rows of teeth. The most beautiful woman I had ever seen stood before me. She was so magnificent that the thought of all other women almost left my mind. I had to fight the urge to ignore everything but her. At five-and-a-half feet tall, she had a slight, delicate form, exquisite curves just visible under her white gossamer gown. Full, golden blond hair cascaded in waves over her shoulder and down her back, and I swore I saw the twinkle of stars among those tresses. Her face was that of an angel, both young and innocent, yet mature and sensuous at the same time.

I wanted to hold her, to kiss her, to *please* her.

I shook my head vigorously to drive the glamour from my mind. She was a fairy, of course. But not a pixie, like the others. She was a *true* fairy, human in size and form, but impossibly perfect in features. And highly magical. It was said that no human could resist her charms. They would throw themselves at her feet and do anything she wanted.

I took a deep breath, and the tug of her magic broke. My mind was mine again. I holstered my gun—I wouldn't need it. In its place, I pulled the iron crowbar from my belt and held it rA frown creased the fairy's face, which did not diminish her beauty in any way. Although no longer under her spell, she was still impressive.

"You're not mine. How odd."

"Neither is Mrs. Gray," I said. "I suggest you let her go."

"I wonder why you are unaffected. You should be groveling before me, like your friend."

I risked a quick glance toward Ross, who had dropped his gun and was indeed on his knees, gazing up at her with a look of awe and supplication.

My eyes rolled as I turned back to the fairy.

"Let them go before I bash your face in."

She eyed the crowbar with suspicion. *That's right, bitch. It's iron. Your Achilles heel.* Just the touch of the stuff could severely injure her.

"My slaves will intervene. Are you prepared to kill your friend?"

Ross rose to his feet. He glared at me with undisguised loathing. I put a few more feet between us, moving slightly closer to the fairy in the process. If he acted against me, I would strike the bitch with all I had.

"You know I'll get to you first," I said with my best poker face.

She regarded me calmly, but her eyes kept flicking to the crowbar in my hand.

"It appears we are at an impasse. Why don't you put the weapon down, and we'll talk." Her voice was light and disarming. Again I felt the tug, and once more I pushed it back.

"Nice try. Release these people, and we'll talk. I'm here to save their lives, not to kill you. Besides, I think we have a common enemy."

She shook her head slowly, and the movement of her hair caused the twinkling stars in it to call my attention. It didn't work. "You may not like them, but you won't kill them. You plan to lock them up and leave them alive."

I saw Liz tighten her grip on the bat. She was planning to strike. Part of me wondered how she wasn't affected by the glamour, but now wasn't the time to consider it. I gave her a stern look and a slight shake of my head, but I couldn't tell if she understood, as she kept her position.

"And that's not enough?" I said, trying to keep her attention away from Liz.

"In captivity, our enemies will endure. Eventually, they will come to power again. They will not suffer enough for what they have done." The facade of beauty and innocence was shaken for a moment, and her anger leaked through.

"And what, exactly, have they done?" I asked.

"They have suffered a blow against my people. Again and again, they conduct their atrocities. They must be punished in kind." The words carried anger and vengeance, yet her demeanor remained calm and peaceful.

"Then, why haven't you killed them? Why attack innocent people when you can target those who wronged you directly?"

"Death is not enough. They must suffer. Their souls must never find peace. And that comes only with remorse, and with guilt." She glanced at Ross.

"Don't even think of it," I said to him as he began to kneel by his discarded revolver. "One more move and I embed this in her pretty face."

He growled at me and looked to the fairy for guidance. The fairy shook her head. He glared at me but stepped away from the gun nonetheless.

"Okay," I said, trying to think of a way out of the situation. "I understand what you're doing. The truth is, I want Gray and his cohorts to go down. I want it badly, and I have no delusions about bringing them in alive. They won't give up without a fight, and I see no way around killing them. So, I wouldn't worry about that."

"Good," she said. "Then, when I have finished preparing their souls, I will let you do away with them. Now, if you will leave me to my work . . ."

"It's not that easy. I can't let you hurt innocent people."

"Why not? It's what you humans do. You're always killing innocents. What's a few more?"

"We're not all killers. For every one psychopath, there are a hundred peaceful people. The psychos just stand out."

She snorted, so I changed my tack. "Hurting these women won't help you. You assume that Sebastian Gray cares about his wife and stepdaughter. He doesn't. Killing them might anger him, but it won't tarnish his soul. The only thing that can hurt him at this point is failure. His only true love is power. Take it away, and it will devastate him. It will eat him up inside to think that someone might be more powerful than him."

She considered my words and then nodded.

"I think you may be right. The others were easy. But this one . . . He is not like the others."

"Then tell me where they do their magic, and my partner and I will take care of them. I'll see to it you get your revenge."

I saw frustration pull at the edge of her red lips and at the slight furrowing of her perfect brow. "Alas, I know not where they work. They have cast a glamour that I cannot penetrate."

"Then I'll find it, and I'll tear down their spell."

She narrowed her eyes. "Why would you help us?"

"Because I don't think you're evil. Dangerous, yes. But not evil. Gray and his Order are. And they have to be stopped at all cost."

I paused to let that sink in for a moment before continuing. "So, please, let these people go. I am bound to protect them, and hurting them won't help you reach your goal."

Her eyes searched mine as she thought about my offer, as though trying—and failing—to read my mind. At last, she stirred. "Very well. If you can find their lair and remove their glamour, then it will be worth sparing these lives. I will release them, but with this warning: make good on your promise, or I will show just how *dangerous* fairies can be."

I nodded, but I couldn't help wondering if I was making a mistake.

The fairy smiled. "Farewell, Simon Kane. I will be waiting. Do not disappoint me."

And with that, she was gone.

Chapter 44

Ross and Mrs. Gray fell to the floor as soon as the fairy had left. It was as though they were marionettes and their strings were suddenly cut. They lay there, confused, looking around like lost puppies searching for sight of their master.

Liz dropped the bat and threw herself into her mother's arms. Mrs. Gray held the girl reflexively, lacking the emotion that a mother should show for her daughter. She whimpered sadly, as though realizing that the fairy was gone for good.

Liz looked up at me. "What did that *bitch* do?" Tears streamed down her face.

"Give your mother a few minutes," I said. "The fairy's charm is overpowering. It'll take a while for her to shake it, but she'll be okay."

I went to Ross and knelt down beside him. I set the crowbar down behind me, out of arm's reach from the detective, just in case this was a fairy trick.

Ross looked at me sheepishly, comprehension still lost from his eyes. I smacked him hard in the face, causing him to fall over. The palm of my hand stung.

The detective blinked and shook his head. He frowned. Then understanding flooded back into his head and he sat up, looking around the room.

"*Shit!*" he said. "She had me. That woman had complete control over me. I would have done anything she said. Kane . . ." He leveled his eyes at mine. "I was going to kill you, and I would have done it."

"I know. But it wasn't you. It was the fairy."

"No, it wasn't. And that's the worst of it. I *wanted* to kill you. She fucked with my mind, and all I wanted to do was make her happy. It was my decision to go for that gun."

"Ross, you have to understand this. Whether the decision to kill me came from your mind or not, it was still the fairy pulling the strings. You would not have done what you tried if she didn't compel you to do it. You weren't in control of your mind, and you would never have done it if you were. I don't blame you."

He looked away from me.

"If that ever happens again," he said grimly, "kill me. Put a bullet right here." He tapped his forehead.

I nodded. "If I can't save you, then I will."

He looked at me then, as though searching my face for sincerity. Finally, he nodded.

"Good," he said.

He stood and took a deep breath. "I'll go call off the troops. I don't think I'm going to report anything—it was just a false alarm."

He recovered his gun, holstered it, and left.

I went to Liz. Her mother had come out of her stupor and sat on the floor crying in her daughter's arms.

I knelt and met Liz's gaze. Tears streamed down her face, but she put up a strong front. She nodded grimly to me.

"Thanks," she said, "I can't thank you enough."

"It's okay," I said.

"Are you really going to kill my husband?" Liz's mother asked. Her voice was small and weak, but there was no anger there.

"Sebastian is an evil man, Mrs. Gray," I began. I didn't think it was a good idea to lie at this point. "He and his friends are doing some horrible things, and I'm afraid he won't give up without a fight. We may have no choice."

She nodded but said nothing. She didn't meet my gaze.

I turned to Liz. "I'll leave the two of you alone. She'll be fine. It could take some time for her to shake off the effects of the fairy's spell, but there's no damage."

Liz nodded and continued to stroke her mother's hair.

"Go *get* him."

I left the bedroom and joined Ross in the kitchen where he was talking to one of the cops.

"So, you're filing the report?" the cop asked.

"That's right," Ross replied. "I called you in, so I'll take care of it."

I wandered around the kitchen as they talked. I decided to take advantage of my access to Gray's house to see if I could find any clues as to where the Order met. I couldn't legally search the house, but if I happened to notice something . . .

Like the rest of the house, the kitchen was spacious,

spotless, and well stocked. The appliances looked new and expensive, the furniture of high quality. All of it fit Gray's tax bracket.

A pile of mail sat on their breakfast bar. I couldn't rifle through them with all the cops around, so I just looked at the few that were visible on the tabletop. There was an issue of *Woman's Day*, a few bills, and a letter lay spread open before me.

The top line read,

> *Mr. Sebastian Gray,*
> *You are cordially invited to a gala at the estate of*
> *Donald Kress. Festivities will begin at 9:00 pm on*
> *Friday, April 25.*

Donald Kress. Sebastian Gray was going to the same party that my dad was attending. And I had an invitation.

"So, what do we do now?" Ross said after the cop left the room.

"We find out where their circle is," I said.

"But how? We still have no idea where to look."

"I think I can find out." I showed him the invitation.

"This is a big black-tie affair. We can't just stroll in."

"You can if you're invited. My father was, and I'm going with him."

Ross raised an eyebrow. "I sometimes forget you're one of the *privileged*. So, what's your plan of attack?"

I shrugged. "I eat and drink, and chit-chat with the guests. And I try to trick clues out of Gray."

"That plan sucks."

"Got a better one?"

He looked around helplessly. "Nope. I'd love to go digging in here, but I'd need a warrant."

"Mrs. Gray might let you," I offered.

Ross shook his head. "If we searched the place, we'd have to let Gray know. And I don't think we're ready for a confrontation. Besides, I have a feeling he would keep that kind of information well hidden."

I considered Ross for a moment. "It must be hard having to tiptoe around a suspect like this. But with all the evidence being magical in nature, you don't really have a case against him. Not officially, anyway."

"It drives me fucking crazy," Ross growled. "I've got the missing baby, Tom Cook's murder, and Powell's murder. And I can't pin any of that on Gray."

"Then I go to the party and schmooze the information out of him. It's all we've got."

"Yeah. Good luck with that."

Chapter 45

My phone rang again as I drove back to the apartment. Ross stayed behind with the other cops, so I was alone in the car. I pressed the answer button on my stereo.

"Simon Kane," I said in my professional voice.

"*Finally!*" came Summer's voice through the speakers. "You haven't been answering your phone. I was starting to think you were avoiding me."

I smiled. Her voice was pure gold to me. "You always called at the wrong times. I'm on a case, you know."

She sobered up instantly. "Has it been bad?"

"You have no idea."

"You're all still alive, right? You? The detective? Liz?"

"Yes, we're all fine. But there have been more deaths, and some—close calls."

"I see. So, when do I see you next?"

"After the case. You've had enough bumps to last you a while."

"I know I should take it easy, but I'm in pretty good shape right now. You're not on the case all the time, are you?"

I snorted. "The case won't let me go. It keeps coming to me. That's why I can't see you until it's over. It's safer that way. Don't worry, I don't expect it to last much longer." Of course, I didn't think *I* could last much longer, but I kept that to myself.

"You said your apartment is safe. It's got spells and stuff to keep it clear of danger. I could come over tonight. We could watch a movie and just relax."

"Why are you so anxious to see me? It'll only be a few days—tops. I'll call you when it's over. Guaranteed."

There was a pause on the line.

"When I've fully recovered, I'll be back to work doing insane hours. We'll hardly have any time together. You'll get bored."

I frowned. "No, I won't."

"Trust me, you will. I'd be like a ghost—there, but so exhausted that I might as well not be. No relationship can survive that."

Now, it was my turn to pause. I understood what Summer was getting at. She wanted to see me soon so that I wouldn't lose interest as quickly.

"Look, Summer. You've already made a big impression on me. I've invited you into my creepy little world, and I don't do that for just anyone. Only you. I'm not going to forget you, and I'm not going to lose interest. You'll have to trust me on that."

"Okay," she said, and there was relief in her tone. "I can buy that. But I still want to see you and catch up on what's happened. So, how about tonight?"

"Can't. I've got a date."

There was a pause. A long pause. *Crap!*

"With my dad," I said. "Sorry, bad joke. It's a big party at one of his friends' place. Well, I doubt he's a friend—just another rich man he does business with."

"Who is it?" Her tone was back to normal. She survived my terrible attempt at humor.

"Donald Kress."

"Really?" She was impressed. "God, you must be filthy rich!"

I shrugged. "Yeah."

"Can I come?"

"Sorry. I wasn't invited. I'm going as Dad's plus-one."

"Oh."

"So, maybe tomorrow night, if the case gives me a night off."

"Okay," she said, but she sounded a little distant like she was lost in thought.

"Well, I should go. I need to get myself ready for tonight, and that's not as easy as it sounds."

"I'll bet. I'll hold you to tomorrow night. If you can't make it, at least call. We can chat."

"I'll do that."

The parking garage was quiet as I pulled in and navigated to my level. I have a floor reserved for my collection—well, a section of a floor, anyway. I pulled the Jaguar into its space beside the Mercedes S-Class and the empty spot where my dead Focus used to park.

I got out, locked the door, and made off toward the elevator. The downside to having my own section in the garage was that it wasn't conveniently near the exits. My footsteps echoed throughout the place.

Something didn't feel right. It wasn't supernatural—at least there was no tingling of magic—but I was nervous. Sure, parking garages creeped out most people, but not me. It took a lot to put me on edge, and walking alone in a dark place wasn't enough. But there I was, walking quickly, like the victim in a crime show before he gets grabbed by the bad guy.

I turned a corner and saw the lighted platform that housed the elevators. I grinned with relief, and then stopped short as a figure stepped out of the shadows to stand in the light.

It was Aleister Crowley.

He smiled. I frowned. I wasn't in the mood for it, but at least I had the time. I continued my walk to the elevators, closing the distance with long, confident strides.

"Hello, friend," the lying bastard said as I approached. "It's time for an answer. What say you? Will you join us?"

He never saw it coming. My hand was around his throat, and his head had slammed against the wall before his smile had a chance to fade. But the fake grin disappeared the instant I put my gun to his temple. I kept my finger out of the trigger guard, but that would only slow things down a second if it came to that.

"One stray hand gesture, or one archaic word, and I'll splatter your brains across this lovely parking lot. Got that?"

His eyes shot daggers at me, but he nodded slowly.

"You summoned it," I spat. "You summoned that shadow to attack me."

Understanding crossed his face, and he replaced the daggers with feigned sympathy. I wasn't about to be duped again.

"It would not have killed you," he croaked, my hand still tight around his neck. "I knew you would defeat it."

"And what if I didn't?"

"I had complete confidence in you."

"And if you were wrong?"

"I would have intervened. Please let me go. I'm not your enemy."

"Bullshit. Sending a monster after me is the *definition* of 'enemy.'"

"You're taking this wrong. I will not hurt you. *Please,* let me go."

The truth was I had no intention of killing him. In fact, I had no plans other than intimidating the hell out of him and telling him to leave me the fuck alone. So, I lowered my gun and let go of his throat. I took a big step backward so I could bring my weapon to bear if I needed to.

His hands went quickly to his throat, massaging the skin there. When he looked at me, all sign of animosity was gone. He seemed disappointed.

"I apologize," he said at last. "What should have been an easy and friendly relationship went terribly awry. I wronged you, and I'm sorry about that."

"The problem is that you can't take 'no' for an answer," I said.

"Too true. I found myself caught up in the desperateness of the situation, and I erred."

"Desperate, eh? How important is it to get me to join your group?"

"Very. My superiors are anxious to bring you on board. I'm afraid they've given me no other option."

"So, if I keep refusing, what then?"

"I'd rather not find out."

"It sounds like your group is prepared to become my enemy if I don't play ball."

Crowley fidgeted uncomfortably but said nothing. His eyes flitted around, like a cornered animal looking for a means of escape.

"Don't worry," I said gruffly. "I won't kill you. Not today. But I'm sending you back to your people with a message: leave me alone, and I'll leave your group alone. Mess with me, and I won't hold back."

The sorcerer nodded grimly. He sidestepped away, and then turned his back to me and walked into the garage. At the edge of the shadows, he turned to face me.

"I don't think you're a bad man, Mr. Kane. I will make sure they understand that."

I nodded stiffly, and then he was gone.

Chapter 46

It took longer than usual to get ready for the party. Blood and subway grime were hard to get out of your hair. I spent an hour at the salon, then had my Ferrari washed. Finally, I had to pick out an appropriate suit. I wasn't happy with anything I had, so that meant shopping. Unlike most of the ultra-wealthy, I hate shopping. If I trusted other people's tastes, I would pay someone to shop for me. Buying a single suit took most of the afternoon. Because I was accompanying my father, I had to make the best appearance possible. I found the right outfit after three hours of arduous work. My father would be pleased—I probably outdid him.

I sent my father a text while at the salon but got no response. That was normal. He was a busy man and likely felt it wasn't necessary to reply. But it meant I would show up on my own and meet him there.

At eight o'clock, I felt the tracker artifact move. Gray was heading out—too early for the party. Anxiety hit me like a hammer. What if he wasn't going to the gala? I could spend the entire evening there for nothing. The party felt suddenly like a distraction, and I wanted to hop in the Jag and race after the magician. But, no. He would be at the party. Anyone as ambitious as Gray was would go if invited. To turn down such an invitation would be social suicide. I had to let Gray go for now and focus on the plan. It was the right plan.

My choice of weapon took some thought. Although this was to be an information-gathering mission, I still wanted to be armed, just in case. But my preferred gun, the Kimber 1911, was too big and bulky. It wouldn't look right under my jacket. So, I had to pick a smaller gun from my collection. I chose the Ruger LCP. It was only a .380 caliber but was small enough to fit comfortably—and invisibly—in a pocket. And besides, a .380 is still lethal, since I wasn't expecting to go after another supernatural creature. I put it in a small, pocket-carry holster that was designed to stay in my pocket when I drew the gun.

My arm wasn't fully healed, but it was doing well. I could move it and bend my elbow without pain, which meant the bone was no longer broken. Twisting it at my wrist still hurt, so I had to be careful with it. At least I didn't need the sling anymore.

At last, I was ready. I put the charm around my neck and hid it under my shirt. In the mirror, I looked just like any other rich brat. Better than most. I grabbed the keys to the Ferrari and left.

It felt good driving through the streets of Boston at night in my favorite car on my way to a party. For a time, I slipped out of detective mode and became a socialite again. Several deep draughts of the crisp air through the car window and the stress of the past few

days began to fall away. I wasn't looking forward to
spending time with Dad. He seemed almost desperate
to work things out with me, which I found unnerving,
to say the least. But if Sebastian Gray was going to be
there, then I couldn't pass up my father's invitation.

Donald Kress lived at the top of a hill in a prominent
section of the city. From there, Boston sprawled out
below, a million twinkling lights. It was nine o'clock,
and already a dozen cars were parked there. Gray's
BMW sat near the entrance. He must have been one of
the first to arrive. I left my car between a Mercedes and
Rolls and walked to the house.

The house—wrong choice of words. It was a
mansion. But even that didn't quite work. My father's
home, where I grew up, was a mansion. This place was
the size of a small English castle and was designed for
one thing: showing off Kress' immense wealth. It was a
gigantic modern monstrosity with lots of glass, shining
metal, and hard angles. It clearly cost a fortune to build,
and the architect probably won an award for it. I hated
it. It was gaudy and looked uncomfortable. Although
I'm all for modern designs, this one just felt cold and
heartless. It was a home for the superficial and the ma-
terialistic.

A shiver ran up my spine as I mounted the steps to
the front door. Clouds drifted slowly overhead with the
spring breezes whipping around me on the top of the
hill. I rang the doorbell. The big black portal opened
before I could count to ten. A man in his fifties stood
before me, stiff in his uniform. He bowed curtly and
held out his hand. I gave him the card my father had

given me. He read it and nodded.

"You are accompanying Mr. Kane? May I ask your name?"

"Simon," I said. "Simon Kane. His son."

"I see," he said and stepped aside to let me in. "Welcome, Mr. Kane. The others have gathered in the parlor. Your father has already arrived."

"This place has a parlor?" I mused. I knew it must, but the term seemed too British for this mansion.

"Of course, sir."

The parlor was big. Like the exterior of the place, it was quite modern, with lots of glass, and every edge trimmed with chrome. One glass wall overlooked the skyline of Boston. A bar was set up along another wall, and artwork hung everywhere—all modern art, no classics. Chairs and couches were positioned strategically to provide a good view of all the most expensive sights in the room.

A couple dozen people mingled about the place. There was not likely to be many more guests coming. A quick survey showed that Gray was not there. *Where could he be, then? The bathroom?* Somehow, I doubted it.

I spotted my father, who stood by the window. He started when he saw me, but then smiled. I strode confidently across the room—appearance and bearing were essential in such events.

"Simon," my father said as I joined him at the window. "I'm glad you could make it. You—you look good."

Compliments never came quickly from my father— at least not toward family—so it sounded strained.

"I wouldn't miss it." It was true, and I decided to let him think it was because of him. I might not trust his motivation, but I appreciated the sudden attempt at being a father.

"So, what's the soiree about?" I asked.

Dad shrugged. "Probably to show off a new multimillion dollar deal he's made. It's what they're usually about."

"You don't sound thrilled. Why'd you come?"

His mouth shrugged. "Everyone who's anyone in Boston is here tonight. It's a social imperative. If I don't go, it'll be like saying I'm a nobody. Besides, there are a lot of important people to interface with. So, as much as I hate catering to the bastard's ego, there's no way around it. It's business."

"And you thought to bring me along. I'm touched," I said jovially as I surveyed the room. I accepted a drink offered by a servant carrying a silver tray of glasses.

"I thought you might appreciate witnessing some of the more subtle parts of my job."

I nodded. "Bring your kid to work day. I get it."

He snorted. "You can never take anything seriously, can you?"

"*Dad* . . ." I cautioned.

He winced. "Sorry." He glanced at his watch. "We should mingle, chat with the more important people here."

We made the rounds, making small talk with one wealthy businessman, then another. I had to admit, my father was a natural. He acted all friendly, as though he honestly cared about his quarry. He'd make small talk and somehow manage to work business in without anyone being the wiser. It was impressive.

"Look who's here," came a familiar voice from behind me. I whirled around, my hand going instinctively to my hip, where my gun used to be.

Sebastian Gray held that affable smile he always had in public. I wanted to bury my fist in it.

"Why Simon Kane, what brings you to this party?"

"I'm here with my father." I motioned to my dad. "William Jonathan Kane. Dad, this is Sebastian Gray, the CEO of Dynamo Software."

"I'm afraid I'm just the COO," Gray corrected me casually. "But I'm sure you knew that."

"You got me," I said. "I was just a little confused. I thought this was a party for Captains of Industry, not their first mates."

His eyes narrowed almost imperceptibly, and he opened his mouth to retort when my father intervened.

"So, you've come with Jeffrey Newcomb?" he asked casually, diverting Gray's attention away from me, and robbing me of a possible slip of the tongue. "I've met your CEO. He's a good man."

Gray shook his head. "We arrived at the same time. I came alone. My wife isn't feeling well."

"Then, I share my son's curiosity at your presence. You appear a little conspicuous here."

Gray afforded my father a wry smile and shrugged. "If you must know, I'm a personal friend of the host."

Movement by the room's entrance drew my attention as my father engaged Gray in idle talk. An older man had entered. He looked distinguished but careworn, as though the business he ran was a source of stress. He was dressed appropriately, in an expensive suit, but he appeared uncomfortable in it. He wasn't used to parties like this, and he expected not to enjoy it.

But it wasn't the old man I was interested in. It was the woman at his arm. The black dress was both stunning and understated, inexpensive, yet somehow appropriate. Her long brown hair was tied in a braid that draped over one shoulder. Her face had just enough makeup to cover the bruises that I knew must be there.

Summer Parke smiled and winked when our eyes met.

"She's beautiful," Gray commented, and I started. "Woefully underdressed, but I'd imagine most of the men here wouldn't complain. What do you think, Simon?" He looked at me intently.

"She's not bad."

He laughed then. "Now I know you're lying. I saw your reaction when the woman walked in. She made quite an impression on you. Could it be you have a soft spot for her? Do you know her?"

It was all I could do to remain dispassionate. I came here to trick Gray into revealing useful information, and now he was doing the same to me. It made me angry. Angry at Gray for getting the better of me, and angry at myself for letting him, and angry at Summer for putting me on the spot.

"She's no one special," I snorted, then shrugged. "Pretty, though."

He eyed me suspiciously for a moment.

"Come on, Simon," my father said suddenly,

placing his hand on my shoulder. "There's someone I'd like you to meet."

He nodded to Gray. "It was nice meeting you." They shook hands.

"It was an honor," Gray said, distracted, still eying me.

I slipped away with my father, and we walked purposefully through the crowd toward the other side of the room.

"So, who do you want me to meet?" I asked.

"Nobody, you fool. I could see he had you at a disadvantage, so I rescued you. You should thank me."

I gave my father a long, thoughtful look. "Thanks." Having Dad with me might have been a good thing, after all.

Chapter 47

I avoided Summer as we all waited in the parlor for the rest of the guests to arrive. Donald Kress remained conspicuously absent. Summer sent me inquiring looks from across the room, but as Gray kept his eye on me, I couldn't respond.

"So," my father said conversationally, as we stood by one wall, admiring the artwork. "Are you not interested in the young lady, or do you just want to keep Mr. Gray from knowing?"

My father didn't miss much. "It's important that Gray doesn't know that I care about her."

He nodded. "You have to be more careful when screwing around with someone's woman."

I laughed, and he gave me a curious look. "She's not his woman."

"His mistress? Same thing, you know."

I shook my head. "He doesn't even know her, and I want it to stay that way."

"Jealous? That's not like you. And especially from this Gray fella . . ." He noticed me staring at Gray, and understanding struck him.

"This is a case."

I looked at him, surprised. I didn't have to say anything—my shocked expression was enough.

"That's why you came here. You're after Gray, found out he was coming to the party, and here you are."

"Dad . . ." I said but had no idea how to follow it.

"It's okay," he said dismissively. "It's your job. It's what I would do." He was disappointed. "You're more like me than I thought."

"So, I'm here because of a case. I used you. But I've been enjoying spending time with you. I didn't expect to, but I actually like it."

It was no good. Dad's walls had come up, and it was all business when he looked at me next.

"So, let me get this straight," he said, and he might as well have been talking to an employee. "The girl doesn't know Gray, but she knows you. You have a relationship. But Gray knows you're after him and might use her against you."

I nodded but said nothing.

"Right. You need to get word to the woman. Tell her to beware of Mr. Gray."

"That's right. But Gray's watching me."

"He's not watching me." And then he was off. He made his way casually through the room, but not in the direction of Summer. First, he refreshed his drink, then he struck up a conversation with one of the guests. They seemed to know each other and were quickly deep in discussion.

I shrugged and turned away. If Dad was trying to help, I wasn't going to spoil it by watching him. I went to the window and looked out over the city. Its lights twinkled innocently. I wondered if the Order was out there casting spells tonight and if any of those lights belonged to cars that were crashing to kill someone else they didn't like. Gray was here with me, but the rest of the Order could be working their magic without him.

"Dinner is served," a voice called politely over the din, and I almost jumped as a shiver ran up my spine. All heads turned to regard an older man, dressed in a black and white butler's uniform, who stood in the open doorway. He looked like a movie-butler, and I half expected him to be named Jeeves.

"If you will all follow me . . ." he said and turned to lead us away.

The babble of multiple conversations shifted to that of moving feet as everyone fell into line behind the butler.

"Done," my father said as he fell into step beside me. I wanted to question him, to find out how sure he was that Gray hadn't noticed, but the magician was right in front of us, with a portly old businessman and his model wife in between. I would have to trust my father's skill at surreptitious communication—an ability I was sure he excelled at in his line of work.

Jeeves led us into another spacious room, this one with white walls and chrome trim. The chandelier that hung from the ceiling was both extravagant and modern in design and managed to cast light throughout most of the room. A long, oak table stretched the length of the place, with over a dozen chairs lined around it. Gleaming dinnerware awaited the guests as we filtered in.

Two people had arrived ahead of the procession and sat now at either end of the long table. One was a woman of approximately fifty years, who managed to look ten years younger. It was amazing what money and unnecessary surgery could do for a person. The other was a man in his seventies who opted to forgo the knife in favor of a distinguished appearance. His short, gray hair was immaculate. His features were sharp and handsome, the lines on his face providing an air of wisdom and intelligence. His piercing blue eyes commanded respect. Donald Kress smiled as the guests filed into the room and took their seats. Each seat had a name tag in front of its plate. Apparently, Kress liked to control everything in his life. I sat beside my father in a spot labeled "Melissa Kane."

I looked at the seat placements. The most powerful men were seated nearest his end of the table, the movers and shakers of Boston, so to speak. My father was at the very end, off Kress' left shoulder. That made sense. My father was nearly as important a person as Kress— arguably the most important of his guests. But he would keep my dad on his left because he viewed him as a threat. My dad was no right-hand man!

Sebastian Gray was on the other side of the table and down at the other end, just two seats up from Mrs. Kress. Summer and her partner sat at the very end, between Gray and the hostess. According to the name tag, she came with Dr. Howard Mullen, whose name I knew to be a board member of Mass General, Summer's hospital. So, when she couldn't go with me, she finagled an invite from Dr. Mullen. She was smart, I had to admit, and determined.

Dinner was just as I had expected. Mr. Kress said a few words of greeting, and then the meal was served. The food was excellent; Kress spared no expense. The conversation, however, fell far short. When you filled a room with businessmen, no matter what the pretense, they would inevitably talk shop. Once the servers came to fill plates, it began—a dozen men started wheeling and dealing, while their wives gossiped. I found it tedious.

I sat at the table and enjoyed my meal as my father engaged himself in discussion with Kress and Paul Urquhart, the man who sat opposite my father.

Another tingle ran down my spine as I noticed Gray carrying on a conversation with Summer. They were both smiling. It looked harmless, but Gray must have had ulterior motives. He suspected I cared more for Summer than I let on, and now he was chatting with her. He was fishing for information. Hopefully, Summer got my father's message, but I was still worried. Gray was an expert at extracting information through idle conversation, and Summer was in over her head. I couldn't stare, and I couldn't hear what they said. I wished I had an eavesdropping artifact or spell. That would come in real handy. I told myself to visit Nick when this case was over.

"So, Simon," Kress addressed me past my father, who was still chatting with Urquhart. "I'm surprised to see you here. From what I've heard, you never chose to follow your father's footsteps."

"I didn't. But he invited me, so I'm here."

"Family loyalty is a noble quality."

He quickly changed tack. "I hear you're a private investigator. That's an unexpected career for someone of your background. What made you choose that line of work? Surely, it wasn't the money."

I smiled. "I guess I like solving mysteries—getting to the bottom of things."

"Sounds exciting," he said with seemingly genuine interest. I had a hard time believing that. Businessmen were all liars. "Does it keep you busy?"

"In spurts. I'm pretty selective about my cases, so there are lulls."

"Are you on one now?"

"Actually, I am."

"Really? I hope it's not about me. I've been faithful to my wife."

I rolled my eyes. So, the man was having his fun. I suppose he was entitled. It was his party, after all.

"I don't do that kind of case. They're not fun."

"So, what kind of case *do* you take?"

I decided to be careful about what I divulged. "Interesting ones."

"I've been told you only take cases involving the occult and the supernatural."

"They're interesting."

"I'm sure they are, but there can't be very many cases like that, I mean, not here in Boston."

"Like I say, it comes in spurts."

"So, what can you tell me about this current case of yours? You're not just here because of your father. You and he don't get along."

He knows something, and he's trying to get me to talk. "Sorry, it's confidential. But my dad and I are trying to fix things."

"I see. Well, I hope this truly is your night off. I've been planning this party for a long time, and I'd like it to go well." There was a clear message in more than just his words. His tone hinted at danger, and his eyes gave me the impression of a cat who casually licks his paw before springing on the hapless mouse. Now, I knew why Gray was invited, and it had nothing to do with the businessmen here. Kress was a member of their Order, and most likely their leader.

And I was the mouse.

The Great and Powerful Kress shifted his attention from me to Urquhart's wife, making small talk.

The rest of dinner passed uneventfully. Both Kress and Gray paid me no more attention, aside from a few looks from Gray. There was a slight lull each time a course of food was served, but nothing could stop deal-making for long. I was relieved when we finally adjourned to the living room. This is where things got more relaxed. The invited guests continued to ply their trade, but the plus-ones all gathered together on the couch, or outside on the deck to socialize.

I followed my father but quickly felt like a fifth wheel, as he continued to deal with Urquhart. Apparently, this was his main reason for coming. I was just there to fill in for Mom.

I glanced around casually to see if I could spot Summer, but couldn't. Frowning, I made my way out to the deck. Several small groups of women and the occasional house-husband stood around swapping gossip. But no Summer. I sought out Dr. Mullen. He had just finished speaking with a tall young businessman with slicked-back hair and an arrogant expression. The good doctor looked tired.

"Weary business, this," I said, stepping up beside him.

He snorted. "You can say that again."

"You don't seem the type to be coming to parties like this. You've got no fin on your back."

That earned me a wry grin.

"I'm here for the hospital. A lot of these people are looking for a good tax write-off. You don't fit in here, either, Mr . . ."

"Kane," I said shaking his hand. "Simon Kane. I came with my dad."

"Ah," he said, and then he looked at me with a start. "You're Summer's beau, right? Don't worry, your secret is safe with me."

I smiled. "She told you?"

"That she did. She said you're on a case and didn't want anyone here to know you're together. Is there danger?"

"Possibly, but I can't say more."

"I understand. Summer talked me into bringing her so she could see you. She's a good woman. Treat her well."

"I will." I scanned the room once more for Summer. Still nothing. "Do you know where she might be now?"

He glanced around. "No. I haven't seen her since

dinner. She went off with that man she met at the table."

I frowned. "Sebastian Gray?"

He nodded. "They seemed to have a lot in common. He followed us in here. I left them talking to mingle."

"I think I'll go find her," I said casually. I didn't want Dr. Mullen to think anything was wrong. "It was nice talking to you. I'll convince my father to make a healthy donation to the hospital."

"Thank you. If you see Summer, tell her I'll be leaving within the hour. I don't think anyone here is going to bite my hook, so to speak."

I smiled. "I will. Good luck."

Summer had left the room with Gray. That couldn't be good. He suspected we were together. The look she gave me when she first came in spoke volumes—and Gray didn't miss a trick. I had no idea what he would do to her, but my gut told me she was in danger.

I stopped a serving woman who was navigating through the crowd carrying a tray of drinks and asked for directions to the restroom. Out the door, turn left, second door on the right. Got it.

She smiled at me hopefully, but I strode off through the doorway. I turned left, as she had directed, but walked past the restroom door and proceeded to the end of the hallway. Officially, I was going to the bathroom. Unofficially, I was trying to locate Summer and Gray.

My spine tingled as I thought about what Sebastian might do to Summer, just to get at me. My heart raced, and my strides grew longer as I hurried down the hallway. The corridor ended at a staircase that opened through a doorway to the left. It presented me with a choice: up or down. Upward led to the second floor, and presumably, the bedrooms. If he planned to rape her, that's where he would take her. But there was something about the downward flight that held my interest. The nervous sensation I had been feeling all evening, which had increased when I found Summer missing, seemed to emanate from the basement, wafting up the stairs like an ill wind.

That sensation. It was a tingle. *It was magic!* I didn't know why I hadn't realized it before. Maybe it was my nerves. Perhaps it was because I didn't expect it here, and Gray was walking and talking, and *not* doing magic. I had been feeling it ever since I arrived, but now I knew what it was, and it wasn't the effects of a spell, like before all those "accidents" hit. Someone was performing a massive ritual in the house, and the buildup of power filled the place like the stench of death.

I stepped into the stairwell and listened. I was alone, so I drew out my cell phone and dialed Ross.

"How's the party?" the detective said after the second ring.

"It's here. The Order. Kress's house is the ritual place."

There was a pause. "Are you *sure*?"

"Yes. They're doing magic now. I can feel it."

"Simon, I want you to tell me truthfully—do you have enough evidence to prove they are breaking the law right now?" Ross spoke carefully, enunciating each word to ensure I understood.

"No. But they're casting. And Ross—they have Summer."

"Jesus Christ," he muttered. "I understand. I'm on my way. But, Simon, I can't bring backup. I have no warrant and no probable cause. I don't even know how I'm going to get in."

"You'll have your probable cause by the time you get here. I can almost guarantee it. Hurry."

"Simon, don't do anything rash."

I hung up. Me? Rash? Never.

Chapter 48

Ross was easily twenty minutes away if traffic was good and he was speeding. I might have been able to get him inside if I waited for him. But they were casting a spell right then, which could have meant a sacrifice.

And they had Summer.

Carefully, I descended the steps into the basement. It was dark downstairs, so I felt my way by running my hand along the left wall. The right wall was left behind as I descended and was replaced by a railing that separated the stairs from the room beyond. Although I knew I was going below ground, the atmosphere didn't change. Temperature control. A finished basement. I fished out the small flashlight I always kept with me, switched it on, and panned the light around the room while standing on the stairs.

It was a large room, with decorated walls, a bar in one corner, a pool table in the center, and a couch and other furniture lining the walls. The place was dark and silent, and empty.

Think, think, think. My mind was a jumbled mess. The thought of Summer being tortured or murdered kept breaking into the front of my mind. No doubt, that was part of Gray's plan. An emotional Simon was an ineffective Simon. I needed to clear my head. The tingling increased as I descended the stairs, but they were not in this room. So, there must be another room somewhere.

The floor was made of concrete covered by carpet. That meant this was the bottom floor. I walked around the room, scanning for doors—both hidden and visible —with the flashlight, but there was nothing.

I stopped and thought. I ran my hand through my hair. If The Order were downstairs, and the tingling I felt said they were, and there were no other rooms, then the only possibility was down again. I walked slowly around the room, scanning the carpet for any cuts that might indicate a trapdoor. The carpet was both expensive and unblemished.

Looking behind the bar, the carpeting was replaced by tile. I knelt and inspected the cracks between them. At the far end in the corner, I found what I was looking for. The grout was gone from a four-by-four section of tile. But there was no latch and no hinges. I pressed down on the tiles in the center and then on each edge, but they didn't budge.

There was probably some kind of release nearby. I searched the shelves of the bar near the trapdoor. There, on the bottom shelf, concealed behind some empty beer bottles, was a button. I reached behind the bottles and pushed it.

There was a slight hiss of hydraulics, and the square section of tiles pivoted open, downward into the hole it revealed. No light issued from it, so I flashed mine down. A narrow shaft descended at least fifteen feet, then ended in what appeared to be some passageway. A series of grooves had been chiseled into the wall, forming a ladder.

I took out my phone and sent a text to Ross.

Trapdoor in basement behind bar. Button behind bottles on shelf.

I turned off the light so as not to reveal my presence and carefully climbed into the hole.

The shaft was barely wide enough for Richard Mann's brawny physique. Still, a claustrophobe would never survive the descent. Step by step, I made my way down, feeling carefully for the next groove with my foot.

At last, I reached the bottom. The air was dank and cold, much different from the climate-controlled basement above. The walls felt rough and made of stone. I stood still for a moment and listened. From somewhere down the passage, I could hear the sound of chanting.

The Order was assembled and casting a spell. All while a party ensued upstairs. That was a pretty brazen thing to do. To think they could slip away and do this while they had so many guests was the height of arrogance. But that fit Gray's personality to a T. Of course, the fact that the ritual place was in Kress' home enforced my theory that he was the real leader. It hadn't occurred to me before that someone might be higher in rank than Sebastian Gray, but if anyone could, it would be Kress.

There was no way the party upstairs had nothing to

do with the spell they were casting. Once again, I sent a text, but this time to my father.

Get out of the house, Dad. Everyone's in danger.

I risked a bit of light as I walked down the passage. The tunnel was clearly of much older design. It had been here long before the house, and possibly before the Pilgrims landed at Plymouth Rock—it felt that old. The walls were roughly cut through the stone, and the ceiling had a slight arch. The passage was only about three-and-a-half feet wide, and I had to be careful not to hit my head on the ceiling as I went. I doubt it was made by Native Americans—it had a decidedly European look to it.

But I wasn't here for a history lesson. I was here to stop the Order, and that meant moving on. After walking for only a couple of minutes, I could see the proverbial light at the end of the tunnel. A door was closed at the end, and red light could be seen filtering through the cracks. The light flickered, causing shadows to dance on the floor and walls near the door.

I put my hand on my hip and felt a moment's shock when I found no holster. Then I remembered. The party. I had my pocket gun. I reached in and drew the Ruger. With gun in hand, I put the flashlight away.

The door was an old, wooden affair, shaped to fit the contour of the tunnel. I had a feeling the hinges would squeak if I opened it, but I had to try.

Listening there at the door, I could hear clearly a single voice reciting some verse in Latin, with the occasional response by several voices at once. My Latin was rusty, and there were words in there that I didn't recognize. I couldn't translate a single line, but I was able to get the gist of it. They were in the power-building phase of the spell if I knew anything about ritual magic—which I did. Although I'd never performed a spell in my life, I'd made it a requirement to learn as much about them, and those who cast them, as I could. They were all too often the subject of my cases. But this sounded far more elaborate and organized than any I had encountered before. They were building up for something big.

I lifted the latch and pushed gently on the door at just the moment when the entire group spoke in chant. It opened easily, without any squeak. I opened it just wide enough to slip through and found myself on a narrow stone ledge that ran around a circular room, the floor of which was about fifteen feet below. A wrought iron railing ran the length of the shelf. A single stone staircase in front of me descended along the wall to the floor below. I knelt down to hide and gently closed the door. Then, I took in the scene below.

The circular room was approximately thirty feet in diameter. The walls were of the same stone as the ledge I was on, and more smoothly wrought than the tunnel I had just left. Torches burned in sconces that hung along the wall at even intervals, bathing the room in warm light. In the center of the chamber was drawn a large, white pentagram with strange writing encircling it. Five men huddled around something in the center— presumably the altar. The magicians wore identical black robes with hoods drawn over their heads. The Order chanted and swayed slowly back and forth as they focused on the altar.

But my attention was drawn to a crucifix attached to the wall on the opposite side of the room. Strung up on the large wooden cross was the naked form of Summer Parke. Her head hung low, and she wasn't moving. There was no blood and no indication that she was hurt. But it filled me with dread. Images of the Powells' dining room came to my mind, and terror welled up inside me. Was I too late?

I had to do something, but what? If I didn't go to her right away, she might die. But if I wasted time with her, I might miss my opportunity to stop the Order. I shook my head. Going to her was out of the question. I couldn't rescue her with the others right there.

So, first things first.

I crept to the stairs as carefully as I could. I put one foot tentatively on the top step, and at that moment, the chanting stopped. I froze and threw my gaze toward the circle.

No one looked in my direction. The Order had ended their ritual. The energy shot outward in a wave that nearly bowled me over. I caught my breath as it passed through me. Either it was not meant for me, or my charm hid me from it, for it left me alone and continued out into the world.

I continued my stealthy climb down the stairs, keeping my eyes glued to the five men in the circle. The men spread out inside the ring and relaxed. Some laughed, and they all chatted, congratulating themselves for the work they had done.

I reached the floor and melted behind boxes that

had been stacked along the wall. Apparently, they hadn't fully unpacked after their move from the warehouse. Good for me—instant cover.

"It shouldn't be long now," said one of the hooded figures in the circle. The voice was unmistakably Donald Kress'.

"And you're sure it'll get him this time?" That was Gray.

"Of course," Kress assured him. "Couldn't you feel it? This spell cannot go wrong. Simon will die, along with everyone else in just a matter of minutes."

"He better . . ." came Richard Mann's voice from a broad-shouldered man who stood near the center of the circle. But he was cut off by a sound, muffled from our position under the earth, but growing in intensity. Everyone looked around in anticipation.

An explosion erupted a good fifty feet above us on the surface of the hill. The ground shook, and I was forced to kneel to keep my footing. A few boxes fell from the long stack, still leaving my cover intact. Armageddon continued above us, with the mingled noises of crashing and rending wood, shattering glass, and large objects striking the ground. Kress' entire mansion must have come down.

And my father was up there. I could only hope he had gotten my text.

I knelt in shock as images of the partygoers getting buried alive ran through my head. By the sound of it, there was no way anyone could have survived. My father. The good doctor. All those businessmen and their wives.

That was it. In one fell swoop, Donald Kress had

managed to wipe out all of his competitors with a single, catastrophic accident. And it would even give him a free pass—for surviving and losing his house, which his insurance will doubtless pay for. It was an accident—no one would ever suspect him.

As I crouched there behind the boxes, the shock wore off and was replaced with rage. It welled up inside me, working its way from my stomach through every inch of my body. They murdered my father. As much of an ass as he was, he was still my father, and I loved him. But I had to control the anger—force it back down. Rash actions would get me killed. There were five of them out there. I had to even the odds some. Would I be justified in shooting them? I wasn't sure. I had to think of another plan.

Peeking out from behind my cover, I could see the men, still robed and hooded, milling about the circle. They would not break the circle. That meant they weren't done yet. Another spell? I now had a good view of the altar they had been huddling around.

On the altar, its arms and legs splayed out, lay the emaciated corpse of a fairy.

And then it hit me. They had tried sacrificing the fairy worshipers because they claimed to use fairy magic. But it wasn't enough. So, they learned to trap fairies and used them for sacrifice. The poor creatures were treated as batteries—cells of magical power. This was why the fairies were mad. This was why they targeted the Order. And I didn't blame them one bit.

A sudden noise drew my attention away from the altar. The din above had gone, and the room was quiet, save for the banter of the men as they relaxed after their exertion. Then, it came again. A light moan drifted from across the room.

Summer was waking up. She lifted her head, which lolled drunkenly as she tried to grasp what was going on.

"Don't worry, bitch," Gray sneered. "It'll be over for you soon enough."

Some say that chivalry always prevailed in moments like these. But I couldn't see how, since your brain switches off and you just react.

I rose and leveled my gun at the man I believed was Gray.

"Fucking bastard," I growled, and then squeezed the trigger.

Chapter 49

I fired two rounds at my nemesis. They were well-aimed shots and would have hit home had he stood still. But he was too good for that. Gray was in motion before I finished swearing, and so only the first shot managed to hit him, striking his right bicep. He dove for cover behind the altar, shouting to his companions as he did so.

"Get him, God damn it!"

I fired two more rounds at an unknown magician that charged straight for me. Both shots hit him in the chest, and he stumbled and fell, first to his knees, and then keeled over into a ball.

Another hooded man had grabbed a ritual knife and pulled back to throw it at me. One shot hit his face. No double-tap this time, as I was almost out of ammo.

A man was at the crucifix, undoing the bonds that held Summer to the cross. She was still awake, but out of it—apparently drugged. I raised my gun but had to wait for an opportunity to shoot without the risk of hitting Summer.

At that moment, the wall of boxes I was half-hiding

behind came tumbling down on me. None of them
were heavy but combined, they managed to drive me
back against the wall. Through the pile of cardboard
lumbered the linebacker figure of Richard Mann. His
hood was pulled back, his face red with fury. He plowed
into me, and I was crushed against the wall, his right
arm pinning my neck. The vice-like hand of his left arm
latched onto my right wrist, and he shoved my hand
with tremendous force against the wall. It took two tries
for him to force me to release the grip of my gun, which
clattered to the floor amid the debris of fallen boxes.

Not for the first time, I told myself to learn Karate,
as I struggled to free myself from the giant's grip. He
pushed his arm harder against my throat, and I found it
difficult to breathe. I kicked his shin as hard as I could
manage, but it only seemed to anger him more. He was
like a smaller version of the ogre, only with a teensy bit
more brains.

"My dear Simon Kane," Gray said from somewhere
beyond Mann's fat head. "You never cease to amaze me.
Every time we try to kill you, you somehow manage to
live. Even now as your father dies above us, here you are.
Alive and continuing to be a pain in my ass. If Richard
had his way, he would have broken your little neck long
ago. Tonight, I think I'll let him. But first, before you
die, I'd like to know how you managed to survive all our
attempts at killing you with magic. Our spells were not
flawed. They should have worked."

So, Gray wanted to gloat. Good for him. That
might give me a chance. My free hand went slowly to
my pocket. I had to have something there—something

I could use as a weapon. I had to keep him talking, keep the conversation going, like in the movies.

"Just lucky, I guess," I said.

Mann gave an extra push against my throat, making me gag. "Answer him!" he growled.

"You'd better do as he says," Gray said casually. "I won't be able to contain him for long." I could see him now, as he stepped up beside Mann. Apparently, he put a lot of trust in his friend's ability to hold me down. That trust might have been well placed.

"Okay," I croaked. "I can *feel* it. I can feel the magic right before it manifests. It gives me a little chance."

My hand was in my pocket. I felt two things: my small flashlight, and my keys.

"You can sense magic? Hmm . . . now that *is* a good trick. That is if you're telling the truth."

"I am," I said.

Slowly, I drew my keys out of my pocket. Gray was close enough that he would need to look down to see what I was doing, but he was trying to read my face to tell if I was lying.

"Fascinating," he said at last. "And how can you do that? Is it a spell of some kind? An artifact? Tell me."

"I was born with it." I figured he wasn't going to live long enough to use the knowledge against me. I gripped the keys with the Ferrari key sticking out like a spike from between two knuckles.

"Really? And how is that?"

"I honestly haven't got a clue."

"Now I don't believe that. I bet you know exactly where you inherited your ability. Not from your father, at any rate. He was painfully mundane—"

A shot rang out in the passageway above and behind me, where I had come from. Both men looked up at the door in surprise, and Mann loosened his grip on my neck and arm—just a little.

I thrust my key into Mann's leg with all the strength I could muster. There was a *pop* as the key tore through his skin.

Mann howled in pain, dropping me as he reached for his leg. I let go of the keyring and threw myself into him, shoving him backward. He tripped on boxes and fell to the ground with a thud, his hands clutching the wound at his leg.

Gray lunged at me, but I was ready for him. I grabbed at him as he grappled me, and we both fell sprawling among the boxes, the magician on top of me.

We wrestled there on the floor for what seemed an eternity. I had to finish this with Gray quickly so I could save Summer. Someone was messing with her, and I had no idea what had become of them.

Gray punched me repeatedly in the face. I heard something in my nose crack, and a flash of pain surged through my head. Blood flowed hot on my face. I grabbed his arm and threw myself to one side, pulling on his arm as I did so. He fell off me as we continued to wrestle. I tried to climb onto him, but he was too good a fighter. His fist kept hitting my nose with each attempt until I finally gave up and rose to my hands and knees. He did the same, and we faced off with only a couple of feet between us.

Then I saw it.

On the floor to the right of Gray lay my gun. He hadn't noticed it, as it was a few feet behind him.

I suddenly threw myself forward and to the right, attempting to stretch outward toward the gun. Gray dove at me, and his fist connected with my kidney. Pain shot through me and my knees curled up to my chest involuntarily. The breath was taken out of me, and my vision blurred. He pounded the small of my back. I was taking a beating and wasn't sure how much longer I could make it. I stretched out my hand and groped for the gun.

He noticed what I was doing and scrambled for the gun as well, but my hand closed around the grip as he crawled across my back. I twisted as violently as I could and brought the gun around to point at the only body part I could reach.

I fired.

His face erupted into blood and bone fragments. He screamed and fell back to thrash about on the floor.

I scrambled up to my knees to see Mann towering over me, his face nearly purple in his rage.

"Freeze!" came a voice from above me.

Ross stood on the platform at the top of the stairs, his revolver aimed at Mann. The oaf glared up at him but put his hands up. He at least had that much sense. I hauled myself to my feet.

"What took you?" I said.

"I'll tell you later."

I nodded and looked around. Summer was gone. So was Kress. I snarled when I noticed the passage that ran off on my level near the empty crucifix. I bolted

after him through the doorway into another narrow
passage, leaving Ross to clean up the riffraff.

"Bolting" was more of a drunken stumble, followed
by painful hobbling, as the various injuries began
to stack up on me. The blows to my face and kidney
were too much. I was in terrible pain, and each step
sent a spike of it up my side. My right arm hurt again.
Although my bit of magic did great work at healing it, it
was still not fully recovered, and the banging that Mann
did to it took its toll. Being a quick healer didn't help
much when you took damage at the rate I did.

The passage was of the same craftsmanship as the
one I had taken into the chamber. It was cold and dank,
and my footsteps echoed loudly as I hobbled along.

I heard Summer's voice from up ahead, weak and
drugged, pleading with Kress to let her go. It kept me
going.

The passage finally opened into a broader tunnel
that ran perpendicular to it. I burst out and looked both
ways.

It was a sewage tunnel. I stood on a narrow walkway
that overlooked an old canal where rain runoff would
travel on its way to the bay. It was mostly empty now,
with only a trickle running along its center.

And, of course, there were creepies. They swarmed
around the canal wall, reaching up in vain to touch one
of us.

Kress stood on the walkway about twenty feet from
me. His hood was down, revealing the face I recognized
from the dinner party. He appeared wild and more than
a little bit crazy as he stared at me with wide eyes and

a desperate grin. But he held Summer in front of him with a ritual knife to her throat.

"Drop the gun, Kane. Sebastian told me you care about this woman. That's why he took her. I see now that may have been a mistake. Undoubtedly, you came looking for her, and thus missed our little surprise." The hint of a sneer pulled at his lips.

Mentally, I counted the shots I had fired. The LCP's one weakness was it only had a six-round magazine. Two at Gray, two at the charging guy, one at the guy with the knife. And one last round at Gray again. That was six.

The gun was useless, so I knelt and rested the weapon on the floor by my feet. Then I rose, my hands palm first before me, in a placating gesture.

"Okay, you've got the power. What happens now?"

He didn't reply right away. His eyes darted about as if in search of anything that would get him out of the situation.

I smiled. "Let's run through things, shall we? If you hurt Summer, I grab the gun and kill you. If you let Summer go, I'll grab the gun, and I *might* kill you. But I might not, since you showed the sense to let her go. If you try to back your way out, I'll just follow along and kill you when you screw up. It's a long way out. So, which is it?"

He took a step backward, pulling Summer with him. She moaned, "No."

Kress ignored her. "Your father's dead, you know. We killed him and all the other scum up there."

"I know. You're a murderer. A cheap, craven killer who can't even kill in person. You're below contempt."

An insane grin pulled at his lips. His eyes shone with malice. "No. It was business. Just a deal. A hostile takeover. I have shares in most of their companies. Now, I'll take control—that's how it works. You eliminate your competition, and then you win."

He took another step backward. Summer's arm floated up helplessly toward his face, the only form of resistance she could muster. But I saw the light coming back into her eyes. The drug was wearing off.

"I think you lost your way. I have no doubt you were a decent businessman once. But you haven't relied on those skills for some time. You've been using your magic to get ahead, and you've lost your edge. That's why you did it. The more you practiced magic, the more your business sense went out the window. The people you killed up there . . ." I paused involuntarily at the thought. "They were better than you. They were better, and you *knew* it. You hated them for it. That's why you killed them."

"You're wrong!" he shouted. He took another step, and it was clumsy. He stumbled a little on a crack in the pavement but recovered quickly. "I'm better than ever. Better than all of them. Better than the late *William Jonathan Kane*." He spat my father's name with undisguised loathing. "And you'll be joining him shortly."

"Mr. Kane is alive," came a voice from behind me.

I whirled about and saw Ross, his gun aimed at Kress. I gave him a questioning look—or was it a *pleading* look?

He nodded. "Luckily he was with me when the

plane crashed into the building. These charms really do work." He smiled grimly.

I turned to face Kress again, smiling broadly.

"No!" Kress cried. "It can't be! Our magic is great! It's powerful. It cannot fail!"

"Oh, but it has," I taunted. "Over and over, it failed. You're a failure, Kress. Face it. You're a loser. And you're going to jail for a long time if you manage to survive the night."

"No! I'll kill you!"

With one meaningful look at me, Summer shoved Kress' knife hand away from her neck and dropped to the floor. Her senses had come back, and she had waited for him to loosen his grip.

I charged. Kress turned and ran, but I was faster, such was my mind. All the pain was forgotten. Everything but my score which I was now ready to settle. I leaped neatly over Summer, who curled up on the floor, and caught Kress by the arm before he had run ten feet.

He whirled around and slashed at me with his knife. I caught it with my other hand, and we strove there on the walkway, his strength against mine. He may have been crazy, and my adrenaline was in overtime, but he was uninjured, and I was in bad shape. And there was something to be said for desperation. At first, it was a stalemate, but then, my energy waned, and he began to overpower me. Slowly his knife arm came closer, and my arm lost ground. My muscles began to shake.

I was going to lose. Why did I run? Why didn't I just let Ross shoot him down? Because this was my fight. He had tried to kill my dad, and I had to teach him the error of his ways. Except that he was winning, and was likely to cut me up.

No.

I couldn't let him win. I had to do something. With the last of my strength, I pulled myself backward and tripped and fell on my back on the ledge.

He didn't expect that, and with my hands clenched around his wrists, he fell forward and landed on top of me. But I was ready for that. I quickly twisted my body to one side and pulled that way with my arms, my hurt arm protesting the effort. Kress toppled to one side, and I let him go.

Over the edge, he went, but as he did, he grabbed my wrist with his free hand. My arm went backward over the side, and I felt it break again. I slid on my back with the weight of the Order's leader pulling me over the side. My head left the walkway and, looking over, I could see him hanging there, clinging desperately to my arm. The creepies had gathered below him and were now clawing at his legs. He looked down, and his eyes grew wide with terror.

He could see them! He was touching me, and so he could see the creepies as plainly as I could, and it filled him with a terror greater than his mind could accept. He dropped his knife and grabbed my arm with both hands. He looked up at me with a pleading look.

"Help me," he moaned.

With my broken arm and compromised position, there was little I could do. I couldn't twist around to grab Kress with my free hand, or I would go over the edge with him.

The creepies grabbed at his ankles, and when they touched his bare skin, Kress shivered and screamed as if stuck by a hundred needles. Sweat poured down his face, and his eyes bugged out. He clung desperately to me, but I only slid more.

I tried to pull him up with my broken arm, but it had finally reached its limit. The muscles twitched like mad, and I lost control of my fingers. It was like a mechanical arm with its wires cut. I just lost all power.

He screamed as he lost his own grip. I stopped sliding, and he fell into the channel below. Immediately, the creepies swarmed all over him. He screamed and thrashed in terror, but there was nothing I could do. I pulled myself back and stood up. Ross and Summer appeared beside me, he had put his coat over her. He looked down at Kress, who thrashed about in agony and frowned.

"What's wrong with him?"

"They've got him. He won't last long. It would be humane if you shot him right now."

"What do you mean? I don't get it. What *they*? He's all alone down there."

I grabbed his hand. His eyes widened as he was suddenly aware of black, featureless humanoids that swarmed the once-powerful magician. Summer buried her face in Ross' chest.

"Holy mother of Christ!" he breathed. "What the fuck are they?"

I shrugged. "Creepies. At least that's what I call them. I don't really know what they are, but they'll suck the life out of him—and maybe his soul—in a few more seconds. Or, you could shoot him. It's up to you."

Ross just stared dumbly. I let him go, and he looked around in surprise.

"Where'd they go?"

"You only see them when I'm touching you. But they are there. Shoot Kress, please."

He raised his gun and aimed, but then Kress stopped screaming. He lay still and didn't move again. Ross lowered his weapon.

"Jesus," he breathed.

"Too late," I said. I really didn't want Kress to die that way, but after all that he did, it almost seemed fitting.

"I guess we're done here. What did you do with the others?"

Ross nodded back toward the passage. "Reinforcements came."

"Then let's get the hell out of here."

Chapter 50

We walked back toward the circular room slowly. Now that the urgency was gone, and my adrenaline had a chance to ebb, I found I could hardly stand. Ross helped me, for Summer's strength was returning, and she was able to walk fine, using the wall to steady herself. She said nothing and focused only on walking and breathing.

"So, now you have the corpse of a fairy to examine," I said to Ross as we entered the passage. "That could help you convince your superiors this shit is real."

"What fairy?" Ross said. "I didn't see any."

"It was on the altar. But I guess you had other things on your mind."

He shook his head. "Simon, I looked at the altar. There was nothing on it."

I stopped short and frowned at him. "It was there, Ross. They sacrificed it. I think they used the poor thing as a battery of magical energy. That was their power source."

"There was nothing on the altar," Ross repeated. "Could this be another creature that only you can see?"

I snorted. "Maybe." I started walking again. "We'll find out in a minute."

Policemen swarmed around the room as we entered. The place was a mess with blood, bodies, and scattered boxes everywhere. The cops left everything as it was as they waited for forensics to arrive.

Two paramedics were huddled around Gray's body. They were working feverishly on his head.

"He's *alive*?" I said, astonished. The medics ignored me and continued their work.

"He was still moving when you left the room. I didn't come alone. I had two officers with me, and they called the paramedics right away."

I shook my head. I felt in my heart that the world would be a safer place without Sebastian Gray.

"So, the fairy . . ." I said and turned to the circle. I scuffed my feet on the salt that had been sprinkled around the circle's edge, just to be on the safe side and ensure all the power was gone. I felt nothing—no more tingles. Then I looked at the altar.

It was empty.

The two-foot-high ritual table was a short stone slab resting on a rectangular stone block. It was made of granite, roughly shaped, but with a smooth top. The whole thing was about the size of a coffee table. I knelt by it and examined the surface. There was no blood that I could see, at least no fresh blood. But I suspected the victims who died on the table were never cut or stabbed—their life force was drained from them. And I would bet they were awake for it. It must have been horrible.

"I know it doesn't look it, but a fairy died here on this altar, only a few minutes ago," I said as I examined the floor around the altar.

"And thanks to you, no more will die here."

It was not Ross. And it wasn't any of the cops or medics, either. I whirled around, rising as I did.

There before me stood the fairy I had met at Liz's house. She wore a white gossamer gown too thin to hide her exquisite form. She was every bit as beautiful as she was the other night in Mrs. Gray's bedroom, but this time there was no tug at my mind, no inner struggle to overcome her magical charms. She wasn't trying to control me. I glanced around the room and saw everyone else frozen in place, staring at her with undisguised lust and awe.

I turned a tired look her way. "I wish you wouldn't do that."

She smiled warmly. "I wanted a private conversation. They won't remember seeing me here, but they will feel *wonderful*."

"I'm sure they will. So, I kept my end of the bargain. I found the Order's hideout and destroyed its glamour. Sorry I didn't leave many of them for you. They resisted."

"Oh, I'm quite pleased with your work. I will hold to the bargain. The families of these men will be left alone. It's these men that we want. And now that they are no longer a danger to us, we are free to have our fun with them."

I chuckled. "Normally, I would object to you messing with humans. But in this case, I think you deserve it. But I'd like you to leave now. My friends have work to do, and, frankly, you make me uncomfortable."

She raised an eyebrow. "I have never made a man uncomfortable before—without wishing it. You are a fascinating specimen, Simon Kane. You are not like any other mortal. There is something special about you, and I'm interested in learning your secrets. I will leave you for now, but I will return. I think we will see more of each other in the future. Farewell."

"Oh, and one last thing," I said. The fairy paused and met my gaze. I felt warm all over in the gentle embrace of her eyes, but it wasn't from magic. "Return the Manns' baby. For his mother."

She nodded, then suddenly burst into a million twinkling lights. They fluttered around the room in a swirl and then scattered through cracks in walls and out holes and doorways. As soon as the last light disappeared, all the men in the room roused. They all looked around nervously, blushing, and then went back to their work.

"I feel weird," Ross said quietly to me. "Like, all warm and happy inside. Kind of like—like I just had . . ."

He grabbed me by the arm. "*She* was here. Wasn't she? The fairy woman?"

I nodded. "The score's settled. The fairies will stop their attacks. Although, I can't guarantee the survivors of the Order will be okay."

Ross snorted. "Yeah, well as long as I get them into jail, I'm good."

The latest—and final—"accident" of the Order's doing was an airplane that crashed into the Kress mansion while I was in the circle room below. Many of the businessmen who had been invited perished in the disaster. My dad got the text I sent and thought it would be a good idea to set off a smoke alarm. Most of the guests escaped, including Dr. Mullen.

The place was a disaster. Aside from the section of the basement where the trapdoor was, the entire house was a massive, smoldering pile of rubble. There was less fire than I had expected, and firemen were working on it, dowsing everything they could find in water. I guessed the charms were responsible for keeping access to the tunnel safe. It was conspicuously cleared, which wouldn't have made sense any other way.

Being at the top of a hill, the plane flew right into the house, rather than crashing down upon it. The building had collapsed, and the plane—a mid-sized twin-engine craft—was buried under it. But the parking lot was mostly untouched, and the deck offered a perfect view of the incoming disaster, thus saving most of the people who were outside.

I let the paramedics treat my nose and arm—they refused to let me go untreated—but not until after they had checked out Summer. She had been drugged, which had mostly worn off, but was otherwise uninjured, so she was back to her old self before long. I pulled my emergency clothes bag from my car, and she dressed behind an SUV. Then, I sat and waited while everyone did their job. Summer was determined to help the medics with the injured, and they weren't about to stop her.

I called Jess as I waited for Summer to finish her work.

"Simon," she said, sounding worried. "I saw the piece about the airplane crash. I had a bad feeling about it. Was it another spell?"

"It was," I said. "But thanks to your charms, Ross and I are fine. And that's going to be the last spell the Order ever casts."

"You stopped them?"

"I did."

"Good," she breathed, relief spilling out of my car's speakers.

"I just wanted to thank you," I said.

"You're welcome, Simon."

"Jess, I'd like to . . ." I hesitated. I was terrible at this kind of thing.

"Don't, Simon," she cut in sternly. "Just don't. We have no future together. We're just acquaintances."

"It's not that," I said quickly. "I just wanted to say I'm sorry, okay. I don't want to get back together. But I'd like to be friends."

There was a pause, then, "I don't know." Her voice was now full of suppressed emotion. "I have to go."

The line went dead, and I sat there thinking. I thought about what could have been and then shook my head. *Jess and I are too different. We don't mesh. It was never going to work out. And I probably screwed up any chance at friendship as well.*

I called Liz and let her know that the job was done and that we'd meet up to settle the case.

"Thank you, Mr. Kane," she said, relief barely evident in her Goth facade. "I owe you one."

"And you'll get my bill."

Eventually, all the injured had been sent off to the hospital, and Summer came to join me. We sat on the hood of my Ferarri—it was going to get repaired and detailed anyway—and watched the firemen deal with the wreckage. We sat in silence for a while, each of us processing the events in our own way.

Finally, I spoke up. "To be fair, I warned you not to come."

She broke a wry grin but continued to stare ahead. Cops and rescue workers were searching the wreckage for survivors—and bodies. "The 'I-told-you-so,' I should have expected it." She didn't sound upset.

I snorted. "It's my trademark."

"And I thought I knew everything about you."

"Has this changed your opinion of me? Tonight that is?"

She sat silent for a minute or two before replying.

"Does this happen a lot?"

"More often than you'd think," I said. "But if you mean, would you be in danger if you dated me, well, maybe. Not so much if you stay clear when I'm on a rough case."

"Those things in the tunnel. The 'creepies.' Can a person survive an attack by them? If we had chased them off or pulled Mr. Kress out, could we have saved him?"

"Are you saying we should have rescued him?"

She shook her head vigorously. "No! Of course not. But, well . . . nobody should die like that. Not even him. I wouldn't have risked any of us to save him, but there must be others who fall victim to those things. I'd like to be able to treat those people, to save them."

I laughed then, clear and loud. What Summer said wasn't funny, but sometimes you just had to laugh—it healed. But she gave me a look as though I had five heads.

"We'd make a great pair," I said, suppressing my outburst. "I catch the supernatural bad guys, and you treat their victims."

She shrugged. "Someone has to. I think it could work."

"I don't know if there's anything you can do. What the creepies do . . . I don't think it's physical. They damage the soul."

Summer shook her head. "The soul is a term used to describe something that science hasn't identified yet. But the soul must have an effect on the body. I think I could be in a good position to study the physical effects of these 'soul attacks.' Maybe I can find a connection. I don't mean to find the soul, but perhaps to see how it interacts with the body. And *that* might help me learn to treat them."

"Okay. I'm not the doctor, so I'll defer to you. But I doubt it'll be easy."

"Nothing worthwhile is. But I've already got a good place to start."

I gave her a curious look.

"Kress' body. He didn't die from any physical

injury. He died from a creepie attack. I'll get permission to attend the autopsy and see what I can find."

"Hmm. Sounds good. So, I guess I haven't scared you off, then?"

She smiled. "Not by a long shot, mister."

Thankfully, my father didn't visit us as we waited. I was exhausted and was in no mood to deal with our baggage. I was glad he was okay, and that was enough. Several of his friends and many of his colleagues had just died, and so he ran around consoling their wives and promising his aid. It was part humanitarian and part business.

When Ross finally had a minute to see me, he didn't have much to say.

"Go home, Simon. You've been through enough shit tonight that I don't have the heart to put you through a debriefing. Get some rest, and come to the station tomorrow."

I wasn't about to argue.

Brad Younie writes books mostly about magic in the real world because he thinks people need a little excitement in their lives. Being an eternal teenager in a man's body, he owns a collection of swords (which he plays with), wands (which he plays with), and spends way too much time studying these things. A man with many hobbies, he plays guitar, reads books, watches movies, and fences with lightsabers and swords that are a bit sharper. But most of all, he weaves tales of magic and mystery that chills to the bone as it makes the heart race.

Visit www.bradyounie.com for more about Simon Kane